Other books by Richard C. Morais

FICTION

The Hundred-Foot Journey

NONFICTION

Pierre Cardin: The Man Who Became a Label

Buddhaland Brooklyn

A Novel

Richard C. Morais

Scribner

New York   London   Toronto   Sydney   New Delhi

SCRIBNER
A Division of Simon & Schuster, Inc.
1230 Avenue of the Americas
New York, NY 10020

First Scribner hardcover edition July 2012

SCRIBNER and design are registered trademarks of The Gale Group, Inc.,
used under license by Simon & Schuster, Inc., the publisher of this work.

For information about special discounts for bulk purchases,
please contact Simon & Schuster Special Sales at 1-866-506-1949
or business@simonandschuster.com.

The Simon & Schuster Speakers Bureau can bring authors to your live event.
For more information or to book an event contact the Simon & Schuster Speakers
Bureau at 1-866-248-3049 or visit our website at www.simonspeakers.com.

DESIGNED BY ERICH HOBBING

Manufactured in the United States of America

1   3   5   7   9   10   8   6   4   2

Library of Congress Control Number: 2012009160

ISBN 978-1-4516-6922-0
ISBN 978-1-4516-6924-4 (ebook)

For my parents,
Vasco and Jane

Buddhaland
Brooklyn

Chapter One

The life of a man is like a ball in the river, the Buddhist texts state—no matter what our will wants or desires, we are swept along by an invisible current that finally delivers us to the limitless expanse of the black sea. This image rather appeals to me. It suggests there are times when we float lightly along life's surface, bobbing from one languid, long pool to another. But then, when we least expect it, we turn a river bend and find ourselves plummeting over a thundering waterfall into the churning abyss below. This I have experienced. And more.

Hard as it is for me to believe, my journey downriver started six decades ago, when I was born with little fuss in the village of Katsurao, high in the mountains of Fukushima Prefecture in Japan. My parents' inn was just eight kilometers from the nine-hundred-year-old Head Temple of the Headwater Sect of Mahayana Buddhism. When I came into this world, the fifteen thousand villagers of this simple trading post on the lower slopes of Mount Nagata still clung to the rocky banks of the Kappa-gawa before it dropped two thousand meters in a series of small waterfalls to the rice plains in the flatlands far below.

The upper reaches of my village consisted of three commercial blocks that ended in a pedestrian shopping plaza, a small bus depot, and a handful of low-rise apartment buildings that also housed a medical clinic built in the 1950s. Simple wooden houses stood in the narrow lanes of the old town down by the river. Flat-topped workshops housed a sheet-metal worker, a wood-carver, and a fish-smoker who plied their wares to villagers.

The town straddled both sides of the roaring Kappa-gawa, its inhabitants connected by two stone bridges. Every day our neighbor, bowlegged Mrs. Saito, left her money in a box at the Mujin-hanbai, a produce stall run on the honor system, and I have fond recollections of her staggering through the town's narrow alleys with her turnips and cabbages, tottering like a windup toy back across the lower cobblestone bridge.

There was something supernal about this stone and wood village in the crags of Japan's mountains. At night, a silky film of dew was laid across every roof tile, bridge, and bush of the village, and when the first shafts of mountain light pierced the thin air, the town smoldered and smoked with rising dew-steam, making it appear as if we were half of this world and half of the next.

My family's inn was called Home of the Lotus and catered to the Headwater Sect pilgrims who came to our mountain outpost to visit the Head Temple. My great-grandfather built the *ryokan* in the 1800s, and it was packed in among the other village houses standing tight at the edge of the rock face that fell dramatically to the river's Town Pool below. The main house was connected by a short covered walkway to a series of additional guest rooms and bathhouses added to the family property in the 1920s. Wherever you were in the inn, night and day, you could hear the river praying.

I was the second of four children, born behind Senior Brother Daiki, and ahead of younger brother Yuji, and baby sister Atsuko. The family's private rooms were in the back of the main house and of modest proportion. We had three small rooms upstairs, in the attic eaves, and two larger rooms on the ground floor separated by sliding *fusuma* rice-paper panels. Both floors of private rooms were connected by a steep wooden staircase worn smooth by over one hundred years of my family's passing feet. Our Oda family altar was downstairs, and in time the Toshiba television set was installed upstairs. Behind the *fusuma* panels were boxes carefully storing our family's history—Grandfather's uniform in the Imperial Army, Great-Grandmother's wedding kimono.

My mother, Okaa-san, was the rock of our mountain existence.

When I think of her now, I recall one hard winter night when a blinding snowstorm and howling winds blew furiously across the mountain cliffs. We were warm and safe inside the inn. I was painting at the *kotatsu,* a table heated from underneath and covered in a futon. The room smelled of ink and wet wool and pickled radishes. My mother was kneeling on the tatami mat across the room as tiny Atsuko suckled inside the loosened folds of her robes. The old-fashioned kerosene heater in the corner burned bright, its yellow heat casting a luminous glow across Mother's face.

Okaa-san was a devout follower of the Headwater Sect and she had a little transistor radio in the corner softly tuned to Shomyo, sutras set to melodies and sung by Buddhist monks. Her skin was smooth and creamy as rice, and her eyes above her pinkish cheekbones were soft with relief, as if the baby's suckling and the monks' incantations were transporting her to some heavenly place far from this difficult world. When I moved my brush across the paper, Mother's eyelids suddenly fluttered open and she came back to the reality of the inn. She remembered I was there and smiled.

I treasure this memory. And yet I also remember, so clearly, that Okaa-san was profoundly exhausted by the long hours of inn work, the clamoring of her children, and the fragility of her husband. She had a fiery temper and a sharp tongue that on occasion got the better of her, and she obsessively nurtured a long list of prejudices and grievances, most notably a profound contempt for the foreigners we called *gaijin.* Buried deep in the worldview she passed on to her children—unfathomable, considering the nature of the family business—was a particularly visceral disgust for Americans, those bumbling barbarians who had somehow defeated Japan. She would rail about how they had ruined our beloved ancient culture, about the evils of their modern technology and the way they introduced twentieth-century consumerism. The few Americans who did make it to our mountain inn seemed to only confirm her worst impressions. "They smell bad," she insisted. "Like horse farts."

3

I can still remember the morning she called my name while I was playing in the small garden that was sandwiched between the *ryokan* and the rocky cliff bank of the Kappa-gawa. I was about nine years old at the time. The golden-ray lilies were in bloom and the Asian rosy finches were fluttering their wings and splashing about the carved birdbath. My mother called again, more urgently, and I put down my stick, dutifully making my way to the *fusuma* door panel that connected the guest rooms to the main house.

Leaving my sandals at the entrance, I slipped inside and walked the waxed and darkened corridor just as a white-haired couple wearing the house *yukata* robes emerged from their guest room. It was Mr. and Mrs. Nakamura, pilgrims from Kyoto, who came every year for prayer and ritual cleansing. They recognized me as the son of the innkeepers and greeted me courteously before separating at the end of the hall. Mr. Nakamura went right to the wood-paneled hot baths for men, his wife to the women's bath quarters to the left.

"Okaa-san. I am here."

Mother and *nakai-san,* our cleaning help from the village, were inside a guest room facing the river, rolling up the futon, dusting the tatami, and airing out the room. "Where have you been?" she snapped. "I'm hoarse from calling your name. Go get the Nakamuras' breakfast tray."

As I turned to fetch the tray, an American couple—tourists, not pilgrims—came strolling leisurely back from the baths. They laughed loudly as they made their way down the hall. The woman was blond and young and very beautiful, while the man was middle-aged and had hair the color of silver mink. For a moment the couple stood at the entrance of their room, where my mother was still bustling about, and cautiously peered in. "Hey," the man said in a friendly way, trying to determine if they were permitted to come inside.

We were all staring at his feet.

He wore the bright green toilet slippers.

4

Inside the house.

Everyone knew you never brought the filthy toilet slippers inside. I will never forget the look on Mother's face as she hissed in our local dialect, "Big bags of rotten garbage! We should hurl them down the mountainside!"

My parents were typical of the generation born in World War II: always working, always harried, always mono-focused on rebuilding the family fortune. My image of them is with their backs bent in two: father bowing repeatedly to the guests, bent over his workbench as he rewired a floor lamp, bent over the roof as he repaired broken tiles. Mother, in her blue-and-white kitchen smock, a kerchief wrapped around her head, bent as she fed wood into the fire that cooked the bamboo baskets of *mochi* rice cakes, bent over the garden as she raked the gravel paths. By the time my older brother had reached adolescence he, too, began to assume the family posture, hunched over as he carried heavy luggage back and forth down the *ryokan*'s corridors.

So perhaps it is no wonder that Okaa-san was angry. Despite all the hard work, my parents never had enough to get ahead, the upkeep of the 150-year-old inn constantly draining them of their funds and life force. But at least I always knew where I stood with Mother, no matter how cross she was. In contrast, my father, Otou-san, was as remote and mysterious as the surrounding mountains—and almost as impossible to read. You never knew what weather was blowing up in those peaks.

I was a very young boy when I first realized my father was different, an understanding that came in a torrid October downpour. Daiki, my older brother, was beside me as we stood silent and shoulder to shoulder in the frame of the kitchen door. Otou-san was in the courtyard, feverishly cutting down the orange persimmons that had been hung to dry from strings tied to the eaves in the back of the inn. Left in the torrential rain, the persimmons would quickly spoil and rot. Turnips were on a slow boil in the kitchen behind us, and the air my brother and I breathed in the door threshold was half from within and half from without, an acrid smell of leaf rot mingling with the vapors of the bitter roots.

The rain fell and fell and fell, hitting the ground in heavy clumps as if a mountain god above had just upended a cistern. Water rushed like a swollen river over the courtyard's cobblestone, streaming in heavy rivulets down Father's reddened face as he gathered the persimmons in his arms. The way the rain ran down his face made it look like he was crying. When his arms were full of the orange fruit, he turned to dash back to the kitchen and off-load the persimmons. His soggy slippers snagged the edge of a courtyard stone and he stumbled. Otou-san managed to regain his footing, but the half dozen persimmons flew out of his arms, scattering and rolling through the dirty rain puddles.

Daiki and I watched Father as he stared at the lost fruit. His face went blank, his eyes two flat, black, and vacant discs. It appeared to me that whatever spirit kept him alive had just washed out of him, was in the gutter river and fast disappearing down the drain. For an unnaturally long time he took the rain's pounding, his head bowed, just staring at the fallen fruit.

When Mother finally came upon us she scolded my father, making such a racket he finally snapped out of his trance and allowed himself to be brought inside to dry off. But before my mother arrived, the three of us stood still for a long time, until I finally felt my older brother, Onii-san, take my hand.

He took my hand. And held it tight.

That is the way it was. It was Senior Brother, Daiki, not my parents, who was the true sun and moon of my world. It is Onii-san who taught me how to fish the Kappa-gawa and its tributaries for the Japanese mountain trout called *ayu*. These mountain outings with my brother were the most joyous moments of my childhood, and just the memory of them today can bring me to tears.

On a spring day when I was seven, Onii-san took me far up Mount Nagata, to the rarely fished Devil's Gate Gorge, near the Kappa-gawa's headwaters. When I was too tired and small to climb the last rock face, Senior Brother carried me on his back.

We passed through the giant boulders cinching either side of the Devil's Gate Gorge, where the water inside thundered and roared, amplified by the stone basin's acoustics. We inched our way along the deep green water's pebbly edge, to the sandbar at the bottom of the waterfall's long pool, just inside the gorge. And there we stood in awe. The majestic water fell 150 meters, thundering to the rocks below. A few bold boulders stood their ground as they were hammered deep in the pool.

Daiki removed two Tenkara fly rods from our backpack. There was no reel, just a leader and line attached directly to the end of the bamboo rod. At first my brother did not fish, just stood over me, patiently whipping the rod back and forth, trying to show me how to dance the fly on the river's surface. I grew bored and hungry and crossly told him to catch us a fish.

My brother stood at the top of the sandbar and cast his fly to a rock in the middle of the current, dappling the dressed hook. The waterfall cascaded behind him, and I can still see his outline against this white wall, a silhouette of a boy in bas-relief.

His fly swirled slowly in the eddy behind a rock, and a shadow rose lightning-quick from the water's depths. Onii-san and I simultaneously cried, "Aieee!" as the line went tight and the water erupted in the boil of a thrashing fish.

"Two-kilo fish," he yelled.

Daiki valiantly hopped from rock to rock as he followed the fighting fish. But it was too strong. The leader snapped, leaving a sickeningly slack line and empty silence. I burst into tears. "I am sorry, Onii-san," I wailed.

Daiki tried to tie on a new leader, but his hands were still shaking from his encounter with the giant trout. His chest rose and fell. My brother lowered his hands and looked at the waterfall, its spray moistening his face. "Don't be sorry, Seido," he finally said. "Don't be sorry. This is fishing. It is also about loss."

Daiki was not at all handsome like my younger brother, Yuji. He was willowy, hunched in the shoulders. Nor was he a particularly good student in school, as I was. But his eyes. They emanated kindness and a natural wisdom, almost eerily so for a mere boy. Mrs. Saito, our neighbor, once called my brother "one of earth's natural noblemen"—and this was the truth.

My younger brother, Yuji, was the opposite of Daiki. He was tough, like Mother, but with an added dash of impish charm. Yuji looms large in my memory, particularly on that day when Mother cooked a large vat of country noodle soup for dinner. She had placed the pot in the yard outside the kitchen door, so she would have enough elbow room to finish preparing the evening's meal. While Mother was distracted elsewhere in the kitchen, Yuji snuck forward to pinch a bowl of soup for himself.

I was coming from the work shed behind the inn, fetching a toolbox for Father, when I caught Yuji red-handed. He was on his haunches next to the vat of broth, one hand reached inside. I angrily clicked my tongue in warning.

Yuji looked at me sideways. When he saw who it was, he visibly relaxed, slyly turning on me a coconspirator's smile. He gently offered me the bowl in his hand. I was older, knew better. But I was helpless against my brother's charm, and I took the bowl, our karmas forever sealed over a shared bowl of stolen soup.

But I do nothing honorable by making my siblings out to be more than what they were. Below the surface there was darkness in our family, and sometimes this darkness materialized, as is normal, in the rivalry of brothers. One year, when I was perhaps eight years old, the family rose early for the annual plum-picking up on our plot of land on Mount Nagata's upper foothills.

My great-grandfather had purchased the small plot from a farmer a century earlier, and had planted a hardy breed of Satsuma plum trees from Kyushu, which were plump and sweet and only ready for plucking, due to the high altitude, in late July.

We had our picnic on a blanket spread out under the plum trees, bees buzzing drunkenly around the sugar-filled fruit. A mountain hawk-eagle circled the pass. Mount Nagata, looming high over us, had fresh snow on its peak, a rarity for that time of year, and the air smelled of honey and faraway ice. Mother tidied up after lunch, washing out the little bowls in the nearby stream, my baby sister tied in a papoose around her back. Yuji, about six at the time, had fallen asleep and was curled up in a corner of the blanket.

I was too young to be of real assistance in the plum-picking, and sorely envied Daiki. He was under a tree, holding a reed tray, gazing skyward. Father stood on a ladder in the branches high above and harvested the year's rich plum crop with a small knife. Periodically he came down to unload his smaller basket into Daiki's tray of fruit, which my brother relayed to crates in the back of the Nissan truck.

I walked over to the tree where they were working and poked at the plums in Daiki's basket. My brother pushed me away, but I came back under the tree, stood my ground, and called up the ladder.

"Otou-san. I want a special plum."

My father up the ladder ignored me.

"Otou-san. A plum. Find me a special plum. Please, Otou-san."

"Shush," Senior Brother said. "Go away. Stop bothering us."

"Otou-san. Please. A plum. Find me the best plum."

"Stop it. You are making Father angry."

I carried on for a half hour, curled around the base of the tree, plaintively calling up to Father, urging him to find me a delicious plum. He never responded. The tree finally stripped of fruit, Father came back down the ladder and told my brother to empty the tray. They were going to start on the next tree in the small orchard.

But before Otou-san grabbed the ladder and carefully withdrew it from the upper branches, he wordlessly pulled a plum from the little basket clipped to his belt and pressed it into my hand. He then moved the ladder over to the next tree and disappeared into its branches—without ever saying a word.

The plum he handed me was not the largest, but it was the color of the finest red-blue ink, and it was so full of sugar sap that crystals had formed a scar over one small injury in the fruit's smooth and taut skin. I sank my teeth into it, and the red flesh squirted deliciously, like watery fireworks, the juice dribbling down my chin. Father had found me the most special of plums.

Daiki came back with the emptied tray. He stopped and stared at me as I wolfed down my special gift. Father brusquely called his name, and my brother finally stirred, moving on to help Otou-san in the next tree. But as he did, he swung close by me at the tree's base and pinched so hard I yelped with pain. For several days thereafter I had a plum-colored bruise, as if the juice of that special gift had somehow stained me on the inside.

"Why, Onii-san?" I wailed. "Why?"

"Because you are his favorite."

This was what Daiki saw. What he believed. But to me, it seemed impossible. Otou-san gave off nothing. He hardly spoke to me. He was nothing more than a distant silhouette at dusk. My most distinct image of Father is from a summer eve when the mosquitoes were out. The sun had just dipped behind Mount Tsukuba in the west. Otou-san squatted on his haunches in the courtyard, smoking a cigarette, snatching a few moments' rest before the next shift of repair work began on the sputtering generator that stood in the shed behind the inn. He hated that old generator, which required constant fine-tuning and coaxing to work. He once said to Mother, on one of the few occasions I remember him speaking, "This machine will be the death of me."

A few pilgrims, back from the Head Temple, moved about in their rooms inside the inn, washing up before dinner. Mrs. Saito's dog bayed in the background. The black tobacco smoke of Otousan's cigarette rose and curled around his head as he squatted over the cobblestones. He suddenly pressed his thumb and forefinger into his eyes, not like he was rubbing them, but hard, almost like he wanted to poke them out. The downward tip of his head in the fading light, the squatting silhouette, exuded a profound exhaustion, to the bone, and this is the essence of my father as I remember him.

But Daiki saw things I could not. Like all lay Believers of the Headwater Sect, we had an altar in our home. We recited the *Lotus Sutra* every morning and every evening, lighting incense and praying for our ancestors. I thought it all tedious and boring, but I did like hearing Lord Shakyamuni's adventurous tales from the sutras, partly because I associated these stories with my mother in her most tranquil state. When she was in this mood, she would sit in the inn's garden with Onii-san and me, and tell us stories of the Buddha's life: How Lord Shakyamuni was born Siddhartha Gautama in southern Nepal, son of King Suddhodana and Queen Maya of the Shakya tribe. How he rejected his pampered life in his father's royal court and, leaving his wife and child behind, went out into the world in search of a spiritual practice that could overcome the four great sufferings of life—birth, old age, sickness, and death. And then my favorite bit, which I made her tell and retell: how, at age thirty-five, sitting under the Bodhi tree, Lord Shakyamuni became enlightened, encircled by a snake.

But then the Buddha's dangerous adventures were over and Mother began, much to my annoyance, to sneak in boring lessons on Buddhist doctrine, about how human suffering was caused by worldly illusions and attachments. When she began to stridently lecture us in this way, my brother would dutifully focus on her every word, struggling to keep up, while I fidgeted and yawned and began chucking pebbles over the cliff ledge. Eventually, sensing she had lost me entirely, she stopped talking and studied the birds splashing in the birdbath. On one such occasion, after a few minutes lost in distracted thought, she ended our session with the wistful remark, "It is my greatest wish that one of you boys will become a Priest of the Headwater Sect. I pray for this great honor. Every day. Why not someone from the Oda family?"

Many years later, on an unassuming April afternoon after I turned eleven, Okaa-san stood glowing with happiness at the entrance of the parental chamber. She beckoned me with her hand: "Come, Seido. Come. Don't be afraid." The palm of her hand was stretched out in invitation.

Inside their bedroom, Otou-san was kneeling on the tatami, his head tipped down so it was impossible for me to read his face. Father's fists pressed flat against his thighs, his elbows splayed out like the wings of a dragon. A half-finished bowl of udon noodle soup and a folded newspaper sat on a tray in the corner of their room.

"We have great honor for you," my mother said, kneeling by my father. "Come, Seido. Sit. Sit by us."

I cautiously crossed deeper into the room and knelt before them. Father did not look up from the floor and I could faintly hear Yuji playing with the baby behind the *fusuma* wall panels.

"Your father and I were at the Head Temple today to meet with Reverend Tanaka, Senior Priest in charge of acolyte training. It is now confirmed. The Head Temple has accepted you as an acolyte for the coming year. Is this not wonderful? This is a great blessing and honor for the family."

I bowed but did not speak.

Mother looked perplexed. "Why don't you say something? Are you not pleased?"

"Thank you, Okaa-san. But I do not want to go."

"But why? This is such an honor."

"I do not want to leave you. To leave the family."

"*Ahso,*" she said with a laugh. "Such attachment is very normal. It will pass. Remember we will be just down the road. The important thing is you have a chance to become a Priest. You will learn the sutras and serve the Buddha and become a very wise man. This is a great honor and blessing for the entire family. You will be the first in our lineage to become a Priest."

In those days such things were decided among the adults—children were never consulted. But my mother downplayed what everyone in the village already knew: boys who joined the Head Temple as acolytes were forbidden to see their families throughout their first seven years of training, but for an annual thirty-minute visit. It was for this reason—and an intuition that something was fundamentally wrong with this turn of events—that I uncharacteristically talked back.

"Why me?" I whispered. "Why not Onii-san? He is firstborn. It is normal that the firstborn become the honored Priest. That is what happened at the Takahashi family. Senior Brother Akihiko Takahashi became the Priest."

My mother faltered when I said this and she looked over at my father for support, but he continued to stare wordlessly at the tatami, unmoved and unmoving. So she leaned forward and gently stroked my hand. "This is true. It is normal that the oldest son becomes the Priest. But it is your father's special wish that you go, not your brother. That *you* enter the priesthood." She clapped her hands, to cheer up the room. "So this is special, special honor Father gives you! Besides, you are the best student of your age in the entire village! This is what Reverend Tanaka says."

My father finally spoke. "You will go."

He never looked up from the floor. He never looked at me.

"You will go. And that will be that."

I bowed. "Yes, Otou-san."

I found Senior Brother standing in the shadow of the hallway. I slowly made my way down the hall, my eyes glued to the floor, but as I passed my brother he said, "He chose you. For the Head Temple. To become Priest."

"*Hai,*" I whispered.

Senior Brother looked down at his brown hands, picked at the scab in the meat of his thumb. I turned and went outside for air. Mount Nagata was shrouded in a gray cloud. I crossed the stone bridge below the inn and climbed up on the moss-covered boulder overlooking the Town Pool.

On either side of the river, washing hung from bamboo poles in the backs of the houses that stood drunkenly over the pool's overhanging cliff face. I lay on my stomach on the moss-cushioned boulder and stared down at the *ayu* in the tail end of the pool below. The deepest part of the water was a dark, almost black green.

I began to weep quietly.

Someone climbed up on the boulder.

It was Daiki. He had followed me.

Onii-san lay down on the rock beside me, chin in his hands, and together we studied the fish below. "Don't be sad, Seido," he finally said. "It will be all right. I will come to the Head Temple and together we will climb up to Devil's Gate Gorge to fish for the *ayu*, like we have always done."

"We both know the monks will not let me spend time with you. Not for many years yet."

He did not say a thing. A trout rose lazily from the bottom of the pool.

"I must ask you a question, Onii-san."

"You can ask me anything, little brother. You know that."

"You want to join the Head Temple. I can tell."

"*Hai*."

"But why? I don't want to go. Yet you do. I do not understand. How can we be so different on this?"

He laid his cheek on the moss. After a few moments he said, very matter-of-factly, "Because I have dreams the inn is going to swallow me."

I considered this for some time and then said, "When I am older I will become a powerful Priest and come and get you. I will save you from this and you will come live with me in my temple. I will make you the temple cook. Yes. The temple cook. And in the afternoon, every day, we will fish together."

My brother laughed. "I'd like that very much, Seido."

"Don't laugh," I said crossly. "I will come and get you. You'll see."

It was nearing dinnertime, so we returned to the inn for our usual evening chores. Inside, my mother was barking orders at the kitchen help as the guests in their rooms were getting ready for the evening, taking baths and shrugging on freshly laundered *yukata* robes. I ran between the kitchen and guest rooms with bowl-laden trays as Onii-san and my father greeted a clutch of late-arriving guests at the main entrance. The inn was full and we were all very busy running back and forth, until we were exhausted.

Late that evening I passed my brother in the corridor. I was moving swiftly through the musty corridor with a steaming tray as my brother shuffled in the opposite direction, his shoulders and back bent under the weight of a guest's heavy bag. He already looked to me like an old man. As we passed in the dark, I whispered, "I will save you, Onii-san. I promise. I will take you from this place."

His eyes widened and we passed without further words. But I will never forget that look my brother gave me. It haunts me to this day. He was no longer laughing at my youthful promise, as he had done earlier on the boulder above the Town Pool. Rather, his silent, wide-eyed look reminded me of Mrs. Saito's dog the day it had hid trembling behind my knees during a thunderstorm. The eyes of the dog had pleaded, *Save me. Take me someplace safe— far, far from this.*

Daiki wore the same pleading look. That night at the inn.

Two days later Father took to his room. He stretched out on his side and stared blankly at the far wall. Refusing to get up, he lay like this all day, his arms tightly folded across his chest. Yuji whispered, "What's wrong with him?"

"Nothing's wrong," I said. "He's tired. That's all."

"But he's like this all day."

Yuji and I stood in the doorway of my parents' room. Inside, Father had his back to us. A fly landed on Otou-san's hand tucked under his armpit, and he flicked the insect away. The fly took off, circled, then returned to the same perch on Father's knuckle. This time he did nothing.

"Is he sick?" Yuji whispered.

The fly rubbed its hands.

"What are you doing there?" It was Mother, bustling her way down the corridor, angrily clapping her hands. "Go play! Go!"

Senior Brother and I were inseparable in the weeks following the announcement that I was to join the Headwater Sect priesthood. We understood that the precious time we had together was dwindling fast and in early June we convinced Mother to let us have a day off for fishing. She packed us a lunch and before the sun rose the next morning we were out, climbing down behind the old Shinto Fox Temple below the village, fishing in a mountain tributary that fed into the Kappa-gawa in the craggy pass below.

It had been unusually warm. Mrs. Saito's yellow dog followed us through the brush and sat on the riverbank, panting as he watched our progression downriver. The dew that had covered bushes and brittle rock in the early morning had quickly burned off in the first rays of sun.

After fishing both riverbanks through the morning, Daiki and I looked at each other, wordlessly communicating as brothers do. We took off our fish baskets, carefully put aside our rods, and went for a swim. The cold mountain river bubbled around us like sparkling sake and refreshed us immediately. After our swim we lay down under a wild-growing mountain cherry tree and ate some bean curd and smoked fish from Mother's lunch box.

Senior Brother fell asleep with his head on Mrs. Saito's dog. I could not sleep, so I watched Onii-san, my nose filled with the smell of the rushing river and the trout we had caught earlier, drying in the warm sun.

When my brother woke we continued to fish our way downriver. It was late afternoon when we reached our favorite hole just below Lady Fingers Waterfall. The *ayu* rose steadily to our flies in the approaching dusk; Onii-san helped me land a particularly fat and hard-fighting fish. "That will feed a few guests," he said.

I slipped the trout into my grass-filled basket, and Onii-san caught his first glimpse of the half dozen fish fatly laid out inside my cane carryall. He clapped his hands and laughed delightedly at my catch, patted me on the back of the head.

"I won't be able to go home, Seido. I'll be too ashamed. You've caught three times more fish than I have. The student has surpassed the master!"

Onii-san turned around and walked back to his own fishing spot at the tail of the pool. I cast a final look in his direction as he took up his fishing rod again on the far side of the rock, his fly elegantly cast out on the water. The setting sun hit the angle of the waterfall spray just so, transforming the fine droplets of mist into an airborne diamond dust, and in this dappled light my brother stood alone, slowly passing into the coming night.

I was eleven years old. It was July and blistering hot. The sun blazed, making Mount Nagata's glacier sparkle, and I now realize that this unusually hot and dry weather was an omen. Early the morning of my initiation into the priesthood, my parents brought me to the Head Temple's main entrance, the Buddha Entry Gate at the front of the monastery's commanding stone wall. Twenty-one acolytes entered the Head Temple that year. I have a vague recollection of white-faced children dropped off by their parents, some from cities as far away as Kagoshima in Kyushu. The parents were instructed to return at noon for the formal initiation ceremony.

Each new boy was appointed a "brother," a senior acolyte of around sixteen or seventeen, to serve as his mentor and guardian. Mine was waiting for me at the gate. He wore the same charcoal-gray robes as the Senior Priests, but with an additional white acolyte sash. I sneaked peeks as he spoke to my parents. He was tall, square-jawed, his heavy brows giving him a rather intense appearance.

He bowed first at my parents and then at me. "Welcome, young Oda. I am Senior Acolyte Akihito Fukuyama. Come with me. We have much to do on this auspicious day. You will see your parents later."

Fukuyama led me through the gate, up the monastery's paths, to a Head Temple back room, where I joined acolytes lined up behind the older monk who was ritualistically shaving the boys' heads. We were measured and dressed in acolyte robes, a white *kesa* patch-sash tied over the left shoulder of the gray robe. We were given our own sandalwood *juzu* prayer beads and a copy of the *Lotus Sutra* personally inscribed by the High Priest. I can still recall the feel of the razor against my head, the buzzing of the flies in the torrid heat, the feel of those silk robes against my trembling limbs.

The ceremony was performed in the courtyard of the Head Temple, on a dais built every year for the Acolyte Acceptance Ceremony. I knelt with the other boy-acolytes joining the priesthood that day. At half-past noon the seventy-seventh High Priest leaned into the microphone and announced my name. The prayer drums kept time with their beat as a chorus of monks in the background incanted the *Lotus Sutra*. I rose and went to the elevated platform and bowed to the High Priest. A dragonfly buzzed about his face but he did not blink, just went about the ritual with calm determination. I turned and knelt with my back toward him, looking out at the audience below.

The senior monks placed *shikimi* leaves on my head, and, as we had been taught, I held a piece of white paper horizontally across my chest. Sweat trickled down my back. The air was swollen with the shimmering heat and rhythmic chanting; below the platform, acolyte families, including my own, were dressed in their best clothes and holding cameras.

After a few prayers, the High Priest took a ceremonial knife and wordlessly pushed the *shikimi* leaves off my head. They fell with a flutter onto the white paper I held at my chest. With this simple ritual the High Priest had "cut" my worldly illusions—and I was an ordained Priest of the Headwater Sect.

After all the acolytes had completed the initiation rite, the High Priest brought the formal ceremony to a close. I looked across the platform at my mother, who was sitting in the front row below us. My parents bowed at me for the first time. It was a momentous occasion. I was now a Priest worthy of respect. I can still recall the way my father looked that day: how the sweat poured off his brow, the shininess of his gray suit, the blackness of his eyes as he thrice lowered his head to the floor in a sign of deepest respect and honor.

After the ceremony, the new acolytes were allowed to talk only a few minutes with their families, to say their goodbyes. I quickly went to my family's side. My father was blank-faced. Mother was uncharacteristically too emotional to talk, and she hid her mottled face, distorted by deep sorrow and soaring pride, behind an embroidered handkerchief she clutched before her mouth. Onii-san kept his head bowed, like he was too afraid to look in my direction. Before I knew what was going on, before I could properly say goodbye to Onii-san and my younger siblings, Senior Acolyte Fukuyama was at my side and making me turn my back on my family. This abrupt parting—it remains one of my deepest sufferings.

Fukuyama escorted me out of the courtyard, through the Head Temple's dark woods, along the Kappa-gawa, up to the long room assigned to eight of the new acolytes. It was a simple chamber at the back of the Temple of Everlasting Prayer, a "Little Temple" near the grounds' East Gate.

I was eleven years old and the ties to my family and my home, even to Katsurao, had been abruptly cut with a ritual knife and a simple cascade of *shikimi* leaves, for the word "priest" means "leaving home and entering not-home."

Reverend Hashimoto roused us at four a.m. Two junior priests banging gongs flanked him. He ordered us, in a clipped tone, to roll up our futons and dress in our robes. A third priest barred us from splashing water on our faces in the adjoining room of communal sinks. Still stupid with sleep, we were led into the adjacent Hall of Worship. On our knees before the Cluster of Jewels Mandala, we promptly started reciting the sixteenth chapter of the *Lotus Sutra* at 4:20 a.m.

To the uninitiated, this might appear like some form of hazing, but this early-morning prayer ritual was based on the soundest of Head Temple practices: it is best to pray to the Buddha in that halfway state between sleep and consciousness immediately after waking, for that is when our inner life is still open and alive with dreamlike possibilities, and the ego is still too weak to make the mind do its bidding.

We prayed for over an hour before Reverend Hashimoto finally allowed us to wash up and have breakfast. This, then, was how my life as a Priest at the Temple of Everlasting Prayer began. It wasn't too bad at first, for those early days were filled with acolyte cama-raderie forged in the heat of our rigid new schedule.

But that all changed the twelfth day after I entered the priest-hood. My duty that morning was to sweep the Temple of Ever-lasting Prayer's outer courtyard. The sun was rising for another scorching day. Carrion crows restlessly swooped in between the nearby trees, cawing their warnings, but I kept my head down and swept the dust to the *tam-tam* of the prayer drums and the nasal incantations of the Priests praying on the other side of the tem-ple's wooden walls.

Chief Priest Kawaguchi and Senior Acolyte Fukuyama sud-denly appeared in the courtyard. They were red-faced, yelling, and it took a few moments before I realized what they were tell-ing me. The family *ryokan* was on fire.

"Go with Fukuyama. Go!" cried Reverend Kawaguchi.

I dropped the broom and Fukuyama and I ran as fast as we could, through the forest, down along the Kappa-gawa, around the Head Temple, and out through the Buddha Entry Gate. It was eight kilometers to Katsurao from the central gate, and as I ran, heart pounding, I could see the fire and smoke rising up from the village, through the ginkgo forest.

When we finally reached the lower terraces of Katsurao, Fuku-yama and I were bent over and grasping our sides, desperately trying to catch our breath. But it was already over. What had been my home was nothing but a heap of charred earth and embers, water-soaked by fire hoses, still smoldering and smoking like some vision from the underworld. I walked stiff-legged around where the police and firemen had the inn's grounds taped off. Back and forth across the bridge I walked, trying to see the devastation from all possible angles, as if a new perspective would somehow help me process what had just occurred. My family was no more. Our entire history, all the earthly mementos of my ancestors, had been lovingly stored in that house. No longer. I was now truly without a home—in the realest sense, not just in priestly terms.

Villagers had lined up across the bridge. Every time I came through they wordlessly parted to let me pass. Fukuyama walked two steps behind me. Standing on the bridge, I saw two policemen in white jumpsuits bend over black lumps, poking at bone ash with their pens. This, I suddenly knew, was the last earthly remains of my family. I leaned over the bridge and threw up. Of the horrors of that day, it is the sound of my breakfast plopping into the Kappa-gawa that I recall most clearly.

According to what the investigators eventually pieced together, my father got up early that day, before my mother and brothers and sister had risen. He made his way to the work shed in the back of the inn, where he kept an emergency supply of gasoline for the generator. No one knows for sure what happened next. Perhaps the failing generator needed another round of fine-tuning and, in the process, an accident occurred. Or perhaps it was a deliberate act. It was never clear, not even when the official investigations were concluded. What I do know is that at some point my father knocked the gas canister over, and a spark, probably from his cigarette, hit the puddle. It could very well have been an accident. But, according to the forensic report, he was soaked in gasoline when the spark hit. This much was clear. But there was no note, no last communication. But Father never said much—ever. And so I will never be certain about what happened that day.

Japanese houses built in the 1800s were made entirely out of wood. The interior walls of Great-Grandfather's *ryokan* were fashioned from rice paper and the floor was made from tatami mats of woven straw. The inn, in short, was nothing but fuel for a fire, and within seconds the flames leapt to the main house from the

21

back shed. The fire warden said my mother and siblings, sleeping on the upper floor, would have had little chance to escape.

The inn and two other houses burned to the ground before the fire was under control. Nine villagers died that day. My only consolation is that our terrible karma did not consume our innocent guests sleeping in the 1920s addition attached by a covered walkway to Grandfather's original house. They were all spared. The wind was blowing west that day.

Our neighbor Mrs. Saito, sitting in the back of an ambulance, spotted me during one of my pacing loops around the scene's perimeter. She had lost her husband to the fire and still wore the soot-blackened kimono she had worn when fleeing her house. She tore off the oxygen mask when she saw me and followed me around the *ryokan*'s taped perimeter, screaming, "His back was on fire! He tried to run! But his back! His back! It was on fire!"

She kept on screeching this at me, over and over again. Senior Acolyte Fukuyama was only sixteen years old at the time, but he turned on the hysterical woman and slapped her, which seemed to have the desired effect. She was instantly silenced. The harried ambulance staff took her away. It was only later I realized that the old woman had not been talking about her husband, or my father, but about Onii-san. This was how he died, screaming in pain, his arms flailing, his back on fire.

Much later, as an adult, I finally came to understand that my father had suffered from clinical depression all his life. Every day of his existence he had fought the good fight, to put his clothes on and go to work in the inn he had inherited, until he could do so no more. In our village in those days, we did not know of such things, clinical depressions and psychotic breakdowns. But now, looking back to that summer, I am convinced my father knew he was losing his battle. Turning me over to the safe hands of the priesthood was his final act of love.

Why was it only me, not Daiki or the other children or even his wife, that my father decided to save? This question tortures me to this day. After many years of endlessly revisiting the events that led up to the tragedy, I have come to the conclusion that my father meant to end his own suffering that day, to take his life, but he never meant to also take the lives of his wife and children and innocent neighbors. I cannot believe such a thing. He loved them, too, in his silent way. I know this. It was simply the unpredictable nature of fire on a dry summer day that swept my family from this earth.

Chapter Two

It is difficult for me to recall the weeks that followed the fire. I know my constant crying kept the other acolytes up at night. There were bullies who made nasty comments, but there were also acts of kindness. One day, when I returned from prayers, I found a "weeping" origami crane sitting on my futon. A fellow acolyte had anonymously left this gift after preparing my bed.

Even the cool and remote Reverend Kawaguchi, Chief Priest at the Temple of Everlasting Prayer, took me under his wing in his way. Every morning for seven days following the fire he wordlessly led me to the Cluster of Jewels Mandala in the temple's Hall of Worship, to incant memorial prayers for my family. Five balsawood stupas were stacked against the prayer room's wall. Kawaguchi had personally painted each stupa with the name of one of my family members, the date and time of their death, surrounded by key phrases from the *Lotus Sutra* and a prayer for the realization of their enlightenment. At the end of the seven days Reverend Kawaguchi banged the last gong of the memorial prayers.

He swiveled on his knees so that we were face-to-face. The temple air was blue with incense smoke. "You must be asking, 'Why did this happen? Why? This must be a terrible dream.' But it is not a dream. It is reality. But remember this, Oda. Your head is the head of your parents. Your feet are the feet of your brothers. Your fingers are the fingers of your sister. If you devote your life to the Buddha, strive for enlightenment, all your efforts will be your family's efforts, and one day the Buddha will reunite you with your family in the Buddhaland."

At the time I did not understand what he was telling me. I was numb. It was also the extent of our entire grief-talk. I never again discussed the tragedy with anyone, for an eleven-year-old acolyte in a Buddhist temple is little different from an orphan in a state institution—coddling was neither offered nor expected.

But the priesthood did console me in its particular way. After the memorial prayers, Reverend Kawaguchi led me into the garden of the Little Temple, where we sat around a stone table under a hinoki cypress, the snowcapped Mount Nagata standing guard above us.

"We will have tea," he said.

The Temple of Everlasting Prayer in the east of the Head Temple grounds was built alongside the Kappa-gawa. At that time of day the light poured through the surrounding camphor tree and ginkgo forests, hitting the river's blue-stone water just so. Over the years I came to deeply treasure this view, a balm for my spirits when they were most troubled. But I will always remember, most of all, the first time I truly took in the landscape around the temple.

The Buddha's Elbow Waterfall stood in the forest, a white-water thrashing of stones that forced involuntary sighs, gulps, and gurgles from the river. Sake-colored froth turned at the water's surface and sent a drunken spray into the air, moistening nearby mats of green moss. The river eventually settled and the exposed rocks in the lower pool jutted up, round and pert, like stone breasts. The water was extremely low due to the unusual heat of the summer, and I remember seeing the *ayu* making rings at the surface, searching for oxygen.

Just meters from the back of the temple the river fanned out into a large glass-topped pool dappled by fallen leaves, before bending gently around Monk's Head. The river gathered pace again, bending around the big rock, before heading roughly over the narrows, where the next waterfall exhaled a new set of prayers into the air.

Such prayers came continuously from within and without. The

junior priests and acolytes were in their second recitation of the *Lotus Sutra,* and through the temple's walls we could hear the muffled hum of their rhythmic chant, the *tam-tam* of the prayer drums. The priests were joined in their incantations by Believers who came at all hours to the Temple of Everlasting Prayer, for it was in this temple that the *Lotus Sutra* was continuously chanted, like falling water, by revolving priests, young and old, every day, for centuries.

On that final day of my family's formal memorial prayers, Senior Acolyte Fukuyama brought us tea by the river. The Chief Priest urged him to sit down beside us under the hinoki cypress, and for some time the only sounds were those of the river, the monks' praying in the background, and the occasional slurp as one of us bent down over our blue-enamel teacups.

Eventually, however, Kawaguchi and Fukuyama began to talk. "Hot weather is drying up the river," said the Chief Priest. "Water very low."

"Yes."

"I am reminded of the ancient poem by Iio Sōgi."

"I cannot recall it."

> *"However low one may be*
> *it is in holding oneself in sway*
> *that is imperative."*

Senior Acolyte Fukuyama sighed in appreciation. "But still," he finally said, "I prefer a bit of humor. Kobayashi Issa—

> *Tub to tub*
> *The whole journey—*
> *Just hub-bub."*

Reverend Kawaguchi smiled. "Yes. This poem is very fine."

In that moment—sitting under the cypress, the breeze sweeping yellow pollen across the river's pooled surface, the air laced with the priests' poetic murmurs—a belief within me took hold with such force that I involuntarily shivered. I was just a boy, true, but in the hellish aftermath of my family's destruction, I was visited by a conviction that a clearing filled with Tranquil Light was waiting for me somewhere, and that one day I would find my way to this clearing, this safe haven patiently awaiting my arrival.

I clung to this vision during everything that followed over the subsequent thirty years, particularly on the darkest of days. Now, looking back, I think this unshakable faith rose from the hum of prayer that had filled me from the morning's memorial incantations, from the scenic beauty of the river and the mountains before me, but it also drew force, most distinctly, from the poetry the priests had recited.

Never before had I heard people talk in this way. My family were innkeepers, and though they read poetry on occasion, it was a revelation to hear this sort of learned talk. My eyes, ears, and heart were for the first time opened to the healing powers of poetry, which I swore would, from that day forward, become an integral part of my own life. To be a priest so calmly able to sum up the emotions of human existence in a few painted words, this appeared to me, even at that young age, as the most worthwhile ambition a person could possibly have. And I instinctively knew it was through such learned efforts I would find the forest clearing that was awaiting me somewhere.

But I can also recall how I made the conscious and forceful decision, at that very same moment, never to cry again. I determinedly locked the tragedy of my family away in the deepest chamber I could find, as if it all had happened to a different person in a different world.

My new life beckoned.

The old life of Katsurao was dead.

The routine I followed as an acolyte had been established over centuries, and for the next seven years it never deviated by one micron. After the 4:20 a.m. prayers we had our first meal of the day, followed by temple chores, such as sweeping the temple courtyard or collecting fresh *shikimi* leaves or conducting a round of ritual *Lotus Sutra* incantations in the Hall of Worship. We were then marched down to the Priesthood Instruction Center for the seven a.m. lessons in Buddhist doctrine. We broke four hours later for lunch in the long hall attached to the Head Temple, which was then followed, depending on the day, by painting, calligraphy, math, poetry, history, music, and martial arts. The final instruction of the day was in the Debating Hall, when we were challenged to verbally spar over a doctrinal point heard in the morning. Back at our Little Temple, we bathed, said evening prayers, and ate dinner. No sooner had we gone to bed, it seemed, than came another four a.m. wake-up call. Every day followed the identical routine.

Our principal teacher, Reverend Tanaka, looked benign, round as a plump plum. He was in fact as sharp-tongued as Mother and had many distasteful personal habits, including, when acolytes had their heads down over the sacred texts, rooting energetically around in his nose and studying the results. For this reason my friend, Acolyte Kenta Kashimoto, nicknamed our instructor Macaque Tanaka, sending us acolytes into peals of laughter as he mimicked our instructor's habit of digging in his ears for wax, which he would then endlessly roll into balls between thumb and forefinger.

Reverend Tanaka's mission was, of course, to drill well past the simple Buddhist fables of our childhood, and no drill officer of the Imperial Japanese Army was more exacting than our teacher. "And here," our instructor said dryly, tapping the wall charts with his wooden pointer, "on this branch of the royal family, we find Devadatta, Lord Shakyamuni's evil cousin. He repeatedly tried to kill the Buddha, including, on one occasion, getting an elephant drunk in the hope it would trample the Truth-Seeker. In this way Devadatta brought great karmic suffering down upon himself. *Immense* suffering."

He introduced into our lectures the concept of the Eternal

Buddha, present in all beings, as distinctly separate from the historical Buddha, Lord Shakyamuni. A couple of flicks of earwax later, and he was explaining how Lord Shakyamuni's teachings were passed on orally for four hundred years before they were laid down in the writings known as sutras. "For the next year we shall study the Pāli Canon, the set of early sutras that spread south and established southern Asia as a stronghold for the saffron-robed monks of Hīnayāna Buddhism."

Our instructor openly loathed such "primitive" branches of the Buddhist diaspora. "Hīnayāna Buddhists believe enlightenment is achieved by following up to five hundred precepts," Tanaka sneered. "Imagine this. The Hīnayāna mendicant purifies himself over several lifetimes, barred from watching a dance or listening to music, barred from sleeping on an elevated bed, barred from eating at 'inappropriate' times of the day. Eventually, they claim, the mendicant is enlightened in a burst of fireworks, catapulted into a permanent state of perfection."

Reverend Tanaka made a face and then spun into a martial arts move, slamming his pointer down on the desk of an acolyte nodding off. We all jumped in alarm. "Of course, this severe Hīnayāna practice meant only ascetic monks living a rigid monastic discipline could possibly become enlightened," our teacher continued. "So what about it, Oda? What about the lay Believers? Are they barred from enlightenment? Is this really what Lord Shakyamuni taught?"

"No, Sensei," I stammered.

"Correct. He did not. Hīnayāna Buddhism is a *provisional* teaching."

I won't recount in its painful entirety the doctrinal drilling Reverend Tanaka put us through, but suffice it to say he then had us track, in color-coded maps projected onto the wall, the Greater Vehicle movement known as Mahāyāna Buddhism. Reverend Tanaka stood next to my desk, peering down at me with his furrowed brows, repeating again and again that the Greater

Vehicle faithful knew the true Bodhisattva, or Buddha, vowed *not* to enter Nirvana, despite striving to become enlightened, and instead swore to stay in this world of suffering to help others.

Compassion was the highest virtue of the Mahāyāna tradition, he insisted, even though we all noticed Reverend Tanaka was conspicuously short of compassion for any other Mahāyāna sect but our own. It was his considered opinion that they were mis-leading mankind from the true path of enlightenment and that they should all be burnt on a funeral pyre. And so he rushed vis-ibly upset through the doctrines of rival Buddhist sects, as if any extended time spent in their doctrinal presence would corrupt our impressionable young beings and send us all, most notably him, tumbling into the Avichi Hell.

Of course, a few acolytes in the lecture hall had relatives who were followers of the Nembutsu and Jōdo-shū, rival Mahāyāna sects, and when Macaque Tanaka discovered this he annihilated the Pure Land sects—and their possible spies in the lecture hall—with all manner of doctrinal insults.

It was the Zen sects, however, that provoked Reverend Tanaka's greatest ire, and when an acolyte dared to express even mild admi-ration for a Zen principle, our teacher's face turned an alarming beetroot. Acolyte Kashimoto so enjoyed provoking our teacher in this way, and often asked in an innocent voice, "Is not the Zen phrase 'A flower falls, even though we love it; and a weed grows, even though we do not love it' revealing of a profound Buddhist principle?"

Macaque Tanaka would become quite apoplectic. When we were finally and sufficiently well versed in Buddhism's squadrons of wayward sects, however, Reverend Tanaka had us bore down into the specific doctrine of the Headwater Sect, and in the safe haven of our own doctrine, our teacher visibly relaxed. The dark-ness of his mood lifted and he was able to sum up our doctrine with something approaching a light heart. We were all much relieved.

Tanaka told us with immense pride that the Buddha of the Infinite Past, as predicted in the *Lotus Sutra*, finally appeared on earth in ninth-century Japan. He appeared, in fact, in the worldly form of the Headwater Sect's founding High Priest, and, inscribing his life and enlightenment in the Cluster of Jewels Mandala, he preached that we could all become enlightened in our *current state of humanity* simply by reciting the *Lotus Sutra* before this Stupa of Worship.

We, the acolytes, were rather relieved to discover Headwater Sect Priests had no behavioral precepts to follow—we could eat meat (in moderation), engage with the world, drink alcohol, marry (this induced much sniggering)—precisely because enlightenment was found in our imperfect state of humanity. This was all quite different from other Buddhist sects, of course, where the indulging of passions and killing of animals for food were karmically frowned upon. But no sooner had I digested this news with relief than a new wave of anxiety washed over me. If we remained imperfect, burdened by our karma, what precisely was enlightenment? I wondered. I couldn't reconcile these inherent contradictions. Acolyte Kashimoto, noticing the puzzled look on my face, leaned over, and whispered, "Imagine a closed oyster, rough and ugly, suddenly opening up to reveal an exquisite pearl long held inside. This is how it is. The Buddha nature is there inside us, always, and can appear at any moment."

"The Eternal Teachings are immutable," our teacher roared from the front of the room. "As the official guardians of Eternal Teachings it is your responsibility as Priests to prevent any dilution of our eleven-hundred-year-old practice. The secular forces of our times are great. Fight back! Resist like great samurai warriors all attempts to bend our Eternal Teachings to the transitory demands of contemporary culture!"

And so, by the time I was ready to attend university at age eighteen, I was a fully indoctrinated and committed Priest of the Headwater Sect, sworn to uphold the timeless tenets of our faith.

I had two friends at the time. That first morning of prayers at the Little Temple I glanced to the right and found Akihito Fukuyama, the sixteen-year-old senior acolyte assigned to look after me, kneeling close by. One hand was entwined in *juzu* prayer beads and held ramrod-straight before his mouth, while the other held up the liturgy we were reciting. I remember how strong his voice was, how straight his back, and how he ever so slightly turned his head in my direction when the Senior Priests weren't looking, and blinked slowly and deliberately with both eyes, in this way sending me a silent greeting from across the temple floor.

Reverend Fukuyama was famous at the Head Temple for two reasons. He was deposited at the gates of the monastery when he was six, the day after his parents were killed in a car accident. Shortly thereafter he was found fidgeting during a painfully long recitation of the *Lotus Sutra* in the Great Hall of Worship. Reverend Tanaka leaned over and gave the boy a sobering smack on the head with his fan.

There the matter should have ended. But ten minutes later Reverend Tanaka lost his place in the *Lotus Sutra* recitation, distracted by another fidgeting acolyte. The six-year-old Fukuyama, hearing the elderly Priest fumble the prayers, rose from his spot on the temple floor, pulled over a footstool, climbed up on it, and then brought his own fan smartly down on the back of his superior's head.

The look of utter shock on Reverend Tanaka's face made the other Head Temple monks roar with laughter—and instantly became part of temple lore. It was universally agreed the child had given his superior a brilliant lesson in "divine karmic retribution"; after being punished for his impudence, Fukuyama was marked by the Senior Priests as a boy of particular promise and steered toward the most rigorous training program.

They were not disappointed. At the age of twenty-one, during a round of formal religious debates, Reverend Fukuyama found himself pitted against a senior and much-revered Priest of a rival Pure Land sect. The distinguished Nembutsu scholar ended his two-hour explication on why the Pure Land's *Amitābha Sutra* was superior to the Headwater Sect's *Lotus Sutra* with much rhetorical style. I was in the audience at the time, holding my breath, silently praying that my friend might avoid a total disaster. Reverend Fukuyama stood slowly, without any sign of nerves, and said, "The honorable Priest's learned comments remind me of the four Buddhist monks who were meditating when the prayer flag on the monastery roof began to flap. The first monk interrupted his meditation to state, 'The flag is flapping.' The next monk corrected, 'Wind is flapping.' The third shook his head and said, 'Mind is flapping.' It was the wisest monk who finally remarked, 'Mouths are flapping!' "

Even the Pure Land Priests sitting in the Debating Hall burst into uproarious laughter, but abruptly stopped when Reverend Fukuyama then proceeded to convincingly use the *Amitābha Sutra*'s own ambiguous phrasing to suggest there was a superior sutra, in the form of the *Lotus Sutra*, still waiting to be preached. He destroyed the famous Nembutsu scholar, in short, and in that moment Reverend Fukuyama's future among the highest ranks of our priesthood was guaranteed.

The point is, Reverend Fukuyama, this gifted Priest, was my personal guardian and could not have helped me more if he had been my own Senior Brother. During one of my most difficult periods, for example, Reverend Tanaka spent months explaining to us acolytes the "ultimate reality" precept of our faith: that the *Lotus Sutra*, properly interpreted, revealed our enlightenment was found in *this* world, in reality, and that the Buddha emerges in the lives of common men and women engaged in everyday life. Enlightenment was not found, as many of our rival Buddhist sects claimed, in some mythic land where perfect human beings paraded around emanating light.

I simply could not get my head around the idea. How could enlightenment possibly be contained, however fleetingly, in the "reality" of everyday life? This life was filled with horrible suffering, irreconcilable to anything I imagined enlightenment to be. Old Reverend Tanaka, determined we would understand this important point, stood before the blackboard and endlessly stressed how important it was we recognize the "ultimate reality" before us—but the concept would not penetrate. I sat in the lecture hall like a blank-faced turnip.

Concern about my grasp of the study material was heightened shortly thereafter by an incident that occurred in Administration Alley. It was a Friday afternoon. We had just come out of our painting class—my favorite subject, besides poetry—and were walking in a clutch to the Debating Hall for our final lesson of the day. My mind was wandering, as usual, when I noticed one of the acolytes up ahead put his arm around another boy and start whispering into his friend's ear. I saw him snigger as the words "his father . . ." distinctly reached me.

After the Katsurao fire I stuck to myself and hardly talked to the other acolytes. I was painfully shy and timid. But that day, before I knew what I was doing, I pushed my way through the crowd and jumped the senior acolyte from behind. I grabbed him under the chin and yanked back his head. The boy yelled, teetered sideways, his arms flailing as he tried to pull me off. We finally hit the side of the library and collapsed in a pile of robes.

The boy had not been talking about me. Or my family. I had concocted the entire scenario out of nothing. As his friend testified during my disciplinary hearing, the older acolyte had been talking about his own father, a Headwater Sect Priest from Sapporo who would shortly be visiting the Head Temple on official business. It had nothing to do with me or my family's troubles.

I had, in short, entirely misread the reality before me. This was the first time I had done so in a serious way, and I had no idea that this habit of jumping to conclusions about the people around me would become the lifelong bane of my existence and lead to much suffering, for me and others.

But this knowledge would come to me only later in life. At the time I lived in ignorance, and my punishment for attacking the boy consisted of hauling the ice-cold temple water from the Pure Water Stone Well for an entire month. One day, on the way back to the Temple of Everlasting Prayer, carrying the water used only in religious rituals, I bumped into Senior Acolyte Fuku-yama. We walked together through the woods for some time, finally approaching the path that led down to the ponds built by the thirty-fifth High Priest. Fukuyama had clearly heard about my troubles. He smiled, like Onii-san might, and said, "Have you seen the lotus ponds?"

I timidly shook my head.

"Come. It is my favorite spot on the entire Head Temple grounds."

"Reverend Hashimoto is expecting me to bring the water," I whispered.

"He won't begrudge us a little side trip. Come. If he questions us, we will simply say it was my fault. I insisted you join me."

We descended the path, entering a clearing where the lotus ponds sat in a stone cradle. Benches had been carved out of the wall of rock to the east, and the brownish pond was choked with blooming lotus flowers. From the flat water pads of green emerged large flowers with pink petals and yellow stamens, spiky purple petals with orange interiors, and, my personal favor-ite, fat-faced flowers of pure white or cream. The frogs, after a shocked silence, proceeded to welcome our arrival with a chorus of joyous croaks.

Fukuyama and I sat wordlessly for some time in this stone basin of flowers, watching the dragonflies and hummingbirds flit, until an involuntary sigh escaped my lips. It was as if a weight had just pressed against my ribs and forced my lungs to billow.

"Seido-san," said my guardian. "Observe this lotus flower blooming before us in the pond. If you study it hard, really look, you will see that below this surface picture, it is the mud and rot of a stagnant pond that is actually producing the lotus flower's pretty bloom."

He bent to pick up a slab of green feldspar, which he turned over and over in his hands. "Right now," he continued lightly, "it must feel like you are stuck in rot and mud. It is almost unbear-able. But trust in the Buddha. It will be precisely this muck that one day will help you burst to the surface in a stunning display of colorful petals."

In this way Fukuyama quietly became my friend and protector. I had one other. Acolyte Kenta Kashimoto and I were assigned to the same room in the Temple of Everlasting Prayer on the day of our initiation, but we didn't become friends immediately. Kashimoto was handsome and well liked. I, in turn, was largely shunned after the fire due to my tendency to follow long periods of inscrutable silence with angry outbursts. One day, after Reverend Tanaka brutally and publicly savaged me in class, Acolyte Kashimoto slid up alongside me as I was making my dejected way back to our temple.

"Macaque Tanaka seems to have it out for you."

"*Hai.*"

"Well, then. We must help karmic ripples reach their intended shores."

Before I could ask him what he meant, Kashimoto had me off the mountain path, into the woods, looking for the tiny rust-brown tree frogs that in the mating season could be found sitting on rotting logs and leaves, stupefied with lust. We caught a half dozen that afternoon and safely stored them in a perforated tin back at the Little Temple.

Reverend Tanaka was a monk greatly partial to rituals and every day he brought a lidded bamboo box to class. When the hour hand approached eleven—and we were reciting by rote sutra passages we might need during the evening's debate—Reverend Tanaka reached for his bamboo box, popped open the lid, and pulled out a bowl of *nattō*, the fermented soybeans served at breakfast. The elderly Priest then put his head down, and, chopsticks in hand, shoveled the foul-smelling beans into his mouth at an alarming speed.

The day after Kashimoto and I visited the woods, Reverend Tanaka as usual snapped open the lid of his box and grabbed his bowl of *nattō*, only to find a half dozen tree frogs, almost the exact color and size of the soybeans, inching their way up his hand and arm. His scream, and the sight of his bowl going airborne before smashing on the floor, made it quite impossible for us to continue our lessons. Macaque Tanaka never found out who played this prank on him, so he punished all of us with extra sutra passages to learn by heart. But all the acolytes agreed the punishment was well worth the entertainment, and, it must be said, from then on Reverend Tanaka opened his bamboo box only with the utmost caution.

This act of rebellion against Macaque Tanaka sealed my friendship with Reverend Kashimoto, and from then on he and Reverend Fukuyama were the only true friends I had in the world. They were the Daiki and Yuji of my Head Temple life, and together they got me through the dark years of my adolescence.

I remember, in particular, a day when I was about fifteen years old. Dozens of acolytes were in the courtyard of the Priesthood Instruction Center. Macaque Tanaka was teaching *The Sutra of Innumerable Meanings* and we had a ten-minute break before our late morning lecture was to resume.

I was sitting in the shade of the eaves, engrossed in a collection of "dew poems"—haiku focusing on the transient nature of life— when something compelled me to look up. The courtyard was jammed with acolytes releasing pent-up energy and the very air shimmered with their laughter and raucous yelling. They wrestled one another, piggybacked, played tag. It appeared to me like they did not have a care in the world.

Food was frying inside the Head Temple's kitchen and smoky puffs of garlic, onions, and ginger were gently rolling under the temple's eaves in our direction. That was when my "separateness" suddenly struck me, as if a permanent cloud obstructing my view were blown away, and in the roar of that playground noise I finally understood I was not like the other boys. And never would be.

Kashimoto was sitting next to me, talking loudly and laughing alongside another boy. I gripped his arm and he turned. I think he saw, in my wild look, how afraid I was of the thoughts in my head. He smiled, playfully rapped my shaved head with his fan, and commanded, in a mock-imperial Senior Priest voice, "Get out of there, Oda!"

A little humor, a little human contact—that was all it took. I forgot the importance of such things for a long stretch of my life, but it is exactly like the poem by Issa says:

> *Heedless of the dew*
> *That marks our closing day*
> *We bind ourselves to others.*

Chapter Three

Shortly after my eighteenth birthday the Head Temple sent me to Tokyo. I had always enjoyed painting, but at age thirteen, when thumbing through books in the Head Temple's library, I came upon a high-quality reproduction of *Catching a Catfish with a Gourd*. It was a mysterious, mist-shrouded painting by Taiko Josetsu, a Chinese immigrant who brought a unique method of Buddhism-infused landscape painting to Japan at the end of the fourteenth century. I was mesmerized by Josetsu's *suibokuga* ink style, and from then on poured all my youthful energy into learning this ancient craft.

Reverend Hashimoto, my academic advisor, urged me to pursue this interest, for which I appeared to have great passion and some small talent. He argued that the advanced skills I would learn at prestigious Tokyo University of the Arts would help fill a vocational need at the Head Temple, increasing the chances that I would be brought back to Mount Nagata for a permanent posting, rather than ordered to some bland temple elsewhere in the country. This appealed to me greatly, for the holy mountain was the rock I clung to in this tenuous world, and so the direction of my academic career was settled.

It was karma that I was one of just twenty-five students nationwide picked that year to join the elite Japanese Painting Unit at the Tokyo University of the Arts. It was there that I became a specialist in *sansuiga*, a rigid form of religious monochrome landscape painting usually devoid of all human representation. The snowcapped Mount Nagata, the Kappa-gawa, and the Temple of Everlasting Prayer in the forest clearing at the very base of the sacred mountain were my inspiration, and I became adept at re-creating their calming influence in the crowded bustle of Tokyo. Guided by my university instructors, I helped revitalize the neglected *sansuiga* painting style with contemporary brushstrokes and color techniques, and was, as a result, invited to teach my technique at the Anglo-Asian Arts Center, a British-Japanese cultural exchange program that took place every summer at my university and at the Slade School of Fine Art at University College London.

My experience teaching the foreigners visiting Tokyo in the cultural exchange program was not a success. The European students were bovine at best, I thought, and the senior administrator did not take it at all well when I presented him with my ten-point plan on how he should restructure the program to make it more effective. I was not asked back after my second year. But it was through living in extremely close quarters with loud and drunk English students, and through the program's language immersion lessons, that I picked up the rudiments of the English language. It was my private English tutor—paid for by the Head Temple but supplied by University College London—who, noticing my love of poetry, introduced me to the Romantic poets William Blake and Lord Byron. More specifically, the gray-haired tutor introduced me to Byron's great poem "She Walks in Beauty."

Alone in my room, I read and reread the beautiful poems of Byron, Keats, and Blake, like a parched man searching for water in the desert. And these verses spurred me to continue my English lessons throughout my university years and beyond.

Byron's romantic poems especially fanned alive emotions and hungers long suppressed by the austere life of the monk, and in the fall of my junior year I found myself standing before the monochrome painting *Reading in a Bamboo Grove,* which hangs at the Tokyo National Museum, trying to learn by copying the great work. Painted in 1446 by the Zen priest Tenshō Shūbun, this revered painting is a masterpiece of mist, mountains, and tree silhouettes. But I was despondent by the end of the morning, for my study sketches fell far short of the required skill, and I dragged myself to the museum canteen in the vague hope that a meal would revive me for a second attack in the afternoon.

The museum's dining hall was hot and stuffy and overcrowded. It took a while before I found a free table squashed in the corner. As I morosely chewed over my canteen lunch box, two attractive women stepped up to my table with their trays. "Excuse us. Are these seats free? Every table seems to be taken."

"*Hai*. Please. The seats are free."

It was so bold for these young women to engage a stranger in this way—but I was mesmerized. The more audacious of the two girls wore black patent-leather boots almost up to her knees, a short black skirt, a ruffled polka-dot blouse, and a red-haired wig with long tresses tied back with ribbons. She had a very pretty white face, with slanted-paint eyes like edible *mochi* cakes. The other appeared more conservative in her long woolen sweater and gold-chain purse. But together they dazzled with Tokyo sophistication, smelled delicious, and, in their presence, I blushed and looked down at my tray. After observing me from the corner of her eye, Red Wig said to me, "Cheer up."

Her friend giggled.

"*Daijoubu desu.*"

I said this, "There's no problem," with an aloofness that comes from being shy. She paused a beat, before dryly replying, "*Hotto shitta!*"—"What a relief."

This time I laughed alongside her friend.

The woman then lifted her chopsticks and very delicately placed a salt-pickled plum on the tip of her tongue. Never before had I seen such a sensual gesture.

So this was how I met Akemi, a name appropriately meaning "lively and beautiful." It turned out Akemi was also a student at the Tokyo University of the Arts, but in the much larger fashion design school. Her father was a high-level banker at Nomura Securities and she was raised in the city's wealthy Denenchōfu neighborhood. I wore civilian clothes while at the university, so when I finally revealed I was not only in the elite Japanese Painting Unit but a Headwater Sect Priest from Fukushima Prefecture, Akemi's eyes widened with interest.

The idea of conquering a provincial Buddhist monk was, I suspect, an amusing challenge to this bored Tokyoite, and from that day forward Akemi reveled in initiating me into the "sophisticated" life I never even knew existed. She frequently appeared without warning at the university's fine arts studios, where I was working late into the night. Pushing open the sliding glass doors of the studio, she cried out, *"Anata-nashi-ja ikite yuke-nai!"* Her catchphrase, "I can't live without you," was delivered with such irony even I knew she was teasing me and probably meant the opposite.

When I called out my position from behind the many easels and canvases obscuring her view, she came back to where I was hiding and covered my face with kisses. She made me put down my brush and shrug on my coat, before dragging me out for a night on the town. We usually went to the red-light district, Kabukichō, and drank to the small hours. Our favorite bar was called the Emergency Room, where waitresses dressed as nurses served us drinks called "influenza" out of beakers and test tubes. Sometimes she took me dancing. I, of course, had never before danced in this way—in a fashionable Tokyo nightclub, no less— and I flapped my arms about the dance floor like a farmyard rooster trying to mount a hen. Akemi and her friends doubled over with laughter.

Akemi was obsessed with all things American and on some occasions she insisted we join a group of like-minded devotees at the Student Union, where we watched subtitled Hollywood films from the 1930s and 1940s. Afterward we retired to a nearby bar to practice our broken English, our knees touching under the swiveling stools. Martinis before us, I'd light Akemi's cigarette and whisper, "Wassa doll like you doing in gin joint like this?" This Japanese-English pidgin was apparently very satisfactory, for she would seductively flutter her eyelashes, rewarding me with a Japanese facsimile of Lauren Bacall's famously smoky look, and say, "You A-okay."

In the early hours of the morning, we often went to the food stalls around the Tsukiji fish market, to eat breakfast as a stream of sixty thousand workers ended their night shift. I remember teetering unsteadily atop the stool of a tiny Tsukiji alley restaurant, shoveling grilled mackerel and turnip into my mouth as I watched the sun just starting to rise over the tile-roofed food shacks. The market workers in blue overalls and white boots lined up for their meal of fish cakes in broth, and when the first wave of city workers finally emerged for their long subway commutes to high-rise offices, Akemi took me back to her studio—and to her bed.

My eyes, as they say, were opened to life. I recall one rainy afternoon, after spending the night with Akemi, when the two of us were doing our homework side by side in her flat. I looked up from my sketch pad, where I was working on a study for a larger painting, and saw Akemi on the bed, with her little feet drawn up against her body, her pad of fashion sketches lying flat against her knees. She was concentrating hard on her work.

Akemi wore faded blue jeans and a red Tokyo University of the Arts sweatshirt, no makeup, and the refined beauty of her face—the way the rain-splattered light from the window illuminated the porcelain sheen of her skin—hit me the way lightning strikes Mount Nagata. I was hopelessly and helplessly in love, the moment so powerful that I was moved to recite aloud a poem by the eighteenth-century nun-poetess Kaga no Chiyo:

> *"Moon flowers!*
> *When a woman's skin*
> *is revealed."*

"You provincials," Akemi said from the bed, without looking up from her sketch. "Chiyo-ni's poems are mush. Overly sentimental."

I should have known then. She gave me many clues. But I did not want to see. One evening while drinking in the leather arm- chairs of the Roppongi Prince Hotel lounge, I asked Akemi, in the middle of my senior year, if, after we were married, she would return with me to the Head Temple in Fukushima Prefecture. Her face went blank before she finally replied we should really move on to the next bar. I never got a straight answer that evening. But that night I dreamt I opened a closet door previously closed and was overrun by millions of cockroaches scurrying out of the dark.

The next party we attended, Akemi disappeared into the bath- room with a few of her friends, and when she finally came out again, she was jittery and sniffling. When I asked her what she had been doing, she snapped, *"Nani-yo?"*—"What do you want?"

Akemi began taking more and more drugs, partying at an ever more frenzied pace, and we began to argue, even in pub- lic. It is painful to recall, but she once threw a lighter at me in the streets behind Shinjuku Station. The crowds coming out of the nearby bars gawked and laughed and yelled at us to "cool it." I was humiliated, upset, and had no idea what was happening. It was one night, not long after this public brawl, that Akemi appeared at my studio and took my arm. Her pupils were dilated, sparkling with an unnatural intensity, and she whispered in my ear, "Come. I have a surprise. Time we flew to the next level."

That evening Akemi led me down a set of dark stairs in Kabukichō. A man who looked like a gangster was standing guard at the steel door in the alleyway basement. Inside, in a rubber- ized room, a woman in a schoolgirl's outfit was sitting behind a glass desk. "Welcome," she said, bowing repeatedly. "We have your room ready. All is prepared. Your hostess will come to you shortly."

As we walked hand in hand down the basement corridor smell- ing of hot rubber, I glanced into a doorway on the left and saw an elderly naked man stretched out on a doctor's table, just as two "nurses" were gently easing shut the door. I realized then we were in a *toruko-buro,* a notorious type of Tokyo "bathhouse."

I dropped Akemi's hand in horror and demanded, "What are we doing here?" She sneered, "*Yowa-mushi!* Where are your balls? You want to marry me? Know me first . . . Now. Are you coming?" I turned and walked back the way we had come. The door of a chamber opened somewhere behind me, down the long hall, and a hostess called out, "Welcome, mistress!"

The girlfriend I had imagined was not really there.

She was an illusion, someone I had made up out of thin air. It was entirely my fault, of course, for Akemi had been clear all along about the kind of person she was. It was I who had mis-read her.

The shock of this revelation was so great I took to bed with a fever. Life outside the Head Temple grounds suddenly appeared deeply threatening and dangerous. I pondered, with great anguish, how I had not missed a morning or evening prayer since I was eleven years old, until I met Akemi, that is. Then, with so many late nights drinking, I skipped prayers, allowing the very lifeline that had saved me as a child to slip from my hands.

No more, I vowed. I rose from my futon, got down on my knees before my dorm room altar, lit a candle and three sticks of incense, and prayed fervently for the next several hours, search-ing for the Buddha's wisdom.

Where was my path? What was I to do?

The voice that came to me in that tiny Tokyo dorm room was clear and bright: Turn your back on this life. Return to sacred Mount Nagata a committed monk, and devote your life whole-heartedly to the Buddha, to protecting the Headwater Sect, and to the safe pleasures of poetry and painting.

This is the life that was ordained for you.

Two weeks later Reverend Hashimoto rang me in Tokyo and offered me his former position of Second Priest at the Temple of Everlasting Prayer. I held my breath. The only requirement demanded by the Office of Head Temple Administration was that I also assume the duties of junior arts instructor for all incoming acolytes. It was a fortuitous occurrence for both of us, he continued, as he himself was finally getting promoted to Chief Priest at his own temple in Kyoto. "Well, Oda? What do you say?" I accepted the offer on the spot. Its very arrival, at that critical moment, was surely an omen that I was on the right path. It seemed so clear to me—at the time.

At the age of twenty-three, after graduating from Tokyo University of the Arts with honors, I returned with suitcase in hand to Mount Nagata. I moved into a modest room in the back of my old temple, and then immediately went next door, to the Hall of Worship, to kneel before the Cluster of Jewels Mandala and offer my life up to the Buddha. Every other diversion I swore to push away, much as I had done after the great fire.

During the next sixteen years I worked diligently at fulfilling my Head Temple duties, eventually rising to master teacher of the arts. These years are marked in my memory by a parade of acolytes shuffling endlessly before my eyes. Each year I stood before the latest crop of wide-eyed novices and demanded from them their very best. "Paint as if you are praying," I told them. "Take up your paintbrush with the same sincerity and pure spirit as you would take up your prayer beads. I do not say this lightly. Any of you foolish enough not to bring this sincere attitude to our lessons will be dealt with severely."

Wholly dedicated to my work and the precise rituals of the temple, I stuck to myself as I had when I was an adolescent. I lived solely for my soothing and predictable Head Temple schedule and the solitude I found in the breezy backwoods of the East Gate. The wooded slope where I resided *was* the Buddhaland, of this I was sure, and it provided me with solace and respite.

Promptly at four o'clock every day, for example, I took tea by myself in the back of the Temple of Everlasting Prayer, under the great mountain's watchful gaze. That was when snow monkeys with sad eyes and sore-looking noses the color of inflamed skin clattered down from the highland forest to feed on the sweet riverside berries and bark across the river from my room. I sat by myself, a pot of green tea at my side, watching this family of macaques gossip and chatter and dine voraciously on shredded leaves, in between picking their noses and scratching their bums. At such moments I was at peace, I would say. And there were other rewards. The Head Temple officially commended me for establishing the English Romantic Poets Association, an acolyte club where English, however broken, was the only language allowed to be spoken. On such morsels of Head Temple recognition I lived.

It must be said, however, that the acolytes themselves had their own view of my teaching abilities. One afternoon, after berating the class for its slovenly execution of a brush technique, I moved to the sink in the studio's alcove to wash some brushes. Two acolytes were talking among themselves around the corner, not aware I was within earshot, and I overheard one fellow disgustedly say to his friend, "Young Oda is just old Tanaka with a paintbrush." I won't pretend this remark didn't sting at first, but the ego-driven mind is adept at neutralizing criticism. No one could say Reverend Tanaka did not care deeply about instructing his students, I reasoned, and so it wasn't long before I was wearing this unflattering comparison as a badge of honor.

Nor was I popular with the general priesthood. There was a great push at the time to drag the Head Temple into the twenty-first century, and when a yellow-awninged gift shop of poured cement was unceremoniously plopped down on the Head Temple's ancient cobblestone courtyard without any eye to aesthetics, I began to publicly and vocally admonish the ambitious Head Temple administrators who, at the time, were aggressively funneling in pilgrims by the busload and pushing such "modernist" changes. There was something off-center about this gift shop smacked down in front of the Head Temple's Great Hall of Worship, and I felt it was my Buddhist duty to speak out, reminding my fellow monks that we served the Buddha, not worldly power and influence, not fistfuls of yen.

One November morning, after I began my public campaign, I came into Administration Alley through the covered archway between the Head Temple kitchen and the library. There was a heavy fog that morning; I was wrapped tight in my winter robe, lost in thought. The only sound in the thick mist came from my wooden clogs clattering on the stone, ricocheting in the archway chamber. Three looming figures appeared suddenly before me in the gray and wet fog, cutting off my passage. I recognized them instantly. They were well-connected Priests of long lineage who had been in my acolyte year but were rapidly promoted to positions of considerable power through their family connections.

"Oda," said one. "We want a word."

The Senior Priests surrounded me and in no uncertain terms ordered me to know my place and pipe down with my criticisms. Important decisions should be left to the more knowledgeable administrative priests; the "fish market atmosphere" I so derided was precisely what drew in new pilgrims and a steady stream of income. I should, in short, be quiet and grateful and just stick to the responsibilities of a lowly art instructor if I cared to keep even this position.

"Is our meaning clear?"

My acolyte years, when I was always the odd one out, distinctly separate from all the others, came flooding back. That unsettling feeling—that I was not like the rest, never would be, and didn't actually belong at the Head Temple—arrived with such force that my hands trembled and a sickening feeling flooded my stomach. But I gathered all my inner strength to simply recite a few well-chosen lines of the great poet-priest Issa:

> "The temple so clever
> At raking in the money—
> It has the peonies!"

Having reduced these Priests to a silent, rapid-blinking rage in this way, I stepped around them and continued my journey through the alleyway as if nothing had happened. Grand Abbot Hamasaki and his top aide, Reverend Fukuyama, let it quietly be known that they endorsed my conservative position, but their support didn't help much. Such "negative" and "overly direct" views convinced the Council of Priests that I was not to be trusted with administrative roles of any true importance. I won't claim, however, that this was a terrible burden to bear. Left alone, I had the freedom to focus almost exclusively on the prayer, religious study, poetry, and painting that were my only true interests.

So my reward during these years was the occasional visit of serene moments, usually when I was alone and painting in my room at the back of the temple. On one such day the glazed tray, the ink stick made of vegetable soot and glue, the water jar, and the blue-veined inkstone on which I ground my paints, sat in proper order next to my right knee. The brushes made from goat, wolf, and marten hair hung from a bamboo rack, while a creamy slice of rice paper washed in an alum solution was secured to the pine board resting flat on the tatami mats before me. To my left, in descending order of importance, were the commissions forwarded by the Head Temple gift shop that I was in the process of executing.

My room's *fusuma* door panels were pushed all the way open to let in the outdoors. I dipped my brush, as the red-rumped swallows swooped down from cliff-face nests to skim bugs off the river, as the *ayu* rose swiftly from below to quick-gulp the fluttering moths and caddisflies caught in the current.

I was entirely transported to the Buddha's Serene World, my right hand in the process of bringing the ink-filled brush back to the board when the wind suddenly came up. An aromatic air of camphor tree and hinoki cypress gusted into the room. My left hand was holding back the sleeves of my robes from smudging the ink as I leaned in to the paper to paint, but I hesitated when I heard that wind behind me stirring up the leaves and making the monkeys chatter nervously—for it signaled a storm was coming.

The storm came a few weeks after my thirty-ninth birthday, when the Priesthood Instruction Center began to shake violently.

I was in the center's ground-floor art studio teaching a roomful of acolytes. It was an earthquake, of course, and we quickly scrambled from the side of the building. We stood in the center of the buckling Administration Alley, nauseous and terrified as boulders and ice tumbled from Mount Nagata above us. The wobbling and shaking seemed endless, the dust-rising roar deafening. I will never forget the feeling of that day. Instability of the most profound kind stood at its center, a sickening knowledge that whatever rocky moorings supported me had in that moment been forever wrenched out from under.

Then it was over. The earthquake hit 7.1 on the Richter scale, a harbinger of the great earthquake that eventually came to Fukushima. One old monk died of a heart attack that day, but all the ancient buildings, including the Head Temple, resolutely stood their ground. It was the Pilgrims Dormitory and a few outer maintenance sheds built cheaply in the 1950s and 1960s that were structurally weakened, and the civil engineers advised us to tear down the buildings and start again.

From then on, whenever I passed the west flank of the Pilgrims Dormitory, I was compelled to stop and minutely study the wall, mesmerized by the crack that ran from one end of the building's edifice to the other. It suggested that total collapse was imminent. Fortuitously, Reverend Fukuyama was put in charge of the reconstruction effort, and he asked me to assist him in this matter. This crack in the dormitory's edifice for some reason so grew in significance in my imagination that it frequently kept me up at night. But it also spurred me to work tirelessly on the dormitory's reconstruction. As a result, the new building was completed in just eighteen months, this time with a better-protected Head Temple energy grid.

But the reverberations did not end there, for two years after the earthquake, we experienced a profound aftershock: Grand Abbott Hamasaki, seventy-eighth High Priest of the Headwater Sect, was blessing a new Toshiba circuit board plant in the city of Iwaki when he suddenly dropped dead from an aneurism.

We were devastated by the news. The old order was no more, and many of us knew something profoundly disrupting to the world was about to take place. The night our beloved seventy-eighth High Priest died I personally dreamt I was standing by the Kappa-gawa behind the Little Temple. I was content among the swaying trees, the singing birds. But then the world suddenly turned upside down. It was another earthquake. Mount Nagata shook and rumbled until the piece of land I was on broke off and began to float down the Kappa-gawa.

I clung to this raftlike clump of earth, frightened, praying all the while as I was taken by the torrent of water. The river became wider, a delta, and then my tiny island was like a ball floating out into the ocean. I looked back at my beloved Japan, longing painfully for home and safety as I was swept out to sea. The earth I was on finally came to rest. I was totally alone and isolated on an island in the middle of the Pacific Ocean.

The silence and barrenness were terrifying.

And so we come to the events that changed my life. I was painting in my room when footsteps began crunching their way across the gravel path outside. I returned the brush to its holder and swiveled on my knees. It was Acolyte Ojisawa, standing at my door under the temple's eaves.

"*Konnichiwa, Sensei.*"

"*Konnichiwa.* Enter, young Ojisawa."

The boy took off his sandals at the door, slipped inside with a respectful crouch, and quickly fell to his knees, head bowed.

"A message, Reverend Oda."

"I see. From the Head Temple?"

"*Hai.*"

It was six months after the seventy-eighth High Priest had died. We sat there, neither of us moving, as the rising wind outside rattled the trees. I sighed. The boy really was *oroka*—stupid as a plank of mountain ash.

"Do you need an invitation to speak? What is the message?"

51

Acolyte Ojisawa bowed again and handed me, with both hands, a note stamped with the Head Temple's gold-embossed insignia, the Buddha entwined by a waterfall and raging fire. "It is from Reverend Fukuyama," the boy said. "He respectfully requests your appearance in the International Division at five-thirty. He said it was most urgent I give you this message personally."

"I see."

The prayer drums pounded the temple's heartbeat.

"Thank you. You can tell him I will be there."

Chapter Four

When I descended Mount Nagata's slopes that afternoon, borders of flowering thistle surrounded the Head Temple's melon, turnip, and radish fields on the upper foothill. In the woods of the next hillock, I passed the stone well where two young acolytes were drawing ice-cold water for the temple altars. They stopped what they were doing and bowed when I passed by on the wooded footpath.

Through the forest and down the mountain the Head Temple came dramatically into view below me—massive, squat, three floors high, and made of ancient dark woods, six sectional wings spreading out from the Great Hall of Worship, designed to take the pilgrims' breath away. Even the Head Temple's swooping red-trimmed roof eaves appeared to reach out beyond the laws of physics to touch the Four Corners Heavens.

I paused for a moment to take in this familiar view of the Head Temple as a *Japonica saepestrita* alighted on a threadleaf bush ahead of me. The butterfly basked in the sun, utterly still, making me recall the ancient haiku that gave me solace when I was a boy first seeking respite at the monastery.

> *Upon the temple bell*
> *A butterfly sleeps well*

Farther down the pass a wide flagstone walkway led up from the temple's parking lot and through the grounds' perimeter stone wall. Street hawkers selling factory-made *juzu* prayer beads and oily incense were not permitted on the official grounds, but sold their cheap wares to the pilgrims as they disembarked from the rows of air-conditioned tour buses outside.

Having negotiated this gauntlet of commercial stalls in the parking lot, hundreds of pilgrims were making their way through the Buddha Entry Gate and up the gently sloping hill surrounded on both sides by mountain cherry orchards. At the cemetery and its Little Temple of Ancestors the stream of Believers stopped to make an offering.

Other pilgrims, some of them chanting the *Lotus Sutra,* continued up the Head Temple's funneling walkways, over the red bridges that spanned the mountain streams, before mounting the stone stairs and passing under the gates that led directly into the Head Temple's central cobblestone court. I avoided this human crush by taking the small gravel path that ran around the side and back of the Head Temple, past the glass-boxed plots of herbs, past the concrete shed that discreetly housed the temple's steel rubbish bins, and finally into Administration Alley.

The seventy-ninth High Priest who replaced our beloved Grand Abbot Hamasaki was none other than Reverend Roshi, the stoop-shouldered leader of the priesthood's "modernist" wing. Some said Grand Abbot Roshi won the ensuing power struggle unfairly; whether or not that was true, he now lived victorious with his family in the alley's High Priest Residence, tucked discreetly behind a row of flowering Japanese lilacs. The administrative buildings from various epochs stood farther along, behind a tidy row of lusterleaf holly and hondo spruce, in line according to order of importance.

As I made my way through the alley that day, the High Priest's wife came from under the scented trees, white gloves and leather purse in hand, heading to the black BMW and driver waiting for her on the cobblestone alley. Several Senior Priests in the lane secretly watched her from the corner of their eyes—with good reason.

When Grand Abbot Roshi assumed power he promptly retired

the battered black Toyota that had shuttled the previous High Priest around and replaced it with this flashy German car. A few of the more outspoken young priests gently remonstrated with the seventy-ninth High Priest at the time, saying his ostentatious Western purchase was perhaps not in the spirit of True Buddhism and might be perceived as "unpatriotic" by the Japanese public at large. Grand Abbot Roshi thanked them for their sincere comments—and then promptly banished the young priests to weed-choked temples in the remotest and coldest corners of Hokkaido Prefecture.

This was the kind of poisoned atmosphere that permeated the Head Temple in those days, a tense unease heightened when Grand Abbot Roshi transferred his great rival and my good friend, Reverend Fukuyama, to the graveyard posting known as the International Division.

Inside the International Division's darkened hall, I took the back stairs to the fourth floor. I pitied Fukuyama his new assignment. The International Division had, from a low base, been growing fairly rapidly, in percentage terms. But the conversion numbers abroad were still relatively small and the threadbare collection of international temples in countries like Indonesia and Thailand were struggling financially because they had little support from the Head Temple and the Council of Priests.

This neglect was, in my opinion, entirely warranted. Over the years I had repeatedly bumped into some of our foreign Believers as they marauded with their fanny packs across the Head Temple grounds. They often behaved like they were in some sort of religious theme park: I caught them dropping stones or yodeling down the Pure Water Stone Well, failing to take off their shoes before stepping across a temple's threshold, or barking their prayers during the formal religious rituals in a way that grated on every fiber of my being. Such unsettling encounters convinced me the *gaijin* did not have the proper sensitivity and intelligence to understand and correctly practice our Buddhist faith.

Reverend Fukuyama was not quite ready to see me when I

entered the anteroom of his office that afternoon, so I took the bench seat opposite his assistant, Reverend Watanabe. Behind him a half dozen nuns and priests sat behind desks, tapping away at their computer keyboards, the air above them dense with black cigarette smoke. I declined the tea offered by a nun. A radio, very low, was tuned to a station dedicated to Japanese crooners. I was of a mind to get up and turn it off and berate the responsible monk. It was entirely inappropriate music for a Head Temple workplace, but just as I was going to engage the fellow, a buzzer sounded and I was ushered into Reverend Fukuyama's office.

Sensei's face lightened when he looked up from the papers on his desk. "Seido-san! It is very good to see you, old friend. I am so sorry to have kept you waiting. A conference call. I am beginning to think some of our priests should take the vow of silence. They gossip like magpies."

"Sensei, it is good to see you. You are so busy."

"Not for you. There is always time to chat with an old friend."

I took the visitors' chair. His desk was piled with document stacks tinged gray and brown from Reverend Fukuyama's inability ever to get his cigarette to the ashtray before the ash dropped. While Sensei and I had talked a few times together at public events over the last few months, we had never been in a position to talk freely and privately among ourselves, and so, now that we were alone, I felt I had to address the injustice of recent events. "It is very disappointing that the late High Priest—"

But Reverend Fukuyama held up his hand, warning me to hold my tongue, and then softened his severe look with a smile and one of his famously mercurial remarks. "All we need in life is good air and regular bowel movements. Everything else is unimportant. Is this not so?"

"But the International Division? Are you finding it . . . rewarding?"

"I am giving the International Division all my energy. There is no such thing as a small job. Only a small mind."

"This is true."

"Which is why I summoned you in this formal manner. I am sorry if it alarmed you."

"I'm fine."

"We are about to start building our first American temple. It is very important that the construction be completed on time and on budget. It is also imperative that the local Priest properly instruct the local American Buddhist community, which is rather lacking in discipline. In short, we need a proper foundation over there, both spiritually and physically, from which to launch our American expansion plans. This can't be done long-distance, of course, and the High Priest has, in his wisdom, agreed it is time to assign a permanent Priest to America. Our first."

"This is interesting."

Reverend Fukuyama stared at me for a few moments through the smoky haze of his office. I stared back, waiting to learn how this all related to my summons. He stubbed out his Mild Seven in the ashtray. "I am reassigning you, Seido-san. I want you to become our Priest in Brooklyn, New York."

To say I was shocked by the news is an understatement. I almost laughed, thinking this was surely a practical joke, but the steely look in Sensei's eye, a look I recognized from when we were boys and I used to watch him compete in debates, told me he was dead serious.

I am not sure what I stammered, something about how I had been stationed at the Temple of Everlasting Prayer since I was eleven years old and couldn't possibly be of assistance to him abroad. Reverend Fukuyama heard me out before dryly observing, "Single-malt whiskey is much cheaper in America. Surely this attracts you."

"This is no laughing matter, Reverend Fukuyama. I will become ill or worse if you take me from Mount Nagata. I am sure of it. You are sending me into exile!"

"Don't be so melodramatic, Seido-san. It's not becoming in a middle-aged monk. You studied English and still read the Romantic poets in their original. What about the Head Temple

57

paying for all those English lessons over the years? Is it not time to pay back your debt of gratitude, if not to the Head Temple, then at least to the Buddha who has provided for you? We now need you to use what you have learned—in America. Besides, this is a promotion to Chief Priest and your own temple. Not a demotion. Where do you get these ideas? You are not being sent into exile. Not at all!"

The ceiling light overhead flashed against the lenses of his black-stemmed accountant's glasses, and so I couldn't see what was in his eyes, but the resolute tone in his voice was unmistakable. "You shame me," I said. I looked down at my hands and whispered, "But I . . . I am afraid."

"Yes. I know."

"I will fail you."

"No. I don't think so."

"I am ill-suited. The Believers make me tongue-tied. And who will instruct the acolytes in the arts? There must be someone else—"

"No one I trust as much as you. Come. Sit. Let us have tea."

Reverend Fukuyama got up from behind his desk and led me to the leather couch and side table under the bay window. As he turned to the hot-water urn and tea tins recessed in the bookcase, I sat dispirited on the couch and stared out at the Head Temple grounds. The panorama of glass before me was filled with the chestnut and ash forests growing up the slopes of Mount Nagata. Above the tree line, I could see the headwaters of the clear blue Kappa-gawa dropping down its feldspar outcrop. Even the top of the Little Temple's red pagoda could be seen emerging from the forest in the far eastern edge of the window's frame.

The sun stood low behind Mount Nagata. It caught the spray rising from Devil's Gate Gorge. This happened only once a day, when the sun's rays met the billowing waterfall mist at just the right angle to fill the air with white and pink diamond dust, a view so beloved and familiar to me, it made me ache. It transported me back to my sacred ground: the humid forest aromatically enveloping the Temple of Everlasting Prayer at dusk, the cicadas joining the Priests as they chanted the evening's round of prayers.

From the bookcase, Reverend Fukuyama complained about the rising price of green tea from Shizuoka, before serving us in the antique jade cups personally given to him by the seventy-eighth High Priest. We sat for a few moments, each of us sipping the tea and appreciating its delicate flavor. But the dread building inside me would not go away, so I firmly put down my cup on the table and pleaded with Sensei to find someone better suited for the New York job.

I argued that he and Reverend Kashimoto were really the only Priests at the Head Temple not put off by my abrupt and quarrelsome manner, and I was, in many ways, totally ill-suited to be a Priest, let alone a Priest assigned such an important task. I much preferred the company of my pen or brush or book to that of other Priests and Believers, and it was well known that the young priests and acolytes had all sorts of disparaging names for me behind my back. This alone should give him pause. I was, in short, not the appropriate choice for this assignment.

"Besides. It is preposterous to say that my interest in the English Romantic poets was somehow suitable preparation for working with modern American Believers."

Reverend Fukuyama smiled and said, "Seido, my friend. It is simple. I need you there, on the ground, in America. You have kept up your English and ably assisted me during the Pilgrims Dormitory reconstruction project, knowledge that will be invaluable for this particular assignment. You really are the only monk for the job. Most important, I can trust you to do your religious duty regardless of Head Temple politics."

Reverend Fukuyama looked away, and in the waning blue light coming from the bay window I saw for the first time the grayness in his skin, the exhaustion, silently undermining his efforts to be the Buddha's loyal servant, whoever the High Priest might be.

Sensei bent his head and slurped noisily from his teacup. When he came back up he lightly said, "You know, Seido, the current

High Priest has handed me a challenge that some might say is a poisoned cup. The Head Temple's five-year development plan calls for seven temples to be built overseas. Should I fail to meet the Head Temple's growth target, the seventy-ninth High Priest will have cause to dismiss me. So I need a few good men to make sure that won't happen. A few good men to help me get the overseas temples built. On time and within the budget."

I owed Reverend Fukuyama so much I could never refuse his official request to do my duty, let alone such a personal appeal, but that did not make the idea of moving to America any easier. I adjusted my mind to the possibility, when it became inevitable what must happen, but leaned forward, saying, "Please, Sensei, perhaps we can agree on this, at least. I will get the New York temple built over the next year, but during this time perhaps you will look for a young priest who could be a more successful and permanent replacement. I will, in short, act as a temporary bridge, to buy you time, but when the American temple is standing I respectfully ask you to bring me back home to my old position at the Temple of Everlasting Prayer. Install instead a suitably ambitious and young priest at the New York Temple. It's a much wiser course forward. Nnn? Can we agree on this?"

Reverend Fukuyama pretended to hunt for his Mild Seven cigarettes while pondering my proposal. He finally found his packet and lit one, dangling the cigarette from his lips like a Yakuza boss. "Perhaps this is a possibility," he said, his eyelids fluttering under the rising smoke.

"Respectfully, Sensei, I know when you give a clear answer and when you give an evasive answer. This is an evasive answer."

"We know each other too well, old friend." He smiled and flung cigarette ash in the vague direction of the ashtray. "All right. If you go and get the temple built, I will look for a New York replacement."

"Then I go and do my duty, Sensei."

"So we are agreed."

"This is not the word to describe what I am feeling."

Reverend Fukuyama puffed on his cigarette. I could tell he was carefully hunting for the right words. "You are wary of human contact, Seido. You avoid the Believers, other Priests, even the quietest of acolytes. This is all true. But whatever you think of your abilities as a Priest, the facts are you have always served the Buddha well. And been my true friend."

I blinked rapidly and turned to the window. A mountain hawk-eagle circled in the hot air above, hunting mice in the Head Temple's melon fields. Down by a stream, two acolytes in gray robes were making their way through the brush with a straw basket, gathering fresh *shikimi* leaves to dry and make into incense in the day's last light.

"To refuse you, Sensei, would be like refusing a parent."

A buzzer rang. It was Reverend Watanabe. The High Priest was looking to review the monthly temple reports with all the division heads at seven-thirty p.m.

Reverend Fukuyama sighed and returned his teacup to the side table. "I'll have Reverend Watanabe send you all the information we have on the New York temple project," he said. "It is well financed, but the reports back about the New York Believers suggest they need a strong Priest to point them in the right direction. One or two of the American lay Believers seem to have an inflated sense of their importance in regards to the temple and our faith. You have never in the past wanted to involve yourself in the affairs of temple administration, but, I am sorry, your religious duty now requires you to get your hands dirty with the lowly affairs of temple bureaucracy. This is the way it is."

"*Hai.*"

The sun set behind Mount Nagata's shoulder and the office turned purple with Sensei's cigarette smoke and the fading light. He gave me a look full of regret and sadness, a melancholia also graced by acceptance of the Buddha's wise if mysterious ways.

In the end we were all just servants of the Buddha, each with his own duties and obligations. And so Fukuyama and I stood, bowed, and with heavy hearts went our separate ways—he to his

61

Head Temple management affairs, and I to prepare for my journey to America. "Seido," he called out one last time as I crossed the room to exit his office. "Have you noticed, to get fresh air into a house after a hard winter, you must sometimes use a little force to open the window that has for too long been sealed shut?"

The next weeks flew by at such speed they seemed to defy the laws of time and space. There was much to do, and in between all the errands to be completed I was driven, whenever possible, to the Great Hall of Worship, to fall on my knees and pray for courage and wisdom and the Buddha's serene guidance during this extraordinary period of change.

Young priests in the wings of the Head Temple vigorously pounded the large prayer drums, as the air was ritualistically purified with *shikimi*-leaf incense. The altarpiece's lacquered doors were wide open, the interior lights illuminating the Cluster of Jewels Mandala and its elegant waterfall of High Priest calligraphy that was the Buddha's life and enlightenment, represented on earth through this sacred scroll of kanji characters. I joined the others, on my knees, prayer beads wrapped around my hands, and silently apologized for my many shortcomings. I prayed fervently to unite my being with the Eternal Buddha and to honorably perform my duty in America.

After finding a substitute for master teacher of the arts—a talented acolyte I had taught in previous years—I opened the New York Temple file sent on by Reverend Watanabe. I was pleased to discover that generous contributions from the Believers in New York had put the project on sound financial footing. A demographic study of the local Believers had identified lower Manhattan and the western border of Brooklyn as the best geographic locations for a temple; a rare opportunity to acquire two adjacent lots in a neighborhood called Brooklyn Heights finally settled the issue. The construction of the temple, due to start shortly, was 80 percent financed by the local Believers and their New York Temple Fund. The remaining 20 percent of the construction costs were covered by the Head Temple Development Fund, the legal conduit for a two-billion-yen donation by the widow of the former Japanese ambassador to Washington, explicitly ear-marked for the building of American temples. Even I, far from gifted when it came to administrative matters, knew this legal arrangement between the local American Believers and the Head Temple was unique. Sensei had somehow negotiated the build-ing of a New York temple at minuscule risk or cost to the Head Temple, in the process putting his indelible mark on the Interna-tional Division.

Reverend Watanabe then had me sign stacks of Citibank forms forwarded by the American bank's International Department in Tokyo, in this way starting the bureaucratic process that would establish my bank account in Brooklyn. Reverend Watanabe explained—in a tone of voice that made it clear he was irritated by how slow I was grasping the details—that the Head Temple Accounting Department would every month wire my American stipend to this Brooklyn Citibank account, which I could then access via a local ATM machine.

I applied for a passport and took it—alongside official let-ters from the Head Temple outlining my duties as its New York Priest—to the U.S. Embassy in Tokyo, to obtain the R-1 nonresi-dent immigrant visa for foreign priests working in America.

When I returned from Tokyo with my papers and passport stamped, there was little more to do but ask Reverend Watanabe to book my flight to New York, which he did with his usual effi-ciency. Holding the airline ticket to John F. Kennedy Airport in my hands somehow made real the surreal changes that were occurring.

In mid-June, a week before my departure, I decided to hike one more time up the slopes of Mount Nagata, to Devil's Gate Gorge. I had a vague sense I must, in this way, say my final goodbyes to Japan, my beloved and sacred corner of earth.

The fog was heavy when I started out in the morning and my knapsack was weighted down with bean curd cakes, tangerines, and a thermos of tea. The cliff path rose through the highland forest, through the Japanese blue beech and stone oak, until I finally emerged above the tree line. The sun burned through the fog rising from the temperate rain forest and made the veins of crystal and feldspar in the rock shine with bright luster.

I looked down the mountain. In the purple air below I could see the Head Temple, the village of Katsurao, and the flatland rice plains in the far distance, stretching out to the horizon. I turned and for the next forty minutes the deer track led me through craggy rocks and giant boulders covered in lichen the color of oxidizing copper. The Kappa-gawa rushed past me on its whitewater descent down the mountainside.

Waterfalls, in Buddhist legends, connect the heavens with earth, and are often poetically used to represent the Middle Way—one foot in this world, one foot in the spiritual world. But for me the Devil's Gate Gorge and the long pool below the fall's thundering ladder had a deeply personal meaning. It was here, so long ago, that I fished for the first time with my brother Daiki.

I shrugged on my Windbreaker. Despite the sweat pouring down my back, the falls' rolling waves of cold mist had started to reach me. I passed through the giant boulders on either side of the gorge entrance. Inside the thundering basin, I walked along the deep green water to the sandbar at the bottom of the waterfall's long pool.

I took off my backpack, removed my Tenkara rod, and began casting my fly. For a brief while I put aside my priestly training and duties and became, once again, just a simple boy from the mountains. I looked down the sandbar and distinctly saw, emerging in the waterfall spray, Daiki's silhouette, struggling with the fish he lost that first day he took me fishing at the gorge.

I heard him, too. *"Don't be sad, Seido. It will be all right. I will come to the Head Temple and together we will climb up to Devil's Gate Gorge to fish for the ayu, like we have always done."*

I had two *ayu* on the riverbank when I stopped fishing. I said a prayer for the trout, for sustaining my life with their death, then gutted them. Shrub twigs and branches that had fallen from the cliff face above had gathered on the pebbly beach of the pool, and I gathered them up for a small fire. I grilled the fish and ate them with the bean curd, washed down with sips of green tea, as my brother and I had done so many years earlier.

Lunch finished and put away, I finally fell on my knees and said my goodbyes to Japan and this blessed corner of earth that was my home and the home of my ancestors. Before saying my closing prayer, I allowed myself the cry of the heart that I had said twice a day, every day, ever since I was eleven years old.

I prayed the Buddha would help me expiate my karma.

For not saving Onii-san.

As I promised him I would.

Reverend Kashimoto, my old acolyte friend, appeared unexpectedly at the door panel of my room the evening before I left for America. He was not wearing his robes, but red golfer's pants, a lemon-and-blue argyle sweater, and white patent-leather loafers. A cap was rakishly pulled over his brow.

"Come, Seido," he said. "I've booked us a table in Katsurao. I am not sending you off to America without a night on the town." I tried to protest that I had much to do still, but he said, "Not another word. Go on. Change. Get into civilian clothes and meet me down on Administration Alley in thirty minutes."

So I dressed and headed out after him on the lantern-lit paths that ran through the eastern woods. The night was overcast, thick clouds blotted out the moon, and the woods were as dark as *sumi-e* ink. I walked with my cap pulled down as a fine mist of rain fell, my hands thrust deep into my pockets. A white Toyota taxi with windshield wipers going was waiting in the alley down below, and I threw myself into the backseat, alongside Reverend Kashimoto. The taxi drove us out along the dark service road, through the Western Gate, and onto the main road that wound around hills and mountain streams before entering the village of Katsurao.

The Cosmo gas station glowed through the rain-spattered taxi window. Uniformed attendants were filling cars with fuel, emptying out customers' ashtrays and filling them with air freshener beads, wiping down windows and chrome car handles. Just past where this Cosmo station was conducting its business, down the side road, my family's inn had once stood. Seeing me study the old backstreet, Reverend Kashimoto quietly said, "Do not think of the old days, Seido. Think of the adventure ahead."

The taxi pulled into the Hotel Sapporo, a neon sign wrapped around the building's rooftop. The restaurant was on the ground floor of the hotel; when we entered, the sushi chef and staff cried out their welcome, "*Irrashaimase.*" The rooms were filled with the comforting smells of black tobacco and high-proof sake.

Reverend Kashimoto had reserved a table for us in one of the private rooms in the back so we could drink without the villagers seeing us. The wood block before us was layered in pink and white sashimi, while the side dishes offered treats like pickled ginger. Most of all, we drank far too many ceramic pots of *genshu,* an undiluted sake, late into the night.

When my tongue was loosened by drink, I said, "You have been to America, Kenta. What can I expect?"

Kashimoto solemnly put his hand on my shoulder. "You have much work ahead of you, Seido. Much work."

I covered my face with both hands and he laughed. "Please," I groaned. "Be serious. What is your advice?"

"I have none. Find your own way with the American Believers. The Americans will challenge you, count on this, and the New York Believers are the most demanding of all. Remember, in Japan, Buddhism is a mainstream religion, but in America it's an alternative religion. This is very difficult for us conventional Japanese priests, because Buddhism attracts the alternative-lifestyle people in America. Outcasts. People with metal in their faces."

"Ugh. I won't be able to deal with these people. Sensei has made a big mistake."

"You are a better Priest than you think. . . ."

"Come, now!" I roared, smacking the table. "You don't really believe that! You have seen me with the Believers and the acolytes. I am awkward. I can't stand most of them. There is no point pretending otherwise. And you know my conservative views. I will make big trouble for the Head Temple. I won't be able to hold my tongue if the American Believers are in any way disrespectful of the priesthood or the law."

Reverend Kashimoto laughed. "Calm down, Seido-san. You know, Reverend Fukuyama once said to me, 'Our friend Seido will one day make a great Priest.' I was, if you don't mind me saying so, rather surprised by this remark. When I asked him to explain himself, he said, 'Seido's problem is not that he cares too little for the Believers. But that he cares too much.'"

Kashimoto and I looked at each other—and then burst out laughing.

When our laughter finally subsided, I wiped my eyes and said, "Sensei has a wonderful sense of humor. We must give him that."

And so I departed from my beloved Temple of Everlasting Prayer. Acolyte Ojisawa brought a trundle cart around to my room, and we loaded it with my luggage. My head pounded from the previous night's drinking and my heart was heavy. I reassured myself again that the Cluster of Jewels Mandala I was bringing to America was safe in the steel cylinder in my briefcase. I slipped one last time into the Great Hall of Worship, bent in reverence, and said final prayers.

When I came out again, Reverend Kashimoto and his wife, plus all the Priests and acolytes and their spouses and children living in the Little Temple, had lined up on either side of the path leading into the eastern woods. As I started down the path with young Ojisawa pulling the trundle cart behind us, they all bowed, wishing me good luck as I passed. I could not speak, such was the emotion inside me, but at the end of the line, I grabbed Reverend Kashimoto's wrist and said, "Take care of my beloved temple, Kenta. Protect it with your life. It stands in the Buddhaland."

"This I will do, old friend. Rest assured."

The taxi taking me to the train station down in the flatlands was waiting for me on the cobblestone of Administration Alley. So, too, were Reverend Fukuyama and his assistant, Reverend Watanabe. As the white-gloved driver and Acolyte Ojisawa loaded the trunk of the taxi, Reverend Fukuyama stepped forward to warmly say his goodbyes, handing me a folder and a wooden box. "This envelope is from my wife," he said. "She asked me to give it to you with her goodbye and special best wishes. It is plum blossoms from the slopes of Mount Nagata, pressed and dried. She gives this to you so at all times in America you have a bit of Japan at your side. So you never have to be homesick. And this, of course, is from me, a bottle of special-aged Juyondai sake from Yamagata Prefecture, so, on the hardest of days, you can taste your country and be fortified."

I bowed. "Thank you, Sensei. Please thank your wife for me. I treasure her gift."

"Be safe, Seido. Be safe. Remember to keep the Buddha in your heart and mind. No matter what happens."

"*Hai.* Goodbye, Sensei. Goodbye. Thank you for this great honor and trust."

I climbed into the back of the taxi. Acolyte Ojisawa suddenly came forward to shut the taxi door, saying, "Goodbye, Master. May you come back to us safely." The boy, I was surprised to see, was blinking hard. "Thank you, Ojisawa. Work hard on your brushstrokes. I will be back to remonstrate with you severely if your technique hasn't improved by the time I return."

"*Hai, Sensei.*"

He eased the door shut and the taxi drove off. I turned around to look one last time at the Head Temple, and saw Reverend Fukuyama standing in the light, exactly where I had left him, his hands clasped behind his back. He was pensively lifting his heels up and down as the Yakuza-style cigarette hanging from his lips fogged up his black-rimmed eyeglasses. Reverend Watanabe was also visible just behind Sensei, holding his superior's black leather briefcase and impatiently looking at his watch, as if they were late for an important meeting. But Reverend Fukuyama stayed put, knowing I would turn one last time, and when he saw my moon-face out the backseat window, he cried out and raised his hand and waved a final farewell. So did young Ojisawa. I moved to raise my hand in return, but before it was fully up the taxi was swallowed by the dark and wet woods of the west.

Chapter Five

$\mathcal{J}$t was strange, like in a dream, to be in Japan one moment and America the next. The plane ride from Tokyo's Narita Airport to New York's John F. Kennedy took fourteen hours, and I officially arrived in America on June 21, the first day of summer. When I staggered off the plane my robes were rumpled and my mouth tasted of dried-out mackerel. I was stupid from lack of sleep. In the baggage area of the airport a group of young black children came forward to stare at my shaved head, gray Buddhist robes, and the special white socks with the big toe split off into its own compartment, like the finger of a glove, so the toes could grip the thong of my wooden sandals. The children seemed to find this highly amusing, for they pointed at my feet, whispered, and then ran off giggling.

I looked back at the carousel. The luggage tumbled from the chute and went around and around. People came and went retrieving their suitcases. The carousel stopped. I stood alone. This was not a good omen. At the Lost Luggage Department a dark woman with a head shaved like a nun and an accent very difficult to understand moved as slow as a slug and told me to circle illustrations of luggage that resembled my own.

I emerged into JFK's international arrivals hall a full three hours after the plane had landed. The woman waiting for me in the crowd was wearing a black T-shirt, jeans, and flip-flops. She was in her late thirties, I guessed, with frost-tipped hair that stood up spiky and ragged. This could not possibly be my official greeting party, I thought, for her attire was entirely inappropriate for formally welcoming a Priest.

But the woman clearly held a placard on which REVEREND ODA was written in black ink. I had read on the plane a long Japanese article about the decadence of American society, about same-sex marriages, and single-parent families, so perhaps this was why, at that moment when we first locked eyes, I thought, *This is militant American lesbian.*

I bowed. The look of relief on the woman's face was great, and she pushed her way through the crowd in my direction. I panicked, not sure if I should bow a Japanese greeting or shake hands Western-style. The woman did neither. She threw her arms around me and hugged me tightly to her bosom.

I stood stiff as a winter cherry tree holding out frozen limbs, as the woman grappled me like a sumo wrestler. It took what seemed like an eternity before she was satisfied I was of flesh and bone, but she finally released me, stood back, and stammered she was the Believer Jennifer Meli. I bowed repeatedly and apologized most profusely, explaining the cause of my delay.

"You poor, poor guy." She commiserated over my lost luggage, and then formally welcomed me on behalf of the New York Buddhist community. "You're here. Finally. We've been waiting so long for this day and we're all totally pumped. Just so you know, I've been appointed by the New York Temple Fund to be your American assistant. So anything you need, I'm your go-to gal."

Then she was again impressing upon me how "ecstatic" and "terribly excited" they all were to have a Priest come from Japan to oversee the building of the new temple. "We'll let you settle in over the next few days and then officially introduce you at a reception in your honor." My mind filled with visions of overexcited Americans hooting and ululating their welcome like I had seen in documentaries about the tribes of Africa. I bowed again, deeper, expressing my sincere gratitude for such a robust welcome.

When this greeting ceremony was finally concluded, I followed her directly out the doors of the airport. Planes roared overhead. The air shimmered, gray and humid, and smelled of burnt diesel, hot tar, and, for some inexplicable reason, deep-fried potatoes.

Rubbish overflowed from the green barrel-cans deposited like land mines across the cement landscape, while tired families dragged their oversized luggage across the pedestrian crossing, dodging car rental buses that seemed eager to run them over. As I followed Miss Meli across the street, a driver stuck his head out of a car window and asked me if I wanted to go to Connecticut, but he did so under his breath, in such a furtive way that I had the distinct impression Connecticut was the name of a notorious "bathhouse."

This was America. After several false starts the woman grew increasingly more flustered, muttering, "But it was here. I am sure of it." We finally located her car in the far corner of the massive parking lot, and Miss Meli bundled me into the Honda's backseat like I was a bag of turnips. We drove off down the highway.

It was incredible. She drove like she had just robbed a bank. Thankfully she did not talk during the trip, but gripped the wheel and sharply pulled it this way and that, bouncing me about the backseat. She merged and switched lanes and weaved in between cars, but always headed in the general direction of the Manhattan skyline that loomed on the horizon.

We finally arrived at 429 Cortina Street, Brooklyn. I opened the car door and almost fell to the pavement in relief. My jaw was clenched like a steel clamp from the way the woman had driven over all the potholes, and I had a throbbing headache. There was a vegetable store on the ground floor of the building, with a wood and glass door to the left of the shop leading to the apartments above.

Upstairs, in the studio flat rented for me, I bowed and thanked Miss Meli most sincerely. I hoped she would leave, but she insisted on demonstrating every item in the apartment, opening and closing refrigerator and closet doors, as if I were mentally slow and might not figure these things out by myself.

"I'll be back tomorrow. Breakfast will be simple. Lox and bagels. Is that okay?" I did not have the slightest idea what she was talking about but nodded, just to get her out the door.

Finally, finally, she left—and I was alone.

I lay exhausted on the cot, staring at the ceiling and thinking, *What have I done? What have I done?*

The first thing I did the next morning, as the early sun came through the window slats of my Brooklyn studio, was remove the Sacred Scroll from the steel container in my briefcase. Burning incense and incanting the *Lotus Sutra,* I took my time to carefully unravel and enshrine the Cluster of Jewels Mandala in the *butsudan* provided by the local Believers. It was a simple but sturdy altar in the northern corner of the apartment, and I prayed long and hard for the Buddha's wisdom and guidance in this foreign land.

The flat was U-shaped, about twenty tatami mats in total. The Believers had furnished the rooms simply but well. It had a sturdy kitchen table under the window, a beige armchair, even a television in the living area. An overhead subway track was visible out the back window, just as it descended into a tunnel behind my building.

Directly below the window was a weedy garden, and a line hung with children's clothes and huge billowing underpants that must have belonged to a very large woman. A crow cawed at me from the telephone wires that ran from the house to a vine-crawled pole out back. As I was studying this urban view, a butterfly briefly alighted on a monstrous-sized brassiere hanging from the clothesline, before fluttering off again. This was a good omen. It improved my mood.

The doorbell rang. I assumed it was Miss Meli coming to cook my breakfast, but it was a man in a brown uniform with my luggage. It appears my suitcase fled to Madrid, Spain, perhaps not an unwise decision on its part. I bowed and thanked the man most sincerely before signing his papers. He was sweating from carrying the heavy luggage up the stairs and he stood before me wiping his face with a handkerchief.

The apartment building's dull brown walls were scarred with

white scrapes from where tenants had trouble turning the staircase when moving in and out with furniture. A battered blue bicycle was leaning against the rail on the landing above. There was a strong hallway odor of rotting wood and dust, which mingled with the smells of onions and overripe melons rising from the vegetable store on the ground floor.

The man blew his nose. Did not move.

I looked at him. He looked at me.

"Is something else?" I asked.

He turned on his heels and pounded down the staircase, saying, loud enough for me to hear, "Fuckin' foreign asshole." This was before I learned about the American habit of tipping, and I thought the man was incredibly rude, perhaps even a little mad. But I had no time to ponder this curious social matter further, because immediately afterward the building shook with the clumping of Miss Meli coming up the stairs.

She burst into the apartment with her arms around bulging paper sacks, filled, it turned out, with plastic-wrapped meat, toilet paper, bottles of fizzy water, and a mop she was dragging behind her, pinned under an arm. She even brought me, quite thoughtfully, a cell phone and a "loaner" laptop.

Miss Meli's attire had improved somewhat from the previous day. She wore a shiny yellow shirt over jeans, with large bug-eyed sunglasses perched on the top of her head in the forest of her spiky hair.

"Hey, boss. Sleep with the angels?"

"Please. In the apartment. Shoes must come off. At the door. This is Japanese custom."

"Yeah. I know. Sorry. Just hang on a moment and let me drop all this stuff in the kitchen first . . . there we go. Shoes off." The woman had a very informal style. She padded across the floor in her bare feet to the small kitchen counter, and turned her back on me as she chattered and clattered about the sink as if we were a long-married couple.

Scrambling eggs and chopping onions, Miss Meli turned to

open the kitchen window and let some breeze in. The wind turned a certain way and we heard what sounded like madmen yelling in the streets, the faraway blaring of fire engines, and crates gratingly dragged across the cement alley. The smells swirling around the flat were of toasting bread and hot tar and moldy fruit and garbage swelling in the heat, all coupled with the tart odor of the vinegary condiment Miss Meli had just placed on the table next to a plate of salmon sushi.

After the long stillness of my life at the Temple of Everlasting Prayer, Brooklyn appeared through the haze of my jet lag as a singularly belligerent attack on my central nervous system. It was the noise and smells of New York that in particular so overwhelmed me, and I found myself wincing or jumping nervously each time a train rattled by the window, the upstairs neighbor came thumping down the stairs, or the pipes in the building began to clang loudly.

Finally, breakfast was ready and I gratefully took my seat. I hadn't realized how hungry I was. Miss Meli pushed a tinfoil packet across the table in my direction and said, "Here's the cream cheese."

"Thank you. I eat sushi without white paste."

We ate in silence. She was my help and I was determined to discourage casual banter and personal intimacies that might prove problematic at some future date. It was important to maintain the proper hierarchy and authority of the priesthood. Thankfully, Miss Meli seemed to take this all in stride and did not push me to talk.

The Formica table under the window was eventually covered in jam jars, sticky knives, and dirty orange juice glasses. It was only then, as we neared the end of our meal, that I said, "May I ask question?"

"Shoot."

"The Head Temple file I read stated there are many, many important figures in the local Buddhist community. I am very grateful for clear picture."

I continued chewing the rubbery bread I could not swallow

while the woman went to the windowsill. She sat on the radiator in a bold fashion, legs spread apart and her scruffy bare feet planted on the floor, the hands resting on her upper thighs for support.

"Can I smoke?"

"*Hai.*"

She pulled a cigarette from her purse, lit it, and inhaled so contentedly it looked as if she were taking in mother's milk. "Okay. This is what you need to know. The only thing the New York Believers are united on is building the Brooklyn temple and having a full-time Priest in the city. Other than that, it's a free-for-all, with basically three competing power centers at the heart of the community."

That morning I learned that Mrs. Gloria Graham chaired the New York Temple Fund, a nonprofit vehicle tasked with building the temple. She had worked closely with the Head Temple's International Division as the fund's assets grew, which explained why New York was the first American city sanctioned to build a temple. "Gloria is throwing the welcome party for you at the end of the week, so you'll be meeting her soon."

Also sitting on the fund's board was the hard-driving businessman Mr. Arthur Symes. He was the largest individual donor of funds to the temple. Miss Meli exhaled a column of smoke out the screen and said, "Gloria has a perfectionist, go-slow approach. That doesn't suit everyone. Particularly Artie. He's a hard-charging entrepreneur and it's pretty obvious he wants to elbow Gloria out of the way and run the fund himself. Artie's actually the one who found the architect and oversaw the land purchase. He even got us the necessary building permits. He's usually two steps ahead of Gloria."

Finally there was Mr. Eddie Dolan, an insurance broker from Staten Island. In the last decade, the New York Buddhist community had grown entirely by word of mouth, with one American Believer informally teaching, to the best of his ability, the basic practice to the next Believer. The Head Temple in Japan, noticing a steady rise in the numbers of American Believers, eventually started sending "touring" priests to New York. Senior Priests like Reverend Kashimoto came to New York for two days every six months, performing a series of religious ceremonies such as enshrinements, and giving brief lectures on Buddhist doctrine.

But many of the Americans craved more doctrinal instruction than these hasty and infrequent visits. It was into this vacuum that Mr. Dolan had stepped. "He runs a regular study group in Manhattan," my assistant said. "About a quarter of the community attend them."

"This is interesting. Have you been to the study meeting?"

"A few times."

"What is your impression?"

She picked a shred of tobacco off her lip and looked out the window.

"I've said enough already."

Miss Meli tidied up the kitchen later that morning and then ran out of the apartment to attend, as she informed me over her shoulder, an Ashtanga yoga class. I was relieved her American "energy" was finally outside, rather than confined with me inside the little apartment, and I used the ensuing quiet to sit at the Formica table with a notepad and pen, organizing my jet-lagged thoughts into a concrete course of action.

A sudden and violent vibration at my elbow made me jump in alarm. It was my new American cell phone ringing for the first time, and when I gingerly picked it up, I found Mr. Arthur Symes, the subject of our earlier discussion, talking in a booming voice through the little phone.

After welcoming me to New York he asked me to come consecrate his altar at his apartment in Manhattan. I agreed, of course, but when I asked for the address, he said, "Stay put. I'll send my driver to pick you up." True to his word, a handsome black car and driver appeared forty-five minutes later down on Cortina Street, and whisked me off in the direction of the Brooklyn Bridge.

How well I remember my first impressions of Manhattan, when the driver opened my door and I tentatively stepped onto the pavement of the American city. For many minutes I stood wordlessly at the bottom of the man-made Devil's Gate Gorge called Park Avenue. Elegant apartment buildings towered high above me like a ridge of mountains, creating a long canyon as far as the eye could see. Park Avenue ran like the Kappa-gawa straight through the bottom of the gorge and the yellow taxis sailed up and down its gentle surges like river rafts. When I looked toward the canyon's horizon, the air above it was soup-thick and gray from car exhaust, shimmering in the summer heat like waves in a physics experiment.

My eyes rose up the sides of the buildings to the blue sky and airplane plumes high above, far beyond the penthouses and spire tops and buttresses. It hurt my neck to bend back like that and I felt quite alone in the world. The buildings looked to me like monsters striding across the earth; I was little more than a tiny and insignificant animal scurrying around in their dark shadows, trying not to get squashed underfoot.

I thought of the great poet-priests Matsuo Bashō and Kobayashi Issa. It was a long-established tradition for the ancient haiku poet-priests of Japan to leave their villages in order to wander the "world," just as Lord Shakyamuni had left the comforts of his father's court to roam the mountains and seek enlightenment. When Bashō traveled seventeenth-century Japan by foot, he took to the road in a disciplined act of renunciation and solitude. The loneliness he felt on the road reminded him of the loneliness experienced by all human beings, and so travel became a means by which Bashō shook off his human bonds in order to fully understand the impermanence of life. Standing alone on Park Avenue, looking up at the towering buildings, I suddenly understood the cosmic loneliness that Bashō captured so well in his haiku.

For eighteenth-century Issa, steeped in Tendai's Buddhist teachings, the solitude of travel had the exact opposite effect. It

constantly reminded Issa of his much-loved family left behind
in his village, and the loneliness of the journey strengthened his
deep attachment to all human beings.

Ripped from all that was home, feeling so isolated and alien
in the New York roar, I could not understand Issa's experience at
all. It was unfathomable. But I had no time to continue this train
of thought, for the white-gloved doorman standing before 1199A
Park Avenue was politely holding open the door.

The lobby was cool and dark and the concierge worked from
behind a large porcelain vase of flowers. I rose in the elevator to
the twenty-seventh floor, where the lady of the house, Mrs. Symes,
stood waiting to meet me at one of the two black-lacquered doors
on either side of the elevator bank. The woman's hair, and even the
tinge of her skin, resembled the color of overripe oranges. She was
short and plump, with numerous gold rings snaking around her
fingers. She wore a tent-shaped dress of black and gold material
that was light and diaphanous, so the overall impression I had was
of someone wearing an expensive shower curtain. She welcomed
me warmly as my eyes constantly drifted to her jewelry, which
seemed to be everywhere, all over her hands and neck, glittering.

Mrs. Symes insisted I call her Harriet and she talked, I soon
discovered, with a drumlike voice over and through everyone
else's conversation. She was very proud of her apartment and took
me on a grand tour, describing in excruciating detail where she
had purchased each statue and stick of furniture. From the photographs in silver frames dotted around the flat I had the impression the couple had several young grandchildren.

Gratefully, we did not go into the kitchen, from which came
sounds of a maid or cook banging pots and scraping dishes, but
the apartment had six bedrooms, running along an entire block of
Manhattan, all of which Mrs. Symes insisted I must see. So I was
shown bathrooms and a sewing room and a media room and several living rooms, including rooms with stunning views, curiously
roped off with a red velvet cord as if in a museum.

The most awkward few moments of the tour occurred in one

such living room after Mrs. Symes unhooked the velvet cord, like we were at a museum, and invited me to step behind the rope. A very large painting depicting Mrs. Symes and her husband, entirely nude and running hand in hand through a dark and threatening wood, hung above a gold brocade couch that straddled the far corner of the living room. I bowed and listened to Mrs. Symes most attentively as she talked about the portraitist and his amusing ways, but I did not know what to say, let alone where to look.

At that moment, most thankfully, Mr. Symes joined us, striding across the room to vigorously shake my hand and welcome me in that booming voice I recognized from the phone. I found it most extraordinary. The couple talked as if I were hard of hearing and standing at the far side of the apartment, even though I was right next to them, and sometimes I even wondered if they were talking to me at all or just between themselves.

"That damned painting. Wish I could burn it. The guy who painted it is a nutcase."

"Artie! Mark's adorable. How can you say such a thing?"

"Please. He's a total weirdo."

The businessman was dressed conservatively in gray trousers; a handkerchief poked up from the front pocket of his jacket. He was in his late fifties I guessed, and was quite freckled and bald on top but compensated for this hair loss with a silver pelt that grew densely around the back of his neck, and a goatee, sharply trimmed, which he constantly tugged and stroked as he talked.

"We're the second biggest elevator manufacturer in the country. I built the company entirely from scratch. Even got the kids working for me now."

"I see."

"Actually, another way to put it is, we are the largest *family-owned* elevator company in the U.S. of A. There's another family-run firm in Germany that, technically, might be bigger than us, but that's only because the dollar is weak right now. And we're much more profitable. . . ."

"How impressive."

"We've also won the U.S. construction industry's 'Best Supplier' award four times in a row. Unheard-of. You'll find . . ."

I eventually managed, in the middle of this corporate history, to steer the conversation to the temple. I told him I was most eager to see the construction site and to personally meet with the temple architect. I had copies of the blueprints and wanted some clarification on some of the things I had seen there.

"No problem. You got it. I'll have my secretary line up our calendars. Now come, Reverend Oda. Let's put you to work."

Their prayer room was at the end of a long hall in the northwest corner of the flat, just past the master bedroom. The walls of the softly lit sanctuary were painted eggshell white and the floor was covered in a thick, platinum-colored carpet that was very soft on the knees. An early Meiji Restoration Period *butsudan* in black lacquer and gold paint and the finest inlaid ivory stood magnificently against the far wall.

It was the only piece of furniture in the room, as was proper, and the altar was set with vases filled with leather leaf greens, white candles in fine candlesticks, and a matching set of bejeweled water cup and incense burner. The energy of the room was focused entirely on the Cluster of Jewels Mandala, the Stupa of Worship discreetly closed off behind the doors of the *butsudan*.

This elegant prayer room made me wonder whether I perhaps had misjudged the Symeses. But then the man yelled at me to "lookit here"—he was pointing vigorously at a large glass vase full of shiny silver balls, which I had somehow overlooked even though it was displayed prominently on the altar.

"Ball bearings," Mr. Symes said proudly, as if that somehow explained their presence on the altar.

"Most unusual," I replied cautiously.

Apparently, Mr. Symes became a Buddhist a decade earlier when his elevator company was in trouble and losing market share. It was a period of painful restructuring, when he had to fire many employees, and, although the company survived, it was "touch and go" for a few years. It was during this fraught time that he turned to Buddhism, introduced to the faith by his daughter, who had joined our sect in San Francisco a year earlier.

"How about that, Reverend?"

"Very interesting. And your former employees?"

His eyes narrowed. "Huh?"

"Where are the employees?"

"You mean the ones I had to fire? Well, I am not sure. Some I rehired. But rest assured they all found work."

"This is good."

"You're missing the point here."

Mr. Symes made a promise during his initiation rite that, if the Buddha assisted his company, he would give twenty thousand dollars as offering for every extra elevator he sold. He did in fact experience a great turn in fortune, and since his fervent prayers for increased elevator sales were answered over the subsequent years, he lived up to his promise to the Buddha—each ball bearing in the jar represented a new elevator sold beyond his baseline on the day of his conversion to Buddhism. He had, in short, donated over $5 million to the New York Temple Fund. "And here we are on the threshold of opening a new temple. Amazing, huh? As I keep telling anyone who will listen—these Buddhist prayers actually work."

He looked at me with eyes wide with expectation, awaiting my approval. I was entirely at a loss for words. How could I explain, just minutes after meeting him, that increased elevator sales were not proof that Buddhist prayers worked. Our practice was about becoming one with the Eternal Buddha at the core of our being and was considerably deeper than a bar chart tracking his elevator units.

"Perhaps we should pray," I finally said.

We knelt before the altar. I cleared my mind and opened the *butsudan* doors to the Stupa of Worship. I took out my *juzu* prayer beads, twisted them around my fingers, and was enveloped in the faint scent of sandalwood. Mr. Symes lit the wick of the altar candles standing erect in the gold-filigree candlesticks, and I leaned over and lit incense in their flames before laying the smoking offering in the ash bed. The couple owned a fine copper bell and it produced a rich and resonating tone when I struck it three times with the leather-padded stick. When I began reciting the *Lotus Sutra,* the Symeses joined in at the appropriate moment of the liturgy.

Never before had I heard a more rushed and sloppy prayer.

Their whole approach was barbaric. No other way to describe it.

I was sick to my stomach.

J made myself green tea back at the flat, and heated up the chicken and rice Miss Meli had left me on the stove. I morosely chewed my dinner and thought about the Symeses and their evening prayers. An image popped into my head of Reverend Fukuyama looking so gray in his International Division office that day he handed me the New York assignment, and this picture of Sensei gave me a heart pang. I rang Miss Meli on the cell phone.

"We must schedule Oko, study-prayer meeting, for all Believers. Americans must work on praying together and getting proper rhythm and pronunciation. And the proper breathing technique. Before the temple is opened the community must be of one mind and have correct spirit. Do you understand? We must pray with one voice."

She said she would make the necessary arrangements for the Oko. In the past, the Oko "tours" had taken place in a rented room at a small Manhattan hotel, and she would make similar arrangements until the temple was completed. I think the woman was chewing gum while we talked, for the sound of a cow was coming through the phone.

"So you understand," I said, making sure I was absolutely clear. "Before the party, before even visiting the temple site, we must pray together as a community and ask for the Buddha's guidance and wisdom. This is highest priority. It is the proper way to start the relationship between the Priest and the American Believers— it is the first building block of the New York temple."

"You got it, boss."

I did not know what to say to this. So I hung up the phone.

But Miss Meli did not understand. Or perhaps she understood, but America itself conspired against the proper sequence of events unfolding. When Miss Meli came by the flat the following evening to cook my dinner, she was very apologetic and said, "Sorry, boss, but no one will let us rent their halls and gather in large numbers on their premises unless we first purchase third-party liability coverage. It's because of a new city regulation that no one really understands yet. I need a little time to figure this out."

"You must stop this."

"Huh? Stop what?"

"This . . . calling me boss. This is inappropriate. I am Reverend Oda."

"Got it. Won't happen again."

And then she said something that made me look away and pretend to study a folder.

"It's a tick of mine. When I am nervous. Sorry."

And so it came about that I was formally introduced to the New York Buddhist community, not at a proper religious ceremony before the Cluster of Jewels Mandala, but at an American cocktail party. I had failed entirely in my first modest objective, but the party was in my honor, had long been planned, and so I dutifully emerged from the building that evening in ceremonial robes. Miss Meli was waiting for me in her car out front.

My American assistant wore a floral dress and I made a formal compliment, hoping to encourage her in this more ladylike direction. As the Honda accelerated down the road, she said, "Could you stand to call me Jennifer? Seriously, Reverend Oda, I'm cooking your meals and washing your dishes. Maybe, on occasion, I'll be sorting your laundry. A little informality is really quite natural under these circumstances."

"Miss Jennifer," I said stiffly. "This I will call you."

We drove through an industrial section of Brooklyn and into tree-lined streets filled with colorful tea shops, clothing stores, and rows of stately private homes. This was Park Slope. My assistant expertly sandwiched the car into a tiny parking space and we walked the short distance to a brownstone with a pretty Japanese maple out front and large bay windows overlooking the street.

The house belonged to the Believer Mrs. Gloria Graham, a literary agent who apparently made large amounts of money representing a dieting doctor. At the door, Miss Jennifer introduced Mrs. Graham as "the chair and founder of the New York Temple Fund." She was a tall and regal-looking woman in a beige pantsuit, with long blond hair and a string of pearls around her neck. Her handsome face was tight and plucked-looking, like skinless poultry, but her hands were covered in spots and skin folds that reminded me of the wattles on a chicken's neck.

She took my arm and said, in a deep voice, "Come, Reverend Oda, let me introduce you around. We so want you to feel at home." As we walked from the foyer into the front room, we passed a flat-screen television wrapped in barbed wire. It showed an endlessly looping video of a man sitting in a chair and eating a boiled egg. He did nothing else. I wanted to ask Mrs. Graham about this curious art installation but there was no time, for we were in the front room already and it was filled with Believers pressed right to the walls.

They clapped and yelled out, "Welcome, Reverend Oda! Woo-hoo!"

Close to two hundred people were circulating between several rooms. Mrs. Graham's husband did not practice and I had the impression he was hiding upstairs, but their teenage daughter was a Buddhist and stood by the long table of food under the crystal chandelier, helping caterers pass around silver trays of "finger food," an alarming description until it was explained I should eat the food on a napkin with my fingers.

A glass of white wine was pressed into my hand. In Japan, I would, of course, never publicly drink in front of Believers I had just met, but perhaps because I was in a foreign land and rather nervous, I gratefully accepted the drink. I am not sure whom I met that evening, it remains a blur, but I remember there was an African-American public school teacher from the Bronx, an accountant, and someone who sold wall-to-wall carpets in Bayonne, New Jersey. I bowed and smiled and greeted the American Buddhists and made small talk.

I was quickly drained of my reserves and still had not crossed even the first room. So I grabbed a second glass of wine. If I had to hear one more time from the Americans that "Buddhism is not really a religion but a philosophy," I believe my samurai ancestors would have risen up from the dead and run them through with the point of a *katana* sword. The Americans seemed to believe, as I had experienced with Mr. Symes, that praying for material benefits and receiving them somehow proved that our religion "worked." Some did not address me respectfully as Reverend Oda, but slapped me on the back and called me "Seido" or "Rev" or "Reverend O," and I had no idea how I should respond to this inappropriate informality, for I had never experienced anything quite like this before.

"You'll find I prepared the community well for your arrival," said Mr. Dolan, the Staten Island insurance agent who introduced himself as the "head study honcho." He had auburn hair and very white skin with cancerous-looking bumps, and such a round hard stomach I had the impression he was hiding a medicine ball under his shirt. "You'll be very impressed," he said. "We meet every other week in a Believer's apartment in Manhattan. I've been giving a series of lectures on the proper Buddhist practice, based on my extensive study. It's very rigorous. Intellectually."

"This is commendable. And the lectures are based on what study material?"

"Ton of books. *The Reader's Digest Encyclopedia of Religion, Tales of Siddhartha, Buddhism for Dummies.* The list goes on and on."

"*Buddhism for Dummies?* I am not familiar . . ."

"Don't let the title deceive you. Heavier than it sounds. Excellent text."

Mr. Dolan had backed me into a corner, behind a potted shrub of some sort, and his face was so close to mine as we talked I felt bits of recently chewed finger food fly through the air and land on my brow and chin.

"I see," I managed to say with a stiff expression. "It is more traditional to base lectures on the *Lotus Sutra* and the Four Sacred Texts, such as *The Eternal Teachings,* but very interesting choice of doctrinal material."

"The Believers here know all about karma. All about it. I spent three sessions explaining the concept."

"This is very efficient. In Japan we believe it takes a lifetime to understand karma. At deep level."

"Yeah, well, you'll find things go a lot quicker in America."

I dabbed my forehead with a napkin and excused myself, just as Mr. Dolan was explaining, "It's like that great line from *Zen and the Art of Motorcycle Maintenance*: 'Peace of mind isn't at all superficial.' "

"I see. Yes."

Miss Jennifer continued the introductions from earlier but was then summoned to the kitchen for some minor kitchen emergency, and a group of men, seeing the opening, quickly surrounded me. They gave me their names, most of which I cannot remember but for the smallest man, a pudgy lawyer of African-American descent, who cheerfully informed me he was "Doric. Like the column."

They were all members of a men's choir. As I was close to finishing my third glass of wine, my English became considerably more fluid, and after a question about the Priests' training, I had the circle of men very interested in my descriptions about living conditions for acolytes at the Head Temple, how all the male acolytes slept in a single room, until eighteen, and how the acolytes did everything together, eating and sleeping and bathing and playing games and studying.

The men were extremely interested in this.

"Do you have a partner?"

"No," I said. Buddhist Priests did not have "partners," for it was tradition, in our sect, that the Priests were the head of their own temples. But we were supported by our "seconds." They laughed as if this were the funniest thing they had ever heard, and then another added, "We're simply dying to know you better, Reverend Oda. I'd love it if you came to our place so we could have lunch and maybe pray a little together. Wouldn't we, Johnny?"

His young friend nodded politely and there was something in this informal exchange that gave me a vague sense that perhaps I did not understand everything that was going on. Then, suddenly, my eyes were opened. All these men around me were homosexuals. I made a dignified bow and said I was "most honored" by the invitation but then excused myself for another drink.

After refilling my glass at the side table I moved toward the garden to get some fresh air, but there I spied Mr. and Mrs. Symes sitting in garden chairs and surrounded by courtiers, like an emperor and empress. This was not appealing. So I turned around and headed back into the main rooms, only to notice that the physical therapist, introduced simply as Laura, was following me.

She was an attractive woman with big hair and a bigger chest over a very shapely figure. She wore a blue dress, which, throughout the party, had been hovering in the corner of my vision, as she doggedly followed me from room to room.

Exhausted, I went and sat on a red divan sandwiched in the corner of the living room, next to a young man sitting with his hands calmly folded in his lap. He was a second-year film student at New York University and had unruly blond hair. I was struck by the color of his china-white skin and the beauty mark on the side of his cheek, all of which reminded me of a nineteenth-century courtesan. His eyes were an unusual gray green, and his voice was pleasing to the ear, not the usual loud and guttural pronouncements I was growing accustomed to in New York.

His name was Michael and I had to lean in close to hear what he was saying. We talked about Japanese film—he greatly admired Akira Kurosawa—and for the first time that evening I began quietly enjoying myself. Until, that is, I asked the young man about his family. He turned white and tense and began stuttering that he hated his parents and had once tried to commit suicide, information offered in a tone of voice far more suitable to discussing the weather.

And there our conversation ended. I did not know what to say. He anxiously looked down at the floor, crushing the aluminum can in his hand, and I swept the room for a sign of Miss Jennifer, hoping she could help, but she was nowhere to be seen. Finally, unable to bear the awkwardness any longer, I expressed my sincere pleasure in meeting Mr. Michael, bowed, and slipped away.

Late in the evening, after taking one look at my drained face, Miss Jennifer took me by the elbow and steered me out of the brownstone, after only the briefest round of goodbyes. We walked silently to the car. I could barely put one foot before the other.

It was not just the wine.

It was these American Buddhists.

They were even worse than I imagined.

Chapter Six

The New York temple was at the time little more than an empty lot on a narrow road near the Brooklyn Bridge. I made my plodding way there in the sweltering heat, fanning myself with a city map. I quickly discovered Brooklyn Heights was more refined and affluent than the Italian neighborhood where I lived. The houses of Nicolai Place had tall windows and elegant black shutters, and as I passed by I caught snapshots of wealthy New York: light filtering through a ficus tree and dappling a grand piano, a modern oil painting all splattered colors and spotlights, a sad-eyed giant poodle staring out the window. This was undeniably an elegant section of the city and the ideal showcase for a Buddhist temple. Reverend Fukuyama would be pleased.

The temple's raw construction site was carved from two empty lots in the middle of the block. Mrs. Graham told me at the Park Slope party that a tired convenience store and diner had previously stood on the adjoining properties, always a bane to the local residents because of the delivery trucks and the greasy cooking smells. These buildings had been torn down for our development. The properties still retained their original commercial zoning "variances," and after the requisite public debate where a few of the local and vocal residents complained perfunctorily, the New York Temple Fund was granted planning permission to build a temple in the architectural style of the block.

"The neighbors mostly took it in their stride, just grateful they weren't getting a mosque," Mrs. Graham had said. "Buddhists don't seem to offend anyone. Just other Buddhists, it seems."

Mr. Symes crudely greeted me from across the street, and my shoulders tensed around my ears when I heard him publicly roaring at me like that. He had no idea I was offended, of course, and simply crossed the street, shook my hand, and told me to follow him into the construction site behind the chain-link fence.

A caravan sat atop the rubble and tufts of weeds at the back of the lot, and inside the site office I was introduced to the Finnish-born architect building the temple. He was polite and brought up three-dimensional images of the temple on his laptop. We sipped coffee from Styrofoam cups while the architect explained, in his singsong accent, the temple's layout.

A Believer entering the temple would find himself in an enclosed foyer for coats and shoes. Stepping through the foyer doors—made of wood and frosted glass—he would cross into the Hall of Worship where the Cluster of Jewels Mandala would be protected behind a custom-made *butsudan* standing against the far wall. The temple would have space for almost three hundred kneeling in prayer; a communal bathroom and Priest's anteroom would be located off the prayer hall. A large study with built-in bookcases could be found up the stairs. This floor would also include a library, an acolyte's studio, and a public sitting room where a Priest could meet Believers in private. The third floor provided comfortable living quarters for the Chief Priest and his family.

I took detailed notes and asked many questions so that I had a firm sense of the construction timeline. Work was to start in two weeks, with the digging of the foundation the first task at hand, and the scheduled completion date for the temple was late May of the following year. The large construction bins meant to cart away the debris were, as we spoke, backed into the lot. I was pleased that the architect took detailed notes, quite prepared to adjust rooms in order to make the temple more suitable for a Priest's daily functions. I suggested, for example, the acolyte's room be closer to the stairway, so he could quickly descend steps to answer the temple door. But I declined their repeated requests to name the New York temple.

"This is not my position," I said. "The name of the temple is symbolically very important. It should be decided by the Head Temple and the Chief Priest who takes control of the New York temple."

Mr. Symes looked at me intently but did not say a thing.

Unbeknownst to me I committed an egregious error that day. "Is it true you visited the temple site this afternoon? With Artie Symes?" Mrs. Graham inquired coldly over the phone that evening. I stuttered that I had, a confession that resulted in a long and stony silence. "I would be grateful," she finally said, "for any future requests relating to the temple—anything at all—to be run through me, the New York Temple Fund's chair, and not through members of our board." How petty and small they were. The Americans. This was what I thought at the time. But it was through such skirmishes I became acquainted with the local Believers, as I simultaneously discovered the neighborhood where I lived.

The fruit and vegetable shop on the ground floor of my building had an Italian name—Vedure di Mamma Colonese—and my landlord was a middle-aged bachelor who lived with his aged mother. He owned both the building I lived in and the green-awninged shop on the ground floor, and I thought it both polite and wise to meet him as early as possible after my arrival.

A fug of potato humus and rotting blueberries greeted me when I entered the crate-filled shop. A few customers stood off to the side, squeezing and smelling muskmelons. Mr. Giuseppe Colonese, my landlord, was at the cash register in the gloomy back, staring at a small TV on the counter while absentmindedly pulling at his earlobe with beet-stained fingers. He was tall and lean like a stalk of celery, but with wiry hairs growing in every direction from his thick eyebrows. His downturned mouth suggested to me he had just eaten something extremely bitter and unpleasant.

It was my landlord who, in his raspy and accented English, made me aware I was in the Italian Brooklyn neighborhood known as Little Calabria. A butcher shop stood across from our building, its window filled with Italian sausages speckled with fat and coiled like snakes in metal trays. The butcher, Anthony D'Amato, stood behind the glass and marble counter in a bloodied white apron; a red birthmark stamped across half his face gave him a sinister appearance, particularly when he hacked apart meat with the big cleaver. A string of bald and yellow chickens hung limply from hooks in the back, looking to me as if they had died of some horrible liver disease, but Mr. Giuseppe explained this jaundiced tint was the result of a corn diet, and these sick-looking chickens were in fact a delicacy. He bunched his fingertips together and kissed them, in a rather curious manner. "*Delizioso,*" he said.

A tired-looking hardware store, its window filled with dusty saws and safes, was to the left of D'Amato's, while Café Sorrento occupied the corner of the block. The café had an etched-glass window out front and a metal-top bar in the back. When I walked by I was convinced a rude customer was hissing his disapproval at me, but I discovered, much to my relief, it was just the steam release of the espresso machine. The café in fact passed into the street a rather pleasant smell of roasted coffee.

The Laundromat to the right of D'Amato's was a social focal point of the neighborhood. Inside, old women with buns of iron hair and dressed identically in black skirts and cardigans sat on the orange plastic seats along the far wall of the Laundromat, watching the clothes tumble. They looked to me like Noi, the fearsome temple guardians, for they said very little to one another, just crossed their hands on their laps and wore angry expressions.

The drums of the industrial-sized washing machines turned back and forth, the round windows filled with gray water, soap foam, and sloshing clothes. Scantily clad young mothers stood before machines, bending over the family wash. They dressed in skintight pants and sparkly tops and showed lots of bosom. The young women talked rat-tat-tat among themselves, cracking gum and rolling their eyes, clearly indifferent to the opinions of their elders sitting against the walls. When they came outside to stand in the street and sip Diet Coca-Colas and smoke long cigarettes, they shrieked with such laughter I had the impression they were enjoying lewd jokes at the expense of their husbands.

The men, meanwhile, seemed to congregate at Joey's Pizzeria, on my side of Cortina Street. I glanced inside and was startled by the raspy yelling, the thumping on tabletops to make a point. A television blared from the corner and flickered strange light. One man I saw ate three very large white-cheese pastries at one sitting. It was astounding how he ate them, as if he were starved, when in fact his stomach spilled out in every direction and appeared to store nourishment for an entire village.

But my early impressions of the Brooklyn neighborhood were not quite right. It was not entirely Italian as I first thought, but much more nuanced, the atmosphere changing subtly from street to street. Mr. Giuseppe stood with me under his fruit-stall awning and explained that the once-dangerous Castor Street, a few blocks east, had during recent real estate booms developed in a totally different direction from the old Cortina Street neighborhood, even though the streets were just a short distance apart. "For young professionals," my landlord said, in a way that suggested such people were deeply suspect.

So I walked over to Castor Street and saw what my landlord was talking about. Within half a block I passed a Belgium bistro with gay yellow trim; a shop selling handmade chocolates; and a comedy club, down a set of stairs, smelling of cigars and spilled beer. On the next block, white tablecloths were set with heavy silver and cheerful marigolds at the corner restaurant serving fine Lebanese cuisine, while a shop specializing in undergarments, each measured and hand-fitted for women of "generous proportions," stood on the opposing corner.

All this I observed with cool detachment, as if sizing up a landscape before starting to paint, and I thought that if I ever painted Brooklyn I would use muted grays, browns, and mauves for Cortina Street, while rendering Castor Street in bolder tones of orange, red, and blue. It was while exploring Castor Street in this way that I discovered, much to my delight, a neon-lit newsdealer selling newspapers from all over the world. Starved for news from home, I went inside and purchased the *Asahi Shimbun*, before heading back to the flat, light of foot, the Japanese paper tucked under my arm. But as I turned back to the studio—passing an art dealer of nineteenth-century French photography—I had a sudden insight into the nature of this robust commercial area. Castor Street was crafted out of a disorienting mix-and-mash of cultures, and I thought, *Brooklyn is not solid. It is unstable.*

This insight would have been quite telling, to anyone with greater wisdom than I had at the time. For the Buddhist concept of *esho-funi* quite clearly states there is no separate and distinct nature between our inner lives and the surrounding environment we live in. They are "nondual," like a man and his shadow, always reflecting each other. But I did not really understand this at the time, this link between "unstable" Brooklyn and myself. Such wisdom only came later.

A few days after my first visit to Castor Street, the police blocked the neighborhood streets off with blue wooden gates. This was no robbery in progress, but the July Fourth national holiday celebrating America's birth as a nation. On a small stage in the center of the Sant'Andrea Park, from which the American flag flew, oily-looking men with banjos, guitars, and violins howled into microphones. I found myself drawn into the local fair by the smell of chickens and ribs roasting over hot coals.

Ambling from stall to stall, I stopped to sniff dried lavender buds sprinkled on beeswax soap blocks, and discovered a hundred things I never knew existed—white balls of cheese sitting in plastic tubs of water, sausages that were red black and bent back like twisted and rusted railroad nails. When I glanced up from such a stall, I saw Miss Jennifer at the far end of the park walking arm in arm with a younger and quite beautiful woman.

The pretty blond-haired friend rested her head lovingly on the shoulder of Miss Meli, who was smiling with deep contentment.

I quickly turned around and left the park, not wanting to have an awkward meeting with my American assistant and her lover. It was best to keep my distance.

I continued down Castor Street to get the *Asahi Shimbun* from my newsdealer, as had become my habit, but he was closed for the holiday. Disappointed, I stopped off for a bite to eat at the People's Republic of Brooklyn, a wood-paneled café. According to the chalkboard out front, the informal restaurant was serving Spanish omelets and Bloody Marys, a most curious-sounding meal.

I lifted *The New York Times* off the peg on the wall, where it was clamped to a heavy wooden stick, and took the paper to a back booth. The unfamiliar food was plopped down in front of me and within just a few bites I had heartburn. It was while I had my head down, digesting the day's news alongside an acid burp, that a shadow fell across the page.

I looked up. It was Miss Jennifer with her blond friend.

"Hey, Reverend Oda. . . . Sorry to interrupt. I just wanted to quickly introduce you to someone special." Miss Jennifer proudly turned in the woman's direction and I rose reluctantly.

"This is my younger sister, Sadie."

I bowed my head—with slightly colored cheeks. Miss Jennifer's sister came forward to earnestly shake my hand with both her hands, and said, "I am so happy to meet you, Reverend Oda. I can't tell you how honored my sister is to be your assistant while you're in America. Even just playing a small role in the construction of the temple means a great deal to her. Honestly, you should hear her. She talks of nothing else."

Miss Jennifer put her hand on my arm. "Please, sit. Go on. We really don't want to interrupt your lunch. But I did want to quickly let you know we're all set up for the Oko study-lectures. We got the insurance squared away. The first meeting will be on Friday."

The Oko was held in a lower Manhattan hotel filled with threadbare carpets, a sour odor, and a constant stream of luggage-wheeling airline staff from South Africa and Malaysia moving back and forth through the lobby. I entered the hotel ballroom on the second floor and found Miss Jennifer and a few other Believers unstacking chairs and dragging them across the floor. The altar was set up on the far wall.

"What are you doing?" I asked.

Miss Jennifer looked up, wiped her brow. "Setting up."

"No chairs. The Believers must kneel. It is part of our formal practice. Kneeling shows we have proper humility before the Cluster of Jewels Mandala."

"But kneeling is a Japanese custom. Americans sit in chairs. Some of the Believers are a little overweight and elderly and really have trouble kneeling. Particularly for such a long time."

"We do not modify the formal practice of the Eternal Teachings simply because Americans are fat."

There was a stunned silence.

"That's a little harsh," Miss Jennifer finally said, "but, okay, you're the Priest."

That day I led the American Believers in prayer, for one hour, as I tried without success to teach them the proper rhythm and pronunciation of the Sutra recitation, even banging a drum during the chanting to help them keep the right tempo. They all wanted to be generals, however, not foot soldiers, and they rushed ahead of my attempts to lead them in prayer, or slowed down, as if drugged. There was no unity. No discipline.

There were maybe one hundred Believers in the room, about half of the people who attended the party in Park Slope, and the room smelled of moldy carpet and sour socks. I began the lecture, formally dressed in coal-gray priest robes over the *kesa*, the white robes, but the Believers before me mostly wore shorts, T-shirts, and flip-flops. They slouched during prayers, absent-mindedly picked at their feet. A man made a big production about sitting in the front row so he could study, he told everyone, but as soon as he sat down his eyes drooped and a short time later he was snoring. Mrs. Graham sat next to him and had the good manners to be embarrassed. She nudged the fellow once or twice, but other than a slight fluttering of his eyelids, he did not respond.

"Proper Buddhist practice is like taking medicine for the many ills that we experience in the course of life. None of you must take this lightly. If you have a bad infection, but do not properly follow the instructions for taking the antibiotics, then you are never cured and the illness comes back twice as strong. This is similar to Buddhist faith. Buddhism has a formal practice, which is the medicine. To become healthy and withstand bacterial attacks, you must first properly follow the instructions on the medicine bottle . . . ."

The Believers rustled in their bags, hauled out tinfoil packets with all manner of foods, even opened up Coca-Cola cans with a pop and hiss like they were at a picnic, not a religious ceremony. I was almost rendered speechless by this behavior. Miss Laura, the physical therapist with the big eyes and bigger chest, wore a bright red dress and followed my every move with great hunger in her eyes, but I was not at all sure her appetite was for the Tranquil Light.

Mrs. Symes's orange hair tower was piled inordinately high as usual and even though I could not see her face behind one of the very large Believers, I frequently saw her red nails rising in the air and then disappearing into her hair pileup, to scratch her scalp. Mr. Dolan, meanwhile, sat near the front and looked over my shoulder. When curiosity got the better of me, I turned to glance at what was capturing his attention. He was studying his reflection in the glass-framed etching on the wall.

I took a deep breath and pushed on. I explained why there was a candle on the right side of the altar, before the *butsudan,* and a vase of greens to the left, and the incense burner and cup of clear water at the center of the altarpiece. I explained that the long-lasting and sweet-smelling green leaves symbolized eternal life. When we approached closely the Cluster of Jewels Mandala we should always do so with a green leaf clutched between our teeth, to prevent spitting, for this small formality shows our sincere attitude of respect to the Buddha's life as embodied and inscribed in the Sacred Scroll. The burning incense, this represented Chudo, the Middle Way between the worlds of life and death.

I was in the middle of explaining the importance of the lit candles—how the light is symbolic of the Buddha's wisdom illuminating the darkness of this world—when someone near the front silently released gas. I had never smelled anything quite like this, like very old and dead cow, possibly the result of too much American fast food. Because I was so resentful of being in New York, I assumed my presence was equally loathsome to the local Buddhists, and so my immediate thought was that a hostile Believer in the audience had just passed his verdict on my Oko in this rude manner.

I defiantly lifted my chin and pushed on as if nothing were wrong. By keeping my priestly bearing and religious decorum, I decided, I would exemplify Head Temple spirit unswayed by the Winds of Impermanence. But the Believer must have been releasing gas bit by bit to avoid noise, because the smell continued to roll endlessly over us in waves. There were whispers and shuffling until Mrs. Graham in the front row made a disgusted face, waved the air, and held a perfumed handkerchief up to her nose, all of which seemed to give the other Believers license to snigger and snort.

There was no point in continuing. I wearily ended the Oko with a short prayer, closed the *butsudan,* and extinguished the candle. The fellow in the front row who had slept through the entire lesson suddenly opened his eyes, stretched, and said, amazingly, it was a "most excellent lecture." There was much grunting and chatter behind me as I turned around to discreetly take off my ceremonial robes behind a screen, fold them carefully away, and gather up my belongings. I assumed everyone was in a rush to get out of the foul-smelling room, but when I turned back to the hall I found they had all lined up as if waiting for a bus.

Miss Jennifer whispered they wanted my "advice." I was stunned. In Japan, Believers came after hours to see the Priest privately and discreetly in his office, and would never talk intimately in public. I did recognize, however, I had little choice but to speak with the Americans like this, as if we were in some open-air market, for there was nowhere else for us to talk until the temple was built.

Miss Laura was first in line, resplendent in her red dress, her big mane of bottle-blond hair teased and shellacked. She licked her lips and talked to me incomprehensibly about "New Age" and "crystals" and "channeling the Buddha's voice" during evening prayer. In an exaggerated feminine voice, girlish and breathy, she informed me she was filled with "Buddha-love," before gently putting her hand on my forearm and suggesting we have a drink together.

I blushed for her. Such silly remarks she was making. And it only got worse from there, for she was followed by a Haitian woman who told me she regularly saw the face of Jesus Christ in the shadows of the Cluster of Jewels Mandala. Then a couple invited me to a dinner party they were hosting; I had a strong sense they wanted to show off their "guru" to friends. Another pushed me to teach at a Tibetan Buddhist Center until our temple was built, unaware this was like asking a Catholic priest to say mass at a Jewish synagogue.

"I can help you," the insurance agent, Mr. Dolan, told me. "You should come to one of my Okos. Really. I can show you how to connect with the American Believers and teach Buddhism from the gut."

"Is this so?" I said stiffly.

I was unsettled further by the way the American Believers unburdened themselves in public. They had little shame over publicly pouring out details of their private lives: about their divorce and how they declared bankruptcy three times, about how the staples in their stomach popped, or how they were having sex with their boss, or that their mother had just announced she was moving in with another woman. Even Mrs. Graham, who seemed to me quite reserved and ladylike, wanted to know if I might be available for some marriage counseling. "My husband won't admit our daughter has ADHD," she said. "It's so upsetting. Perhaps you could have a word with him?"

I said very little of substance, but that did not appear to matter, because the Believers seemed to interpret my blank face as confirmation they could head in whatever particular direction they wanted to go. The American Buddhists simply did not grasp the fundamentals of our faith. They seemed to think enlightenment was a place where one was very nice and very rich and free of all problems.

Of all the peculiar experiences I had during that early period of adjustment in New York, none surpassed that unusual morning when, after breakfast, Miss Jennifer and I descended to Cortina Street together. My assistant was returning to her flat in Cobble Hill, and I was off for my newspaper purchase before settling down to write Reverend Fukuyama. But as we exited the building's front door, I caught a glimpse of a vaguely familiar shape in the periphery of my vision, lurking among the boxes of lettuce and red beets and cabbages of my landlord's sidewalk stall.

"Reverend Oda! Is this where you live?"

It was Miss Laura in her usual high heels and tight-fitting dress. Every instinct in me said this was no coincidence, to find Miss Laura shopping where I lived, and I did not know how to respond to this awkward situation. But Miss Jennifer stepped forward and lightly said, "Hey, Laura."

Miss Laura was visibly startled and instantly looked to the front door from which we both had come. You could see, in her face, her brain racing with questions, but she managed to reply, "Hello, Jennifer. I've heard so much about Vedure di Mamma Colonese. For years. Thought I'd finally give the store a try. Glad I did!"

She then turned back to the shop attendant and handed him a twenty-dollar bill from her purse. "That'll be all, honey. Thank you. I'll settle up now." The boy dashed back into the store with her money, while my landlord, Mr. Giuseppe, stood at the shop's entrance with his arms folded, looking out at Miss Laura with an expression of open distaste. Miss Laura dismissively turned back in my direction, and said, "Are you settling in, Reverend Oda? Moving is so difficult. I can't stand it."

"I am settling in. Slowly."

"And you're being properly taken care of?"

My assistant stiffened at this remark and so I responded slowly and carefully, "Miss Jennifer is taking excellent care of me, thank you, even though my helplessness in the kitchen and with general housekeeping must be troubling to her."

Miss Jennifer was chewing gum so hard I could see the muscles clenching and unclenching in her jaw, but she responded lightly, "I have three brothers. Trust me. You're no trouble at all, Reverend Oda."

The boy returned with Miss Laura's change. Smiling, resting her hand gently on my forearm, the woman whispered in my ear, "Must run now, Reverend Oda. But remember, you promised me a drink. Here's my number. I'll get my feelings hurt if you don't call." There was some yelling across the street, which momentarily distracted us, and Miss Laura used the moment to press a card, with her telephone number, into my hand. "Bye, sweeties," she cried as she trotted off in her high heels in the direction of the subway.

From the doorframe where he was leaning, Mr. Giuseppe spat out a word that to me sounded like "pootana." I did not know what this meant, it must have been Italian, but in tone I understood it was not at all complimentary. Miss Jennifer and I started walking down Cortina Street together. I kept replaying in my head the conversation with Miss Laura. "What does this woman want?" I finally blurted out. "I do not understand why she gave me her telephone number."

"Get out of here! She slipped you her number?" Miss Jennifer rolled her eyes. "Well, it's pretty obvious Laura wants to jump your bones. Subtlety has never been the woman's strong point. She once made a pass at Artie Symes. Can you imagine that? Harriet almost tore her apart. It was ugly."

"Jump bones? What is this?"

Miss Jennifer paused briefly before she said, much more gently and slowly, "Laura is hoping to see what you have under your robes, Reverend Oda. Do you understand? Am I being clear?"

I blushed a deep red, curtly excused myself at the next corner, and headed over to Castor Street, allowing Miss Jennifer to continue down Cortina Street by herself.

Imagine my shock at hearing such a thing. Just imagine.

Chapter Seven

As Reverend Fukuyama predicted, I became, out of necessity, intricately involved in the minutiae of American temple administration. Miss Jennifer came by the flat in the heat of late summer, her arms as usual bursting with bags. She had me sign legal documents that registered me in New York State as an ordained priest, so that I could perform state-recognized Buddhist weddings. All the time she was telling me to "sign here and here" she was chewing that infernal gum in my ear. When the paperwork was complete she told me that a squabble had broken out on the temple's fund-raising board. Mrs. Graham was taking issue with Mr. Symes's efforts to control the temple funds and she wanted a board restructuring, with a new slate of directors, particularly now that I was available to assume the position of New York Temple Fund chairman. I entered the date of the emergency board meeting in my calendar.

This was when I realized Miss Jennifer had some very worthwhile qualities. The blunt and informal way she talked was sometimes difficult to digest, this was true, but I also had to admit she had a gift for helping me understand what was going on with the New York Buddhist community below the surface of events. I increasingly came to rely on her astute observations.

One day she appeared unexpectedly at my apartment door. "Reverend Oda," she said, "I hope you don't mind me coming by like this, but I am not standing here as your assistant. I am standing here as a simple lay Believer. I have a very personal request."

"If I can be of help," I said warily, "I will help."

"My fiancé died a month before our wedding, a very long time ago. Died in a motorcycle crash in Connecticut. During a rainstorm."

This was the moment I realized how badly I had misread her, and, despite my shock, I managed to say, "I am very sorry."

"Yeah, me, too, but it was a long time ago." She looked at me evenly, dry-eyed. "Could we perform a memorial service for Jimmy? Next Monday it will be exactly ten years since he died. He was twenty-eight."

"Yes, of course. I will prepare a memorial stupa." I held out a pad and pen. "Please. Write down his full name, date of birth, and the day of his death. I will make the proper preparations."

I studied my diary and we agreed to perform the memorial at four o'clock the following Monday. I suspect my cheeks were a bit red, ashamed as I was by my early assumptions about my assistant, and that evening this significant misreading of Miss Jennifer led me to perform an extended *zange,* sincere apology, before the Cluster of Jewels Mandala.

In the coming weeks Miss Jennifer only grew in my esteem. I began to notice, for example, that whenever she asked my advice, such as the proper sequences of reciting chapters of the liturgy during everyday prayers versus formal ceremonies, she would listen hard and then incorporate whatever I said without fuss. I also began to notice she was never without a book in her purse, something dense-looking on philosophy or psychology. It was a new bit of intelligence that did not fit into my earlier conviction she was a simple housekeeper.

My eyes were finally opened in the worst of the summer heat. New York had turned oven-hot and a sticky heat rose mercilessly from the pavement. Born and raised in the cool mountains of Fukushima Prefecture, Brooklyn in August was, for me, the Avichi Hell. The air itself had a meaty substance to it. Whole families sat deflated on their side-street stoops, sipping iced coffees and Coca-Colas and fanning themselves. Couples woke me up late at night, their drunken brawls provoked no doubt by the sweating sheets and throbbing walls that would not cool down. During the day, anger was everywhere and the slightest thing— water drops hitting me as I walked under air conditioners—was enough to send me into an irrational rage. Even the giant water bugs seemed oppressed by the merciless heat; they emerged at dusk to hunker down beside garbage cans overflowing with waste.

One such blistering August afternoon I went for a walk, the heat in my apartment unbearable, trapped as it was under the tin roof. The old air-conditioning unit hummed in the one room but it did not cool the apartment. I escaped into the streets. I walked to the bakery at the corner of President Street, where I had recently discovered Italian ices made of pistachio nuts, cream, and lemon. An impatient woman behind me drummed her fingers on the counter; the shop girl scooped lemon ice out of a barrel, snatched my money, and said "next" in that abrasive nasal manner that I had begun to recognize as Brooklyn's dialect.

On my return I passed the Sant'Andrea Park, the concrete play-ground where old men in fedora hats smoked cigars and played a game called bocce under the shade of a chestnut tree. Not wishing to rush back to the boiling apartment, I ate my ice on the shaded bench and watched the ball-clattering game. Miss Jennifer was by chance shopping in the neighborhood. When she spotted me in the park she crossed the street, slid with her bags along the bench, and gave me a white-toothed American smile. She wore cutoff jeans, flip-flops, and those bug-eyed sunglasses. I courte-ously nodded back and said, "Is hot."

"Sure is." She took a long drink of water from a plastic bottle.

It was too hot to put up my usual defenses and so the conversa-tion naturally moved in a more personal direction. I discovered, for example, Miss Jennifer had a PhD in Italian literature from Columbia University. She was, in fact, an expert in Medieval Ital-ian. I was astonished.

Her informal way of dressing and talking initially led me to believe she was a laborer of some sort, but that afternoon I learned her father, a partner in a conservative Wall Street firm, had "belligerently liberal views" and for years made her and her siblings attend the toughest public schools in Brooklyn. When her brother was badly beaten up, her mother overrode her father's objections and transferred them all to private schools.

When I politely queried her about her work, she said she translated Italian writers into English for American publishers, and had recently completed a grueling four-year project translating Boccaccio's *The Decameron*. For this reason, she was "totally burnt out" by translation work and had volunteered to become my assistant.

I disposed of my lemon ice cup in the green bin as a steel bocce ball flew through the air and clacked off a cluster of balls in the alley of dust.

"Have you been to Eddie Dolan's study meetings yet?" she asked.

"No. I have not."

She looked away, but I could see, in her fluttering lids, she was irritated and disappointed by my response. She said, "Yeah, well, I wish you would," and took another gulp of water. Miss Jennifer then suggested Mr. Dolan, the community's study leader, really didn't know much about Buddhism at all. He was, she said, a "charlatan," and that was the true reason why she had become my assistant. "We're starved for the real thing," she said, "and I was secretly hoping you wouldn't mind privately recommending some Buddhist texts for me to study. A lot of the key writings have been translated into English, but I need you to guide me, to point out what texts are important and which aren't."

This was the first sign of proper Buddha-Seeking Spirit I had seen in America, and I instantly responded, "Miss Jennifer, I will be most pleased to put together a study schedule for you and help you pick out the right reading material. This is very encouraging to me, that you want to study the Buddhist canon."

Moved by her simple expression of faith, I did not speak again for some time, and so we sat in silence, side by side, in the shade of the chestnut tree, puffs of cigar smoke from the bocce game drifting our way. "You know," she finally said, "if it's that hot in your apartment we really should get you another air conditioner. The one you have is probably shot. Come on. Let's see what they have at the hardware store."

My assistant jumped up, the bag of groceries under one arm, and darted through the traffic of Cortina Street to the hardware store opposite the park. I tried to follow her but cars were stuck in traffic, both directions, and she had not crossed at the lights. The metal hoods of the cars shimmered with heat and their sound systems were at such high volume that the very cement I stood on pulsed with the bass thump of the pounding music. Every time I put my foot on the street to follow Miss Jennifer, an SUV or truck lurched aggressively forward a few inches, a horn somewhere blared, and I jumped back to the safety of the sidewalk. This simple monk from the mountains could not, in the engine-revving and hostile traffic of New York, go forward or back or knew what to do.

All this Miss Jennifer saw from the far pavement, and she made her way back across the street and wordlessly took my hand. Like a mother duck swimming across a river current, ducklings following safe in her wake, Miss Jennifer bobbed and weaved her way through the cars, gently turning left around the eddy of a front bumper, pausing to let another car roll by, turning right around a back bumper, until she had safely guided us across the road and we were standing on terra firma before the hardware store.

"All right," she said. "Now let's get some chill on you."

I realized then, if I ever wanted to find my way back to Mount Nagata, that I had to take this woman's hand and let her show me the way through the rough-and-tumble streets of America.

The New York Temple Fund board meeting lasted three hours and resembled the eighth and lowest circle of hell-torture, the cauldron of incessant suffering forty thousand *yojanas* under the earth. Not even the location of the meeting could be established in advance without a dozen phone calls and endless emails back and forth, until Miss Jennifer made the commonsense argument that most of us lived in Brooklyn, closer to Mrs. Graham's house than Mr. Symes's Manhattan apartment, and for such practical reasons the emergency board meeting should be held in her home.

When Mr. Symes finally arrived from Manhattan in his chauffeur-driven Town Car, he seemed quite humble compared to the exuberant person I had previously met. The rest of us arrived at the townhouse well before him, and we were politely sipping tea on Mrs. Graham's odd sectional couch, which looked to me like it had been melted in an oven before finding its way into the woman's living room. Suddenly, through the bay window, we saw Mr. Symes climbing the steps of the Park Slope brownstone and ringing the doorbell. Mrs. Graham strode across the house and opened the heavy front door. From where I sat, I could see her peering coldly down the steps at the man she had, just a few minutes earlier, dismissed as "that elevator salesman."

Mr. Symes greeted Mrs. Graham with dignified reserve and sincerely thanked her on behalf of the entire Buddhist community for so elegantly hosting the party in my honor the previous month. Mrs. Graham appeared mollified, shook his extended hand, and then guided us all to the dining room next door. I was instructed to sit at the head of the mahogany table, next to the gavel. Miss Jennifer sat to my right and slightly behind, taking the minutes. Opposite me sat the fund's lawyer, whom I finally recognized as "Doric. Like the column," from the night of the party. I gave a benediction and the meeting was officially opened.

Mr. Symes promptly took a sheaf of papers out of his briefcase and plunked them down on the table. He had a whole new set of bylaws and directors' slate drawn up by the lawyer who was also on the board and sitting in the room. I was uncertain as to what this meant, but Miss Jennifer leaned over and whispered, "Artie just tabled a motion, seconded by Doric, that we immediately vote on his new slate of directors."

Mrs. Graham had red blotches on her neck. "We are here to *discuss* changes to the board," she said. But proceedings were already formally under way, whether she liked it or not. It was unanimously agreed that I should be made the New York Temple Fund's chairman, with the deciding vote. The documents also proposed that Mr. Symes would assume the newly created position of vice chairman, as well as the head of fund-raising and asset allocation, in effect bumping Mrs. Graham out of her previous responsibilities. Miss Jennifer was to be reappointed as the secretary, while Mr. Doric was again made head of legal affairs. The fund's outside auditor, Deloitte Touche, was to be reappointed for another year, while Mrs. Graham was demoted to "public relations director."

"This is a hostile takeover," Mrs. Graham said acidly, before going on about how the proposal was riddled with "serious conflicts of interest" and, as a result, the temple "could very well lose its nonprofit status."

The things she said had me quite on edge, but the lawyer and Mr. Symes calmly refuted her claims, one by one. "That's a blatant falsehood, Gloria," said Mr. Symes. "We have the checks and balances in place stipulated by law." The arguments went back and forth, endlessly and hotly for over two hours, each comma of the twenty-seven-page legal document before us painfully combed over and analyzed by Mrs. Graham, Mr. Symes, and Mr. Doric.

I held the gavel and looked grave but understood only half of the fast-paced conversation, mostly because it was so technical and revolved around American nonprofit statutes. Many of the details I learned afterward, when I asked Miss Jennifer to explain what precisely had transpired during the board meeting. During the meeting itself, however, my assistant kept her head down while writing furiously on her yellow notepad. Her job appeared to be limited to documenting the arguments being made, not actually participating in them, and however I pleaded with my eyes that she take a more active role, she kept her head down and performed her given task. I was very disappointed. I had, at that point, come to value her advice.

Things turned when the three warring board members suddenly demanded that I vote on their respective positions. Each pushed me to "carry the motion," but I had no idea what this meant. Perhaps I was meant to carry the papers to the room next door? Reading the confusion in my face, Miss Jennifer again leaned over and whispered in my ear. "Ask some questions. Find out who would be the person best equipped to help you oversee the temple's construction. Just take control. Use common sense."

I took a deep breath. "Excuse me."

They all stopped talking.

"Mrs. Graham. You have done very, very good job building the New York Temple Fund. But now we are entering new phase. Nnn? It is physical construction of building. For this reason I must ask question. Have you ever built a building of this size before?"

"No, I can't say I have, but . . ."

I turned to Mr. Symes. "Please answer the same question."

"Three factories I built were all several times the size of this project."

"And you are the single largest donor of funds to the temple?"

"Yes. By a wide margin."

Miss Jennifer's whispered advice—"Use common sense"—again reverberated in my ear, and I said, "Mrs. Graham, I think it is good for the temple that Mr. Symes now take the position of vice chairman. It is wise to switch jobs around sometimes. I have seen this done many times at Head Temple. Such movement keeps administrators fresh. So, I thank you sincerely for past efforts, but must ask you now to take up new public relations position."

We voted. The new slate of directors was passed. The pressed-lipped Mrs. Graham then tabled a motion of her own, which was unanimously accepted: 80 percent of the temple's funds would be immediately put in escrow, in reserve for the actual construction, the funds solely invested in U.S. Treasuries. "We do not want the fund's new asset manager speculating in the stock market," Mrs. Graham pointedly said.

The first call of the next day brought even more distress. The construction of the temple had ground to a halt, Mr. Symes informed me. An official of the city was forbidding any further work without reopening some previously settled zoning matter. He suggested the inspector might be fishing for a bribe.

I was horrified and said so. This was not a cause we could make. We were building a temple. It had to stand on pure ground.

$\mathcal{J}$f these developments with the temple's construction were not difficult enough to manage, the unstable New York University student, Michael, was demanding an increasing amount of my energy and time. I had not spoken to the boy since the Park Slope party, although he had attended every Oko since then. He always sat quietly in the back of the ballroom, never seeking to engage me after the study meeting. But one night he called me at two in the morning. I was asleep and stumbled to find my cell phone. The boy was so upset he could barely talk, and at first I did not understand a word he was saying. It was quite clear, however, he was extremely anxious and begging me to come to his apartment.

"It's a matter of life or death," he whispered.

This I understood. I staggered around the studio hunting for my clothes. I managed to find a taxi after just a few minutes, which was a sign that the Buddhist gods were protecting the boy, for it is not easy to find a taxi in Brooklyn at any time of day.

I was at his apartment on West Eleventh Street only forty minutes after his call. He was waiting at the door in a silk kimono, fluttery and shaky, talking impossibly fast. I followed him into his studio and was met, full force, by the sour odor of American student life. Dirty clothes and books were scattered across the floor, a half-eaten cheese sandwich lay on a chair, and the bed in the corner was a jumble of dingy sheets.

"She wants me."

"Who wants you?"

The young man glared. "Don't say you don't know!"

I swallowed hard and took a breath. "I assure you I do not know who you are talking about. It is not clear. My English sometimes fails me."

He seemed to accept this explanation, and again began to pace, talking half to himself, half to me. It was disconcerting. But an inner voice sternly told me to get ahold of myself. So I removed a sweater from a director's chair and sat down, planting both my feet firmly on the floor.

Michael paced back and forth across the studio's hardwood floors, past the wall of pine bookshelves, constantly pulling a white linen handkerchief through the fingers of one hand. He paced, chattered, and every time he swept by, dust balls rolled across the floor. After sitting still awhile and listening to his manic rambling, I slowly understood there was some presence he was deathly afraid of physically taking shape in the room.

I wordlessly went to his altar and knelt before the Cluster of Jewels Mandala. I lit the candle and three sticks of incense, gathering my beads and centering my thoughts. He continued to pace the apartment behind me. I fervently prayed that the Buddha and all the Assembled Gods of the Treasure Tower come here, to this Manhattan apartment, to protect this young man. I prayed he be able, with their support, to find the courage to fight whatever he was afraid of, that he find this strength face-to-face with the Buddha, on his knees before the Cluster of Jewels Mandala. I prayed that his life would fuse with the Eternal Light Wisdom of the Buddha. I prayed from the depths of my being. After a while I heard him slow down, kneel beside me. Soon we were united in one voice and forging through time and space during the mysteries of prayer. I left his apartment at four in the morning, exhausted but content that I had done the best I could as a Priest.

Michael called again two nights later, and we repeated the previous evening's events with little deviation. The following day I was bone-weary, run-down. My obligations to the Buddhist community at large were starting to materially suffer from Mr. Michael's nocturnal demands, and so when he called a third time I decided I would not forgo another evening's sleep.

I could at first hear only breathing at the other end of the phone. "Hello? Hello?" It was a few moments before Michael, his voice cracked and hoarse and exhausted, finally whispered, "The Buddha is sitting in my armchair."

I rubbed my forehead. "Put him on the phone. I want to talk to him."

"What?"

"I want to talk to him," I said firmly. "Please ask the Buddha to come to the phone. I have need to talk with him."

The "Buddha" apparently decided to leave. I called later that morning, after a deep sleep, but there was no answer at Mr. Michael's apartment. I became afraid. What if my action had pushed him to do a terrible thing? I paced my studio, wringing my hands like Mr. Michael himself had done, until I had the idea to call Miss Jennifer. I was much relieved when she told me, after she made some phone calls, that the boy had checked himself into a state mental hospital.

That afternoon I had a strong need to paint. Since arriving in America two months earlier, I had returned to the rituals that helped fend off painful pangs of homesickness when I was a student in Tokyo. Under the pressed plum blossoms from Mount Nagata, given to me by Mrs. Fukuyama and propped up on the mantel of my Brooklyn wall, I laid out across the Formica table a pad of paper, my inkstick, brushes, and mixing stone. I then poured myself a generous cup from the bottle of Juyondai sake given to me by Sensei.

I painted from memory my beloved temple grounds, and my imagination was again able to taste and smell the temple's *shikimi*-leaf air, the chanting waterfall, the forest mist suffused with sap from the camphor tree and hinoki cypress. In my Brooklyn studio, I felt the moist forest earth beneath my feet, my favorite patch of Japanese soil on the slopes of sacred Mount Nagata. I painted that spot again and again: the ocher melon fields of the foothills, the waters of the Kappa-gawa, the ash and ginkgo forests rising vertically up Mount Nagata's raked slopes. Always in the corner of the painting, my sanctuary, a faint outline of the Temple of Everlasting Prayer and its red pagoda.

The Head Temple scene I was painting came in as usual, full of delicacy and tranquillity, and I comfortably slipped into the trance of the active imagination. The brush took on a life of its own, dancing across the paper, from paint pot and water, to cream of paper, and back again. Suddenly very tired, I put down my paintbrush and went to the kitchen in search of an apple.

I returned to the watercolor pad with my teeth sunk into the flesh of the tart apple—and froze in horror. I had, in my trance, painted a figure, an anonymous man bent over in the corner of the painting. I moved my face close to the paper to get a better look, and was shocked to discover he was setting the Head Temple's dry melon fields on fire with a torch.

I sat down at the laptop and sent Reverend Fukuyama an email, again urging him to find my replacement. *It is imperative,* I wrote. *Please.*

Michael signed himself into Bellevue Hospital, a large city hospital in Manhattan, but his parents, informed of his mental collapse, moved him to a private clinic just outside of New York, behaving not at all like the cold devils he had described. Miss Jennifer and I of course visited the young man at the first available opportunity.

The private clinic was in Westchester County, in a leafy suburb just north of New York City. There were no walls or fences surrounding the redbrick clinic with white columns, just a courteous guard who advised Miss Jennifer to park her Honda alongside a silver Mercedes. Old oak trees on the property swayed in the gentle breeze and they provided a sense of tranquillity and solidness to the property.

The young man's private room was on the second floor, and he was pacing back and forth in front of a commode when we arrived. "Hi, Jennifer! Hi, Reverend Oda!" he said cheerfully. We warmly returned his greeting, but just as we were about to sit in the room's two chairs, the young man stopped in his tracks and shrieked, "Don't sit there!"

We froze. He looked down at his feet. "If you sit there, I can't see you," he said. He did not look up, but radiated a hot anxiety off his tipped head. "Please. Sit on the windowsill."

Miss Jennifer guided me by the elbow to the window, where we gingerly rested our buttocks on the sill. I felt I must say something, so I cleared my throat and said, "I am very pleased you are in such a fine clinic. You have a nice room. Is the food good?"

"It's okay."

"I see. And are you treated well?"

"Sometimes they are here."

"Ahh," I said. "This is your parents?"

"No, no. Them. Them."

"This is good. No?"

The boy gave me a fierce look and picked up a heavy book. I think he was about to throw it at me. "I'm pretty sure Michael is talking about the presences he is afraid of," Miss Jennifer quickly interjected.

I was totally and utterly confused. But I saw how tense he was and knew I must do something to reduce the tension in the room, or someone was going to get hurt. "I am ashamed that I said an inappropriate thing," I stammered. "It is my English. I do not always understand what Americans are telling me. Please forgive me my lack of understanding, Michael. I am very ashamed I have said something hurtful. This was not my intent."

There was a long and awkward silence as we all stared at the empty chairs. I was at a loss as to what I should say or do next, and, as the silence persisted, I grew increasingly irritated and wanted to leave. It was at that point Michael blurted out, "Prayer gives me courage."

"You probably want to pray with Reverend Oda. Will that help?" Miss Jennifer asked.

The young man finally raised his eyes to look at me and I saw for the first time the unmentionable horrors. There raged, in the flicker of his eyes, a fiery blaze and small arms flailing and I was suddenly afraid of getting swallowed by this thing in the boy's face that I knew wanted to consume not just him but me.

I tore my eyes from his gaze, pulled my prayer beads out of my briefcase, and tied on my ceremonial robes. "Where do you pray?" I said.

"I usually pray as I pace."

"From now on, you must kneel and pray toward the East. Collect yourself and focus your mind toward the sun. Where is east?"

"The window faces north."

"Then where the armchairs are is east. So sorry. But we must move the chairs."

Before he could object, I had brusquely pulled the armchairs to the other side of the room, and replaced them with a two-foot-high table taken from next to the bed. I smacked the top of it with my hand.

"This is your altar. Listen to me. This is sacred space, Michael. When you kneel here and pray, you will be protected. Your demons will turn into Buddhas, your poison into medicine. This is what the Buddhist texts promise those who have faith." I went to the sink, rinsed a spare glass, and filled it with tap water. I placed this offering of pure water in the center of the makeshift altar.

"The *Lotus Sutra* is your lantern in the dark. Recite it here with deep sincerity, and it will show you the way home to safety. Miss Jennifer, please make sure Michael is sent incense for him to offer the Buddha. And if possible, we should bring up his *butsudan* and his Stupa of Worship. But if this is not possible, it is not important. Michael, you must understand, the Buddhaland emerges when there is sincere spirit and effort. This is what beckons the Buddha and all the Assembled Gods. Nothing else."

Miss Jennifer made a note in her pad. Michael seemed to devour every word I said, like a parched man suddenly offered water. It was then that I heard Sensei's voice. I recalled an instance when Reverend Fukuyama firmly told an arrogant acolyte that Buddhism was "taught with the back." That is, it was a Priest's duty to lead a Believer to pray directly to the Cluster of Jewels Mandala. A Priest who too often faced the Believers, rather than offered his back, interfered with their direct connection to the Buddha.

So I silently led the three of us in that room to the makeshift altar, where we knelt in unison to pray. Michael and I said our goodbyes an hour later and I saw that his blue-gray eyes were nighttime black at their center, so very deep and black, with just a tiny spot of light in the pupil. I fixed my attention on that light and realized it was a tiny reflection of the light of my gray robes.

Chapter Eight

Not in my wildest imagination, while sitting on the slopes of Mount Nagata, would I have imagined that my New York life would require that I regularly participate in American society rituals. But the invitations to this and that party or opening were constant. Immediately after my encounters with Michael, I had to attend a party at the Hotel Waldorf Astoria in Manhattan. Mr. Symes had invited me and several other guests to a charity fundraiser to finance the private education of bright and ambitious immigrants, generously paying the forty-thousand-dollar "donation" for our table. I felt it would have been bad manners to refuse, even though I sorely wanted to.

The ceiling of the Waldorf ballroom was painted blue and its floor was covered in round tables formally set with white tablecloths and heavy silver. The hall looked like a field abloom with white flowers under a beautiful sky. I sat next to an American woman, reed-thin and wrinkled in a chocolate-colored suit. She talked nasally as if she suffered from inflamed sinuses, and she kept sending back her food. "Oh, no, no, no, no," she said when her salad arrived, thrusting the plate back at the poor waiter and angrily staring at him over her bifocals. "Didn't you hear me? I asked for olive oil and vinegar on the side."

My neighbor to the left was a white-haired little man. Mr. Richard Heller, as he was introduced, wore horn-rimmed glasses and listened to the table's conversation without looking up from his plate. When Mr. Heller heard something that seemed to interest him, he swiveled his head and listened so intently he reminded me of a mountain hawk-eagle hunting for mice. Mr. Symes informed me, quietly and off to the side, that Mr. Heller was a greatly respected editor of an American political magazine and website.

The highlight of the dinner was the auction to raise funds for the immigrants' education. Such curious items were for sale: a weekend for two at a resort in Vermont, complete with a private yodeling instructor; one hundred hours of flying lessons with the head pilot of Bank of America's fleet of planes. Mr. Heller's firm was auctioning a lunch for six, personally hosted by the editor at the media company's Upper East Side townhouse. The hammer for that event finally came down at $186,000, which was, to my mind, a lot of money for lunch.

I had never been to anything like this before and said only a few words all evening, preferring instead to sip wine and abstractly watch the events unfolding around me. As frequently happened to me during those early days in New York, my body was at the table but my mind was somewhere else, floating high above the room, observing all with the landscape painter's eye. I remember in particular the American executives with the red faces at the adjacent table. Their ties were loosened, they banged the table and hooted during the bidding, and reminded me in a hundred different ways of my macaque family back at the Temple of Everlasting Prayer. The women at the table laughed along with their men, but occasionally their faces stiffened, and one wife even put a restraining hand on her husband's arm when he began shouting with excitement.

During the dinner itself, the editor on my left and the woman to my right tried to engage me in conversation, and I was forced to descend from my airy observation post to partake in the reality at the table. Our attempts at conversation resembled the mangled iron of a train accident; I allowed sighs to escape my lips during embarrassing pauses and then nodded vigorously at inappropriate moments. They gave up on me after just a few attempts, and thereafter talked among themselves. I can't pretend this was a disappointment.

A turning point in the evening came when the Englishman across the table began to talk about the hidden cultural costs of illegal and excessive immigration. "It's not right that we in Britain have lost whole cities to Pakistanis and Indians," he said. "I want to buy kippers in Watford. Not Balti spices." There was an appreciative laugh around the table. Mr. Symes, glancing over at Mr. Heller, said, "Dick has quite a different view on the subject. Don't you?"

The editor had dropped his preoccupation with his cuticles and was intently staring at the Englishman. "Ah," he said. "The protectionist view so beloved in Europe."

The gentleman from England stared coldly back as if he had just detected an insult and said, "Your Republican Party seems to endorse my position." The editor dismissed the "unthinking mob" of the Republican Party with a wave of his hand and talked of how immigrants served an important role in society, by providing "labor-market flexibility." Or something to that effect. I am still confused as to what the heated argument was all about.

But I knew they were having an important conversation because an elaborate dessert was served in the middle of the discussion and the woman to my right did not turn back the plate, scold the waiter, or level one single criticism at the staff. She simply stared over her bifocals at her dinner companions, before leaning across my plate to spar directly with Mr. Heller. "Oh, no, please," said the nasal woman. "Dick, you're sounding like a fruitcake." The editor gave the woman such a tongue-lashing, while constantly thrusting his fork in the direction of her bosom, that I became quite concerned for her safety.

It was at this point I began to realize that America was about extremes, the pull of opposing forces, undoubtedly because of the very different social experience I had immediately following this high society event. The next morning I went out for my usual walk, but, restless and wanting a change from Castor Street, I turned toward the Brooklyn waterfront.

As I walked briskly down Sant'Andrea Avenue, passing the redbrick Catholic church, St. Mary's of the Sea, the parish priest came out the front doors in his ceremonial robes and ducked around the building into a side door. Beyond the church, a row of single-family homes and a few tired-looking garages stood. A man scuttled down one of the garden walkways on the far side of the garages and yanked open a wrought-iron gate.

"Hey. You."

I jumped in alarm.

It was my landlord, Mr. Giuseppe Colonese. On this day he wore black trousers and a brown pullover; his eyeglasses were covered in a fine powder of dandruff from his bushy eyebrows. He smiled, a rare occurrence, and I got my first good look at the gold tooth in the side of his mouth.

"Hello, Mr. Giuseppe. Is this your house? Is very big."

"Yes, very big," he said, opening the gate farther and waving at me to enter. "*Vieni qui.* Come. You must have a coffee. See our house and meet Mamma."

Unable to turn down this forceful invitation, I followed my landlord through the iron gate and up the white gravel path of his front garden, lined by spiky-leafed bushes. A statue of the Virgin Mary, in white alabaster, stood under a crab apple tree, hands outstretched, as we headed up the path.

The house inside smelled of mothballs and a vinegary stew. I tried to take off my shoes once inside the foyer, but Mr. Giuseppe would not let me, insisting the marble floor was too cold. This quite revolted me—so unsanitary—but I bit my tongue and did as he instructed.

A tiny woman in a blue housedress and slippers, hands gnarled with arthritis, shuffled forward from the back of the house and barked in Italian, not even looking at me. My landlord yelled back at her.

"*Basta, Mamma! Mah. Che cosa!*"

The old woman stopped talking, her black eyes bright and flinty, her face covered in a lacework of wrinkles. Her white hair shimmered luminously in the overhead light. She wordlessly took me by a finger and led me back to the kitchen, her son silently bringing up the rear.

The kitchen was large and simple, lined by glass-fronted cupboards filled with mismatching crockery. A cast-iron pot with a heavy lid sat atop a low gas flame, bubbling away, belching that unpleasant vinegary smell that I had detected upon first entering the house.

"Rabbit," my landlord said, as he contentedly lifted the heavy pot lid and fanned over the fumes so he could inhale deeply the odor I found so unpleasant. His glasses steamed up and he gave me another one of his crooked, gold-toothed smiles. "I am sorry for the yelling. Mamma no speak the English well and she get excited with me because she have no warning you come visit. She want to make things special for you. She say it is not proper to have priest come to house and not make special food in his honor."

I was, I admit, impressed by the old woman's formal courtesy, a way of behaving that I had not really seen since I'd left Japan. I bowed. "Please thank your mother. Is great privilege to be invited into her home. This is special enough." Mr. Giuseppe translated and she nodded, as if this were the proper response. She indicated I should take the honored end-seat at the Formica table.

As my landlord pulled out the adjacent chair with a scrape across the linoleum floor, Mrs. Colonese shuffled to the kitchen cupboard in her slippers, to pull out tiny china coffee cups and saucers and silver spoons. The white refrigerator hummed in the corner. Mr. Giuseppe tapped my wrist and began to tell me how big the house was, and how he snapped up the property at the right moment in the housing market recession, when the Catholic diocese in Brooklyn was involved in a financial scandal and desperately needed to raise funds.

"Come, I give you a tour while Mamma set the table."

Mr. Giuseppe's corner of the house was entered through a dark passage off the main staircase but opened on generous rooms with large windows and heavy wood paneling. Framed boxes hung crowded on the walls while the museum-like display cases filled every room, all exhibiting an endless variation of beetles and moths and butterflies, meticulously collected and preserved and pinned to cork. Mr. Giuseppe was an amateur insect collector, which I had not expected at all, given how rough he was in person. I was amazed by his extraordinarily delicate collection, which was spread across several rooms, and I could have spent all day examining the specimens and listening to him as he talked about catching butterflies in Long Island's wetlands, how he caught them on their single day of life, fluttering from bush to bush, before they faded and died.

He knew all the insects' Latin names and was reciting them softly but with great feeling when we heard Mrs. Colonese's cry summoning us downstairs. When we returned, the kitchen table was covered in sugar biscuits, rice pudding, and what they told me was *torta della nonna*. In case I did not like sweets, there were savory dishes with anchovies and olives, oily sheep cheeses and thin slices of dried meat. And when I thought she could not possibly bring more food to the table, she pushed a pear into my hand before placing the large bowl of fruit before me in the center of the table.

"Bravo," she said, and patted my face.

A battered metal pot finished sputtering on the gas burner and the elderly woman poured the oil-thick black coffee into the dainty cups, each no bigger than an inkwell. Only then did she sit down opposite me and cross her arms. She did not eat or drink anything, but studied me intently as I talked to her son. Unsettled by her intense gaze, I sat up straight and sipped the too-strong coffee as Mr. Giuseppe told me about how they had come to America when he was just eighteen, and how he and his mother now owned 429 Cortina Street, the Old Rectory, and two other buildings in neighboring Baltic Heights that they rented out to Hispanic immigrants working in construction. "You are good, quiet tenant," he said. "Not like that woman and her children downstairs from you." It looked to me like he might spit.

When it became apparent I was taking little food, Mrs. Colonese forcibly put a slice of cake on my plate while her son rose from his chair and returned with etched crystal glasses, almost like thimbles, in which he poured a clear liquid he called grappa. We lifted our glasses. The drink made my eyes burn and water, but I tried not to show it, just sucked in my breath, and the two of them laughed.

This, then, was the point when the old lady patted my hand and spoke softly to me in Italian. Her son grew quiet—I had the impression he was embarrassed—and looked down at the floor. I had my eyebrows up, pretending I was listening, but wore an expression that I hoped made clear I did not understand a word she was saying. She just talked and talked, softly and urgently, until she finally said something to her son, who rubbed his face and said, "No."

She again spoke to him, softly, with tears in her eyes, and he looked sick and finally said, "My mamma, excuse me, she is old-fashioned. She wants me to translate. She say this: That her husband, my papa, he die on the railroads when I was young. So I must work, since I was sixteen, to take care of her. But I not find good work where we live in southern Italy, which is why we follow our cousins to America. And here I work hard and do well. But because of all this hard work I never have time for normal things like other boys, and so here I am in my late forties, with no woman to call my own and no grandchildren for her. It is because of her I not have my own family, she say, and this is her greatest suffering in this life. She cannot die knowing I am a bachelor living on the top floors of this cold house, and she can see in your eyes you are a good man, a good priest, and that you want to do well. She say the sad look in your eyes is like Jesus Christ, and so she beg you to help me find a good woman."

When he finished, Mr. Giuseppe leaned forward and said, from the corner of his mouth, "Just nod like you understand and will help. And then forget about it. She is an old woman. She not understand how things work in the modern world. In America."

But his mother's English was good enough to understand this, for she slapped her son's arm and let forth a torrent of abuse. Mr. Giuseppe rubbed his arm where the outline of her hand was already visible, his face quite red. From then on he tipped back on his chair and rocked, his expression hidden in the shade of the dimly lit kitchen, but continued translating her message.

"She ask again, will you help her, a widow alone in the world, who cannot die until her son has found a woman? Will you help her? She say she try everything. She pray to God every day, light a candle in St. Mary's, ask her friends, but nothing. The women I meet, they not like me or I not like them, and her priest at St. Mary's, Monsignor Trebaldi, he is useless. Of no help. He only wants to buy our house back for the diocese."

I did not know where to begin but took a deep breath and said, "Mrs. Colonese, I have only been in America a few months now. I am far away from my home country, so I am like a baby discovering a new world. This is a practical issue. I am so ignorant of America and its ways, I do not know how I can be of help in this matter. But I recognize your sincerity and the respect you show me and I cannot do nothing. So I will go back to my altar and pray deeply, not just for my own wisdom in this matter but for you and your son, that you might find the Tranquil Light in this world and in the next."

The woman stared at me as Mr. Giuseppe translated. After a pause she said this was all very nice, but what she really wanted me to do was introduce some decent women to her son. This Tranquil Light, less important, she had her son translate. She pinched her fingertips together. *"Una donna. Capisce?"*

Mr. Giuseppe then said something in Italian and the two of them burst out laughing. The tears in their eyes were now from laughter, and the emotional swings in mood since I entered the Colonese house were so extreme that I was exhausted by it all. I stood and said, "Forgive me. I have overstayed. I must depart now." I bowed, thanking them most sincerely for the coffee and hospitality and privilege of visiting them in their home.

My landlord walked me to the door and as I was about to leave the old woman tottered forward and handed me a plastic bag. I peered inside, unsure. She had given me three greengage plums. "This is offering, Mamma say. For your god."

I bowed and thanked them again and then was out on the street.

I instantly felt a great weight lift from my shoulder, not having to sit sandwiched between the old Italian woman and her son, everything I did chased by her bead-black eyes. But when I continued my walk toward the waterfront, I was haunted by the unsettling feeling I had unfinished business. A few listless steps later I returned home. Back in the apartment, I made the woman's offering to the Buddha, setting the three plums in a white bowl on the altar. I knelt and prayed for old Mrs. Colonese and her son, that they find peace and contentment and tranquillity in this life and the next.

For words are not empty. They are karma.

And I had made the old woman a promise.

The next morning Miss Jennifer came by the flat to collect the annotated notes for the Buddhist text she was studying under my tutelage. She voraciously devoured the assignments I gave her, and the next sacred work in our reading series was the *Flower Garland Sutra*. She seemed quite excited and was only a few minutes inside the apartment before she blurted out Mr. Eddie Dolan was telling Believers they could get more from his "Okos" than they could possibly get from listening to my dry recitation of Buddhist doctrine. Dolan was setting up a rival Buddhist community.

"Are you sure?"

"I heard him myself."

"This is not good."

"You can say that again. You've got to stop him."

Initially I did not want to believe things were quite as bad as Miss Jennifer claimed, but, one afternoon after an Oko, when I was behind a pillar packing my briefcase, I overheard Mr. Dolan telling an elderly Believer, "But why do you come all the way down to lower Manhattan to these meetings? I've got a study meeting on the Upper West Side, right near you. You should come. Try it out. Everyone says my meetings are really satisfying."

I was furious and from then on seized every possible opportunity to study this self-appointed Buddhist "teacher." There were, I admit, some unexpected surprises. I discovered that besides leading the Buddhist Study Group, Mr. Dolan ran a charity pairing insurance executives with underprivileged teens missing a father figure. This threw me a little. I had in many ways misjudged and dismissed him, when he clearly was more competent and admirable than I had originally assumed. Still, the more I heard his Buddhist bafflegab and learned of his underhanded efforts to lure Believers away from my study-lectures, the more certain I became that a public confrontation between us was inevitable. And so I made up my mind. I would attend his next meeting and confront him in public debate.

As soon as I made this determination, however, Miss Jennifer sent me an email that my presence was first and foremost required for another emergency board meeting. I audibly sighed at the news; one such meeting had been quite enough for a lifetime. But this was my duty and at the appointed time I made my way to Eleventh Avenue in Manhattan, as Miss Jennifer's message instructed. I double-checked the email when I arrived at the address, for a red satin banner was flapping over a revolving glass door that was disgorging streams of bag-laden shoppers. Apparently I had arrived at the World Food Emporium, which was, I thought, a totally inappropriate location for a temple board meeting.

Out of the white-hot glare of the street and into the chilled chamber of the warehouse, my eyes adjusted to the ebb and flow of shoppers moving through the cavernous hall. I smelled birds roasting on a spit and the briny odor of fresh seaweed and oysters sitting on crushed ice. Employees in white aprons and shoppers with carts moved in fits and starts around colorful displays of jam, olive oil, and dried South American chiles that looked like ropes of clotted blood.

I was at the wrong location, I was sure of it, but as I dialed my assistant's number, I bumped into Mrs. Graham trailing a young Brazilian couple I recognized from the Buddhist study meetings. Mrs. Graham seized my arm and said, "There you are, Reverend Oda! Wonderful. Now we're all here. But you look lost. This way."

The Brazilians with Mrs. Graham shyly bobbed their heads in greeting. It was quite peculiar. The couple spoke English poorly and was not to my knowledge involved in any of the temple's administrative affairs; it was unclear to me why they should be invited to an emergency board meeting. Unsettling, too, was the fact the Brazilian woman was extremely pregnant, and it looked to me like her baby might arrive at the merest tap of the chairman's gavel.

As the four of us circled a pyramid of pineapples, I suddenly became aware of the chambers built into the food hall's north wall. The World Food Emporium had converted the old factory cellars into themed dining rooms. In the Italian cellar, platters of grilled vegetables, bowls of pasta, and thinly sliced cuts of cured meats were set upon by what appeared to be the voracious staff of a fashion magazine. Next door, in the Japanese cell, Dai-ichi Securities traders, according to the chalked blackboard out front, were noisily sitting down to a lunch of sushi and sashimi. In the Swiss chamber, with the big wheels of cheese and a giant cowbell hanging from a pillar, fifty New York Buddhists sat under a banner. HAPPY BIRTHDAY REVEREND ODA! YOU'RE 42 TODAY! it read.

I am quite sure I groaned aloud, but the roar of commerce coming from the main food hall prevented anyone else from hearing my involuntary cry. Mrs. Graham, perhaps misreading the pained expression on my face, leaned in to my arm and whispered, "The Japanese room was already booked. Switzerland was the only option left. I *told* them to start earlier."

My assistant, knowing me better, hastily took me aside. "Look," she said, "Harriet Symes demanded we throw you this surprise lunch. I know this isn't your thing, but it was unavoidable. Your date of birth was on all those nonprofit forms you had to fill out." So there was nothing I could do. I smiled stiffly and allowed myself to be pulled to the seat of honor in between Harriet Symes and Eddie Dolan—the joint organizers of the event—while also managing to gulp down a glass of Swiss white wine.

The tables filling the cellar formed a horseshoe, and as the Buddhist community exchanged greetings and chatted and lifted glasses, the World Food Emporium's catering staff served us cured beef thinly cut on wooden blocks and a salad with some sort of yellowish dressing. I formally thanked Mrs. Symes and Mr. Dolan for the surprise birthday party, but they chatted at such speed, each talking over the other, I had trouble following the conversation, which seemed to flit randomly from subject to subject. I looked out at the faces around me. Mr. Symes was laughing uproariously at something Mr. Doric said, Miss Jennifer was listening intently to a young girl with metal studs all over her face. For the first time I caught a glimpse, just a suggestion, of the camaraderie and sense of community among the Believers.

The luncheon's main course consisted of pots of melted cheese heated over copper flames, a Swiss national dish, I was told. It was a tradition in Switzerland that any man who lost his bread in the melted cheese had to buy a round of drinks for the table, announced the waitress, and any woman who did likewise had to give all the men a kiss. There were a few grumbles by the women present how "incredibly sexist" this all was, but such remarks soon gave way to squeals of laughter as we tried to feed ourselves with the yakitori-like steel skewers and the baskets of cubed bread sitting at each table.

I did not have the knack for stirring the melted cheese—my crust ends were repeatedly left floating in the cheesy goop—and my week's stipend from the Head Temple went very quickly buying rounds of drinks. But we all laughed uproariously every time a piece of bread sank into the morass, and I did have an unexpectedly enjoyable birthday after all.

It was while I was warily eyeing my next piece of bread, deter-mining how best to thread the end piece down the needle in a secure way, that Harriet Symes and Eddie Dolan next to me began discussing the Engaged Buddhism Movement.

"What's that?" asked Mrs. Symes. "A prenuptial for Asians?"

"Ha. Ha. No, that's not it," replied Mr. Dolan. "But a great question, Harriet. So glad you asked. The Engaged Buddhism Movement is something we *must* embrace at the Headwater Sect. It's one of my primary objectives. Buddhism, you see, is based on contemplation of the inner self, what some cynics might call navel-gazing. But it is true, when you visit Buddhist temples you usually find the monks contemplating the rain dripping from a branch and praying and doing, you know, whatever, on their isolated mountain outposts."

Mrs. Symes's eyebrows arched and she pointedly looked over at me.

"Buddhists are rarely proactively engaged with the real world," Dolan continued, missing our exchange and proceeding to dismissively wave away the entire priesthood. "So *Engaged Buddhism*—a movement spearheaded by a Vietnamese Zen master—addresses that problem head-on by deliberately trying to apply contemplative Buddhist prayer to the activist hot-button social, political, economic, and environmental issues of our times."

"Excuse me. This premise is incorrect," I said, gently setting my spear down on the table. "Engaged Buddhism is not applicable to our faith."

For a moment I actually felt a little sorry for the fellow, the way his face contorted as he tried to digest the fact he was being challenged. But he managed to say, "Oh? And why not?"

Whatever sympathy or grudging respect I might have had for the man evaporated the moment he spoke in that arrogant tone, and I instantly recalled what Reverend Fukuyama had said during our last phone call, when I had briefed him on the temple's construction delay and Mr. Dolan's maneuvers. "Cut off the fellow's head," Sensei had said.

So I explained very clearly to the Americans at the table that the Engaged Buddhism Movement was only relevant to Buddhist sects built on extreme forms of introverted practice. Zen, with its core practice of silently looking inward during endless hours of zazen meditations, was just such a deeply introverted Buddhist theology, which explained why the Engaged Buddhism Movement was created by a Vietnamese Zen master.

The Headwater Sect did not fall into this category of Buddhism. "Mr. Dolan," I said, "you only think Engaged Buddhism is relevant to *our* practice because you have not properly learned the tenets of our faith."

I had in effect just called him an ignorant fake and he was smart enough to know it. He bristled with hot indignation as I calmly and coldly pressed on. "The *Lotus Sutra* specifically states, 'No affairs of life or work are in any way different from the *ultimate reality*.' If you had studied Buddhism formally and really understood our doctrine, Mr. Dolan, you would know that term 'ultimate reality' actually means *enlightenment*. So Engaged Buddhism is irrelevant to our faith because we already believe enlightenment emerges when we are fully engaged with the world."

I said this all while retrieving my clump of bread from the enameled fondue pot, and I suspect this is what enraged him the most, the casual ease with which I had put him in his place. He blanched and pressed his lips so tightly together they appeared to be bloodless, and we sat tensely for a few moments more, each waiting for the other's next move.

Mr. Dolan gave me a bitter look I had seen before, that time when the Headwater Sect monks had surrounded me in Administration Alley and I had quickly cut them down to size by citing Issa. He then abruptly turned his back on me and began talking with the person sitting to his other side. I knew in that instant he would never again risk being in the same room with me. But such is the way with bullies and charlatans. They scurry under rocks at the merest challenge.

There was a roar of laughter from across the room. Mr. Symes came over to our side of the table, none too steady on his feet, and threw his arms around his wife and kissed her noisily, wetly, and repeatedly on the neck. Harriet Symes squealed, which made everyone laugh, all but Mr. Dolan, who said very little for the rest of the afternoon. And when the layered cake riddled with candles was finally carried over—and the Buddhists robustly sang happy birthday, much to my mortification, with even passing strangers joining in—I turned with embarrassment to engage my neighbor, only to find Mr. Dolan's chair empty.

He had slipped from the room when no one was looking. But he had also left a gift by the side of my plate. Inside the white cardboard box, I found a bronze copy of the Statue of Liberty. There was a small card: *Happy birthday, Reverend Oda. I pray you might find peace and liberty in America. Sincerely, Eddie Dolan.*

I gently placed the lid back on the box. Harriet Symes finally realized Mr. Dolan had left the Swiss cellar without saying goodbye and that I had subsequently become subdued. She leaned over, patted my hand, and said, "Don't you mind Eddie, Reverend Oda. It had to happen this way. There's only room for one sheriff in town." I did not want to discuss the issue further with her and was greatly relieved when she became distracted by the "schmear" of cheese down my front and began fishing around in her enormous purse for something called Tide to Go.

So Mr. Dolan, the renegade "teacher," was dispatched without much difficulty. He never again appeared at any of the Buddhist meetings, even though I later heard he had a website. But that did not mean my battles with the wayward members of the American Buddhist community were over. Far from it.

Sister Marie was the Haitian woman who cornered me after every study meeting. Beaten down by her incessant requests for special attention, I finally agreed to pray with her and her friends at her Upper West Side flat. I did so with considerable unease; she was the woman who repeatedly claimed she saw Jesus Christ in the shadow of her altar.

On the following Saturday, in a dark hallway smelling of fried food, a tiny black woman swung open the battered metal door of an apartment. She wore a platinum wig and a red dress. Her nostrils flared as if she were trying to sniff me, but I must have passed, because she suddenly gave me a gold-toothed smile and waved me inside.

"Reverend Oda! Glad you could make it."

It was Sister Marie herself standing before me and I was once again amazed that every time I saw her she looked like an entirely different person. I slipped off my shoes and gingerly stepped inside the apartment filled with laughter and loud talk. Sister Marie had a live-in aunt, a bowlegged old woman in a white turban, and there seemed to be some sort of party under way. The women smartly clapped their hands to get their friends' attention, drinks were put aside, and we were led into the adjoining room.

The dining table had been pushed to the far wall so all the Believers could huddle around the Buddhist altar. Just a few feet away from our simple Buddhist shrine stood another altar. Jesus Christ, carved from what looked like wax or tallow, stood at the center of the table, eerily lit by a spotlight draped in red gauze.

Now, looking back, I can appreciate a little bit the liveliness of this Caribbean altar, the colors and sheer force of earthly life it represented. It was so different from the austere elegance of our Buddhist altar. But at the time I was horrified, revolted by the strange and alarming artifacts surrounding the imploring Jesus: a cardboard coffin decorated with rhinestones; a bottle of vintage rum, sealed by wax; black-faced rag dolls in peasant dresses; a heart-shaped box of chocolates; a glass bowl of sunflower seeds; a dozen colored glass jars filled with candles that flickered; and a framed photo of what I presumed was a dead relative.

I knew, instantly, the table was dedicated to Haitian voodoo. More disturbing still was the fact that the altars were so close together the greens of the Buddhist shrine blended into the voodoo altarpiece, as if the two religious practices were easily interchangeable. Their easy proximity gave me the strong impression that the women of the house actively practiced both faiths simultaneously, and I finally understood why Sister Marie saw Jesus Christ in the shadow of her altar—he *was* in the shadow of her altar.

But at that particular moment I could not respond appropriately because a dozen American Believers were already on their knees, packed in tight around the Buddhist *butsudan,* eager to start evening prayers. I hastily tied on my robes and began the service. Sister Marie knelt behind me when I began the evening liturgy; she prayed in a high-pitched nasal tone that sounded nothing at all like her natural voice. The temperature of the room rose ever higher as Believers worked themselves into a fit. The elderly aunt jiggled up and down, barking in an odd, manly voice.

I brought the prayers to an end as quickly as I could and swiveled around to look Sister Marie and her group of friends straight in the face. I sternly said, "If you are Buddhists of the Headwater Sect you must humbly follow the Eternal Teachings, not selectively, when it suits, but wholeheartedly and consistently and purely. If you want to belong to some other religion, such as voodoo, then join that religion. But do not mix the tenets of our faith with another practice. You cannot mate a horse with an ox."

There was an uproar. I can't recall exactly what happened next, because everyone talked over one another in the heated exchange that followed. I sat as calmly as I could, rebutting remarks when I found an opening, but I was seething inside and frustrated by all this yelling. Eventually a young man bellowed, "Just get the fuck out of here!"

This was the most constructive comment I'd heard the entire evening, and I packed up my belongings in a tight-lipped fury. Sister Marie walked me to the front door, and, before I left, I peered one more time down at the small-boned face, the platinum wig, and the red dress. I was again going to remonstrate with her, but she peered back at me, open, blank-faced. I realized then the woman had no understanding of the gravity of her trespass. She probably wasn't entirely there.

After dinner the following evening, I sat at my kitchen table in

Brooklyn, sipping tea, while Miss Jennifer was at the sink washing the dishes. My assistant's back was to me as she soaped and
scrubbed the broiler pan in the sink. The ceiling fan's vibration
rattled the apartment's bad wiring and periodically the overhead lights flickered. I could hear the woman downstairs thumping through her nightly chores, feeding her brood while the TV
blared.

While scrubbing the pans in the sink, Miss Jennifer appeared
for a brief moment like a nun with her back to the congregation,
her shoulders and hands moving rhythmically as though she were
deep in prayer. It was this fleeting vision of Miss Jennifer as a nun
that led me, I believe, to tell her about Sister Marie's voodoo altar
and my unsettling experience at the Upper West Side apartment.

For a few moments the only sound was that of plates clinking
underwater, until Miss Jennifer said, "Well, at least now you *know*
how badly we need you to teach us authentic Buddhist doctrine.
You'll just have to help us understand. Help us get it right."

My hands circled the china cup in front of me and I stared
at the bright yellow tea releasing steam trails. "I am not a good
teacher. Not at all, Miss Jennifer. It is not my position to be here
long. I am much better with paintbrushes and poetry books than
with people. It is perhaps wise that a more able Priest, perhaps
someone younger, with more energy, come here to instruct the
American Believers."

I immediately regretted my remarks, for they undermined the
relationship between master and disciple. But there they were.
They were out and I could not take them back. Miss Jennifer,
dishes washed, turned around from the sink and pulled off her
pink rubber gloves.

"Yeah, well, we'll see," she said lightly. She took a cigarette from
her purse and sat on the window's sill. I watched her shake her
wrist to extinguish the match, then blow a powerful column of
smoke through the window's screen, out into the night, as a train
rattled by.

"Let's face it," she said. "It's your karma to teach us. Those are your orders from the Head Temple. It is ours to have nowhere else to turn. So we're kind of stuck with each other. Don't you think?"

I did not answer. Afterward, Miss Jennifer sat down at the kitchen table for our daily study of the *Lotus Sutra*. I had been skipping certain chapters, on my way to the doctrinally crucial Chapter 16, when Miss Jennifer stopped me and said, "What about Chapter Three? It's such a curious chapter."

I stiffened. "Do you have a particular question?"

She replied that she specifically wanted to understand the Parable of the Burning House, a fable buried in the chapter. "How I am supposed to interpret this story?" Miss Jennifer pressed. "A father watches his house burn down while his children innocently play their games inside. What does that signify? It's really quite a disturbing image. And what does this strange remark mean: 'Though the fire is pressing upon them and pain and suffering are imminent, they do not mind or fear and have no impulse to escape'?"

I closed the book and poked my thumb and forefinger into my eyes. "I am very tired, Miss Jennifer. Please. Let us finish with the evening prayers and continue our studies another day."

We fell on our knees before the Cluster of Jewels Mandala. Miss Jennifer followed me solemnly in prayer and the room quickly filled with the ancient chant of the *Lotus Sutra*. In front of me, incense curled to the heavens as the altar candle illuminated the room. Behind us I could hear the roar of the subway as tired New Yorkers hurtled at breakneck speed through tunnels and past city lights.

And that was when the Third Voice joined us in prayer. For the first time.

I looked about me, but no one else was in the room.

Where did this voice come from? I did not know. I shook and trembled and fought the rising tide of fear, earnestly bowing my head and praying for the Buddha's wisdom and guidance in this strange land.

Chapter Nine

The sun chased the last sugar into the grapes that hung from trellises in the back of Brooklyn homes. The last fire hydrant of the season was opened for the children. It spewed water into Fourth Street and the children screamed with delight as they ran through its torrent. The fiery September sun and the fire hydrant spray met somewhere over the street and created a school of rainbow trout swimming across the Brooklyn sky, reminding me of the Devil's Gate Gorge at that precious time of day.

But it was all coming to an end. The U.S. stock markets fell. The first leaves erupted in a fiery burst of russet and red before fluttering dead and exhausted to the pavement. I was told it was the Canadian maple, that gash of angry fire, that made a New York fall what it was. For me it was the testy wind, pensive one moment, then raging away irrationally until it forced tears to roll down my face. It was a bully, this wind, and it rattled garbage cans and whipped the torn, dried leaves into a trembling state of anxiety.

The end was near and everyone knew it. New Yorkers who argued violently on stoops and fire escapes just weeks before were now subdued, chastened, and seeking out the bosom of their families. The rough-looking father promenaded with his wife and children past the Longshoremen Union Center, enjoying the last nights of balmy weather, stopping on President Street to buy ices for the children. The mother in plastic flip-flops and a blue skirt, a cardigan across her shoulders, walked arm in arm with her man, soft at long last. Even the children were well behaved. No cuffs around the ears, for once.

I, too, could not resist this salute to the dying summer. One day, when the September sun was sinking in late afternoon, I emerged from 429 Cortina Street in a pullover and took a seat on a Sant'Andrea Park bench, a plastic cup of red wine at my fingertips. I read the Japanese papers, sitting next to the old men playing bocce, and when their roars were particularly loud, I glanced up from the papers to see what was happening. When I did, my eyes drifted over Brooklyn, over the rooftops, to where the black clouds were gathering, the threatening storms of winter preparing to run us down.

And was reminded of the Bashō poem:

> *There is no sign in the cicadas' cry*
> *That they are just about to die.*

This was when it dawned on me that I was Mr. and Mrs. Symes's preferred social escort when one of them was indisposed. When I informed Miss Jennifer of my suspicion she laughed, and I rather crossly told her this was no laughing matter. It was, in its way, an insult to the priesthood, and I was determined to correct this state of affairs the next time I saw the Manhattan couple, which occurred at the next Oko.

Mr. Dolan's abrupt departure had, as I feared, rid the hotel ballroom of not just him but more than a dozen other Believers who followed him out the door. Still, I was starting to recognize the core of regulars, the "trunk," as Sensei might call them, and in the midst of this tenacious group were the Symeses.

After the official meeting was over I took the couple aside and delicately suggested "official escort" was perhaps not an appropriate duty for a Buddhist Priest. They looked at me, blinked, and then talked between themselves about all they were doing for the temple. I understood their meaning. It was clear. When Harriet Symes turned back to again include me in the conversation, she let it be known she needed an escort for an upcoming fashion show. Would I mind terribly? And so, a few days later,

I dutifully showed up with my embossed invitation at the Peter Brooks spring-summer collection at the Carlton-Brown, a newly opened hotel near Madison Square Park.

The hotel's side entrance on Twenty-Fifth Street was covered in a white tent for the much-anticipated Peter Brooks event and I followed the throng of arriving guests along the velvet ropes that led into the canvas cupola. Inside, the crowd pushed and shoved and I soon found myself in the middle of the bottleneck that had developed under the tent.

Guests around me waved invitations and yelled, some even using their purses and steel camera cases to force their way to the head of the crowd. Not for the first time since my arrival in New York, I found myself slowly lifting out of my body and observing the surreal events around me with cool detachment and a painterly eye, while my corporeal self was down in the crowd, roughly pushed about and pummeled.

Floating in the sea of heads across the tent emerged the odd orange pagoda of Mrs. Symes's hairdo. "Reverend Oda!" I heard her cry. "Stay there! I'm coming. I'm coming." It was a remarkable lesson in endurance to see this little woman punch her way through the crush of coats and capes, and, once at my side, she said, "So happy you could come. Now, let's get our seats, shall we? Should be good. The title of the show is 'Eco-Warrior.'" Before I could inquire what this meant, the woman had snapped open her purse and retrieved her invitation just as another surge in the crowd jostled us off to the side. "I'll lead the way," she yelled. Her fingers locked onto my forearm and soon she had us past the long-haired guards, up a flight of cool and dark lobby stairs, and into a large room filled with chairs and spotlights and a stage.

"Harriet! You look wonderful. Do I detect a Marc Jacobs?"

"It's Peter's! When he was an unknown FIT student."

"No! I would never have guessed. It's such a knockoff. I must tease him about that."

I was brought forward and introduced, with a faint handshake, to the designer's business partner. His eyes were constantly wandering the room. "I put you in the front row," he finally said. "Next to Bernadine."

Even I could see Mrs. Symes was not pleased by this news, but the man missed the look because he was already off to greet another client. So we moved up to the front of the runway, past the rows of cameramen with their immense cameras and telephoto lenses, and took our seats.

"Oh, no. No, no, no. That just won't do."

I turned to the familiar nasal voice. It was the woman from the Waldorf charity dinner, the one who had constantly returned her food. When she finished berating the photographer in front of her she turned and peered at me over her bifocals. "Oh . . . Reverend Oda, isn't it?"

I bowed. "I am afraid my English is not good. I did not quite understand how to pronounce your name that night."

"Bernadine. Bernadine Horovitz. Fashion editor for *The New York Times*."

"Ah, yes." I repeated her name, stumbling a little over the *r*'s. "I am pleased to make your acquaintance again."

"You do get around, don't you? Bit of a social butterfly?"

She knew the haiku image for transitory life. The butterfly. I was oddly touched. "*Hai.* Yes."

The two ladies on either side of me leaned forward to look at each other. They said hello and vaguely kissed the air in the direction of one another before leaning back in their seats without another word. After a few moments, I felt Mrs. Symes's hot breath on my ear. "Watch out for that one," she hissed.

I nodded politely but did not allow any expression to show on my face.

Mrs. Horovitz was soon leaning toward my other ear.

"Interesting conversation that night, wasn't it?"

"Ah, yes. Very interesting."

"Dick Heller is brilliant. But he can also be a schmuck."

"A shmuk?"

Just as I was about to inquire about the meaning of this curious word, the lights dimmed. Music that sounded more like a car crash blasted over the loudspeakers, making conversation quite impossible, and a woman with half a plant attached to her head strode onto the stage.

I blinked. I cannot remember much of what followed. The details are a blur. But I recall the women were long-limbed and the materials they wore clung so tight to their bodies little was left to the imagination, or were so soft they fluttered in a trail behind their arms, like insect wings. There was also lots of foliage and moss scattered about. Perhaps it was because of the collection's naturalist theme, or because an image had been planted in my mind during the earlier conversation with Mrs. Horovitz, but the ephemeral and fluttering nature of the show made me recall a long-forgotten moment when I walked into the Head Temple's daikon field. I was just a boy and it was that migratory time of year for a rare species of mountain butterfly. When I entered the daikon field a thousand red-spotted butterflies lifted and fluttered and filled the air.

The lights came back on.

"Well? What do you think?" asked the flushed Mrs. Horovitz.

"*Hai.* Like butterflies. Very rare and beautiful butterflies that disappear without trace." But I did not have time to properly say goodbye to the editor because Harriet Symes already had her grip on my arm and was again hauling me through the crowd. But now there was pushing to get out of the breathlessly hot room, the guests pressing anxiously toward the two exits.

Outside on the street I sincerely thanked Mrs. Symes for the experience. She snapped open her purse and pulled out a tissue, exclaiming, "Oh, I so hoped you were going to like it, Reverend Oda. I was a bit nervous inviting you, to be honest. You know, a Buddhist Priest at a fashion show? But it was fun, wasn't it? Tell me you liked it."

"I did. To have a profound knowledge of this world is Buddhism. So, the Buddha's Land is here, too, not just in the temples."

"Well, see, that's just why you're so great, Reverend Oda. You just make Buddhism sound so enlightened."

It was nighttime. It had rained while we were in the fashion show and the rain puddles reflected the city's lights. As we waited for a taxi I asked Mrs. Symes why she didn't like Mrs. Horovitz. The woman seemed pleasant enough this time around.

"Oh, she's a piece of work," said Mrs. Symes, as a taxi came to a screeching halt before us. "Terrible mother. I can't stand the way she treats her children. Bye-bye for now, Reverend Oda. See you at the next study meeting!"

The evening did not end there. Mrs. Horovitz's review of Mr. Brooks's spring-summer collection appeared in *The New York Times* the following day, and in this article she wrote I was "a high-society Buddhist monk," a description so upsetting to me I didn't quite know what to do. She then described me a little before quoting me as having said Mr. Brooks's designs were "beautiful butterflies that will disappear without a trace."

I did not mean that at all, of course, and soon afterward Mrs. Symes called to say my comment had created a furor. The designer's business partner was in a rage and claiming I had destroyed the season. Apparently, despite the critical acclaim, few department stores were purchasing the Brooks collection. It *was* disappearing without a trace.

"Don't you worry about a thing," soothed Mrs. Symes. "You're made. You'll be one hot dinner guest after this. Trust me. Everyone will want to meet the Buddhist Priest with the good fashion eye."

It was all rather disconcerting and the mail that day did contain a fat envelope. Thankfully, it was not an invitation. It was a letter from Japan. The acolyte Daisuke Ojisawa had sent me his painting of the Buddha's Elbow Waterfall, the view from my room at the back of the Temple of Everlasting Prayer. I found myself blinking back tears when I saw my river, the ginkgo forest, the waterfall.

The enclosed letter read, *Greetings Reverend Oda. I hope this note finds you well. All the acolytes at the temple are praying for you, the successful completion of the New York assignment, and your safe return to Japan. In the meantime, I thought you might like this reminder of home. As you can see, I am working hard on my brushstrokes with our new art instructor, but, permit me to say, he is not quite as accomplished a teacher. Respectfully, Acolyte Oji-sawa.*

This unexpected and touching gift from Japan stirred things up inside and that night I awoke with a start. I could not sleep further. I went to my closet and pulled on a thick wool sweater before going to the window and throwing it open.

I needed fresh air. I needed all my windows opened.

It was sharp and cold outside and the hard air felt good. The rooftops of Brooklyn appeared stiff and brittle in the chilly night. A roar of heavy clouds swirled across the sky until a gap momentarily opened up, a silver rim and halo first announcing the cloud cover's imminent opening. Shafts of powerful moonlight poured through the roof hole, illuminating the city below. Moonbeams streamed across Brooklyn's tar roofs, creating a swirling palette of purple, gray, and platinum out of the night. I heard the rattling steel of the subway on its overhead tracks before the train shot past my view, but I was still unprepared for its beauty. Surely a comet, I thought. Surely an omen. A haiku came to me then, my own haiku, a humble offering to the itinerant poet-priests of old:

> *Over Brooklyn*
> *The sliver moon of silver*
> *Reveals the jagged roof.*

That fall Reverends Fukuyama and Kashimoto passed briefly through New York. They first flew to London to visit the temple in Highgate, before flying on to San Francisco for a round of temple negotiations with the local Bay Area Buddhist Community. In between they stopped off in New York for less than twenty-four hours, arriving late one night.

Reverend Fukuyama rang me from the airport hotel in Queens and said since the temple site was really nothing more than an empty lot at this point, they would much rather spend their few hours in New York shopping.

"Shopping?" said an incredulous Miss Jennifer. "Before they've met any of the American Believers? Or seen the temple site? Sorry, but that's just too weird. And not a little disappointing."

"They will see the temple later. After shopping."

Fortunately, Miss Jennifer kept her opinions to herself when we all met up, and was, in fact, charming and solicitous, the perfect tour guide for the Head Temple Priests. After listening to the long list of purchases they wanted to make, she smiled, nodded, and took the Head Temple Priests directly to the Golf Annex on Broadway.

Knowing what she was thinking, it was, I admit, rather embarrassing to watch Reverend Kashimoto push his way into the golf emporium with such feverish excitement. Reverend Fukuyama was nicknamed the Silver Fox with good reason, and he quickly slipped away with Miss Jennifer, leaving me to keep Kashimoto company as he tried on an endless number of golf gloves, Lacoste shirts, and polyester trousers. I finally had enough when he got in line for the computerized "virtual club swing test range," and told him he should meet me in the store's interior courtyard when he was finished.

A skylight allowed natural light to reach the ground floor, where middle-aged men were toting newly acquired golf bags back and forth. I looked up at the Tiger Woods Café and saw Reverend Fukuyama sitting next to the second-floor railing. Barred from smoking, he clutched an empty cigarette holder in between his teeth, while his left hand toyed with the handle of a teacup on the table before him. Sensei wore a stony-faced expression as he concentrated hard on what Miss Jennifer was saying, mulling over her comments, his eyelids rapidly beating behind the black frames of his glasses. She sat opposite him in her leather jacket, her head tipped forward, talking in a heated rush in the general direction of the teapot and dish of biscuits between them.

Reverend Kashimoto, carrying four bulging bags of purchases, was suddenly at my side. His face was flushed and he said, "I know I should not say it, but I must. The Buddha's Heaven is here. I have found it."

That day we visited an Apple store and a jeweler in the diamond district, followed by whirlwind tours of Bloomingdale's, Barnes & Noble, and Saks Fifth Avenue. It was exhausting. When the Head Temple Priests finally had all the gifts they wanted for their families and friends back in Japan, we took them by the Nicolai Place site for a drive-by viewing before rushing them back to JFK.

"Very fine woman, your assistant," Sensei said at the airport curbside. "Strong seeking spirit. Miss Meli would make an excellent nun."

After this whirlwind visit from my friends, the ache for the Head Temple became acute, and I determined, with renewed vigor, to pour myself with single-minded purpose into getting the New York temple built. It was the quickest way back home to Japan.

For several weeks, every time I brought up the temple's planning permission impasse, Mr. Symes had said, "I am trying to get it resolved. I'm trying." I had had enough of this. The morning after the Head Temple visit I called up Mr. Symes and told him, in no uncertain terms, we had to get the zoning matter resolved and the construction ban lifted.

"We are at a critical juncture," I said. "The cement foundation must be poured before the ground freezes. Or else we are lost."

"I know. But I can't get this key bureaucrat to budge."

"Make an appointment, please. I will go see him with you."

To reach the plans examiner's office in downtown Brooklyn, we had to walk through the long corridors of a municipal building. It was so cold, so dark, it reminded me of a mausoleum with the dead buried in canisters in the walls. The examiner's frosted-glass door opened to a gray room with high ceilings, the only color coming from family photographs and children's paintings, hung so the heavyset man behind the desk could see them while sitting in his creaky chair.

He was just finishing his lunch when we arrived, some form of home-cooked chicken in silver foil. "One of your underlying plots was on a rare 'fixed-term' variance," he said. "It technically expired a couple of weeks before the public hearing."

The examiner and Mr. Symes talked back and forth for some time, and despite the highly technical nature of the discussion, I understood the examiner's department had failed to spot that one of our plots had reverted to "residential-only" use, at the time of our original approval, and he was trying to correct this error by forcing us to go through a new public hearing. "Your planning permission argument, that the existing 'commercial use' variances were in excess of the 'community use' variance needed for a temple, just wasn't true at the time at the time of your hearing," he said.

"This is just outrageous," said Mr. Symes. "Are you implying we got someone to look away? That somehow—"

"Don't go there, man! That's not what I am saying at all."

The examiner wiped his hands and fingers with a napkin and glowered. I noticed that he spoke with an educated accent when talking about technical zoning issues, but when Mr. Symes made him angry, he slipped into New York street talk. "This development, as stated here in these filings, can't go ahead as is," he said, reverting to his professional demeanor. "I am sorry. But you need to go through a new ULURP public hearing and get an up-to-date variance for 'community use.'"

Mr. Symes exploded and I knew then that if I did not act decisively the New York temple would never be built on time. I would fail my assignment and Reverend Fukuyama would be punished for my shortcomings. But just as my anxiety was building to an intolerable level, I had a vision of Sensei—smoking, lids fluttering, standing with his sly smile—and a serene calm settled over me.

In that moment I believe I experienced, for the first time, the mysteries explained in *Master and Disciple,* a sixteenth-century religious text all Head Temple acolytes were forced to study during their training—and few of us actually understood. According to this theory, when a teacher and his disciple practiced with every fiber of their being to uphold the Buddha and the Law, the profound bond between them could mysteriously cut through time and space. The talents of one became the talents of the other. The enlightenment of one became the enlightenment of the other. In this case I suddenly possessed Reverend Fukuyama's remarkable gift for bending bureaucrats.

I pointed at the family photograph on the wall. "How old is your daughter?" I said. The girl wore a black velvet dress, her dark skin pretty against the white-lace collar. She stood by her younger brother. Their mother, a wide woman in a wider hat, had a sparkling white-toothed smile, mirrored in the smiles of her children. The examiner turned his attention back to me and said, with a threat in his voice, "She's twelve. What's it to you?"

This time I pointed at the watercolor of the Williamsburg waterfront, just above his head. "She did this?" The man nodded warily. "This is a very good painting, particularly for a child this age," I said. "See how she handled the glass in the apartment building windows? This is a difficult concept to grasp in watercolor because it is counterintuitive. The illusion of glass is created by 'not-painting,' by allowing the paper to be its true self. She has done so with great finesse. I am a master teacher of the arts back in Japan, so please believe me when I say it is very difficult to teach even much older children this skill of 'not-painting.' Very few of my senior students reached the level your daughter has already attained."

"The girl's painting all the time. Self-taught. Her mother's people, they're artistic."

"She has a gift. You must get your daughter proper art instruction."

"Yes, Reverend. We're applying right now to the gifted child program at the School of Visual Arts."

"If you are not successful in this, I will personally give her lessons until you find a proper school solution, because it is very important your daughter continuously improve her skills and reach her true potential. It would be a tragedy if this did not happen for a child of this talent. She needs proper teaching at very high level. Nnn? Do you understand what I am saying?"

"Yes, Reverend, I do. Thank you."

The inspector turned his attention back to the papers in front of him, lost in thought. There was silence in the room. He exhaled slowly. "Jeez, what a mess this is. What are we going to do here? Look, give me a couple of days to think this over. I need to discuss this with my supervisor. Hard to dispute that the initial screwup was within our department and a little flexibility on our part is now not entirely out of order. I'm not promising anything, mind, but if there hasn't been too much political noise on this, we can probably settle this among ourselves and avoid a full Planning Commission hearing. Can appreciate this is no time to be adding unnecessary costs, particularly not to a house of worship. I can appreciate that."

And so, finally, the fate of the temple was in the Buddha's hands. I had done my best.

Chapter Ten

As we awaited word from the Brooklyn planning office, a decision that would seal the New York temple's fate, I preoccupied myself with the Believers and their issues, which, though tiresome, provided welcome distractions from the tension of the pending planning decision. This was an unexpected development for someone so particular about his solitude, but without my all-consuming Head Temple routines to occupy me, tectonic plates deep within began to subtly shift and lurch without my realizing it.

What I did know was that I was going stir-crazy sitting in that Little Calabria flat waiting for the examiner's binding decision. Unable to stand it any longer, I pushed myself to formally enshrine altars in the Believers' homes, to visit the sick in the hospital, to give spiritual guidance to the unemployed members of our community.

One day, exiting from 429 Cortina Street, I again found the physiotherapist, Miss Laura, hovering around my front door, pretending to shop for vegetables at the Colonese store. She wore a pink and hairy sweater under an unbuttoned raincoat. Pink strings were tied crisscross around her bosom, undoubtedly designed to provide her formidable chest with even more dramatic lift. "Good morning, Reverend Oda," she said. "Just buying some squash. Don't you love fall and all those delicious gourds? The meat is so orange and sweet on the tongue. . . ."

This time I said, straight out, "What do you want from me?"

"Oh," she squeaked. "I . . . I . . ."

"Come. You came to my door for a reason. Speak now."

"I guess I was hoping we could get to know each other a little better. Have a cup of coffee, maybe?"

Mr. Giuseppe arrived holding a bag of her purchases. He glowered at her and barked, "There anything else?" The woman shook her head, opened her purse to pay, and I saw then that her hands were trembling. I was unexpectedly touched, seeing her vulnerability in that way. I softened my tone and said, "Then we have coffee. Come. Follow me."

I crossed the street to Café Sorrento. I heard her behind me, the rustling of the paper bag in her arm and the click-clack of her heels as she ran across Cortina Street. We took seats in the back of the café, at the round marble table under the mirror. The waiter brought us brown coffee cups.

"So. We have coffee now."

She licked her lips and made some small talk, about a film she had just seen, but our conversation did not get far when it became clear I had not seen the film and did not know anything about it. She fell silent for a moment. Then she talked about her work, about her new superior, who was actually much easier to work with. When I was starting to wonder where all this was going, she said, "I am curious. Can Priests have partners? What are the rules on having an affair?"

"Such things are not approved. Neither are they forbidden. Celibacy, marriage, adultery—these are worldly experiences that are immaterial to experiencing a treasured moment of enlightenment."

"How modern and fantastic."

I sighed. "It is an illusion to think we can do whatever we want, without consequences. It is wise you study and better understand what is karma. But I sense you want more from me than the answers to these questions. Is there something else? We are here now. Speak. What is on your mind?"

Miss Laura played with the tissue in her hand and looked at the floor before she hesitantly said, "Reverend Oda, when you put me on the spot like this, I don't know what to do or say. All I can tell you is how I feel. And that is . . . lonely. I'm constantly hungry for men. I can't help it."

"What are you saying? Man is like peanut. You cannot stop eating peanut?"

Tears topped the rims of her eyelids and rolled down her face. She hung her head in shame and whispered, "I just want to be in a man's embrace. All the time. It is the only time I feel . . ."

"So you come to my door for what? To have sex with me? "

"No. . . . Well, yes, I guess . . . . Oh, I don't know."

She was now crying openly into a tissue.

I sipped my coffee. It was very disturbing, when people cried in my presence, and the subject matter, well, it was not at all pleasant. "Look at me," I said. "This void. This emptiness you feel. Men will never fill it. Sex will never fill it. Only your own true Buddha nature can satisfy you in this deep way. Seek the Buddha first and foremost and I promise you everything else will take care of itself. Do you understand?"

She wiped her eyes. "Yes. I think I do."

I took out a piece of paper and together we drew up a personalized practice and study schedule for her to follow. "Pant after the Buddha like you pant after a man," I said. The horrified expression on her face made it clear she did not approve of the image I used to help her understand the nature of prayer. But we agreed to meet again on a regular basis, and before we parted, Miss Laura gripped my hand and kissed it, like the Catholics do their bishop, and I blushed terribly. Such a peculiar Western habit.

At that time I was also preoccupied with my unfolding and complicated relationship with Michael. He weighed on my conscience and I again went to visit him in Bronxville, a leafy suburb, as I had promised I would. This time I went on my own.

Shortly after I arrived at the clinic, a nurse informed me he had a new room on the ground floor, because Michael was on a suicide watch list. My spirits instantly plummeted on hearing the news.

Michael's new room was overheated and on a hall patrolled by around-the-clock staff, with a nurse and muscular orderly sitting near his door. But Miss Jennifer had on a previous visit picked up and brought the Cluster of Jewels Mandala and *butsudan* from Michael's apartment, and his altar was all appropriately center stage against the wall of his room. This, at least, I was pleased to see.

I took a seat in an armchair near the window and halfheartedly opened my book of Coleridge poetry, awaiting Michael's return from a group therapy session. He arrived twenty minutes later and the first thing I noticed was that his energy was different from the last time I saw him. In many ways he seemed more sane, not so intense and manic. But he also spoke in a monotone and there was an unmistakable heaviness to his movements, as if he dragged around the weight of the world.

"I am sorry you are doing poorly," I said.

Michael dropped onto his bed. "Praying doesn't seem to help much anymore."

"I see. This is unfortunate."

We were silent as I collected my thoughts and tried to determine my approach, but before I could speak, he added, "And my parents are back. Full-time." Michael, on the bed, leaned back against the wall and seemed to look past me, to the scene outside his window. "Do you know a parent's terrible love?"

It was so unexpected, this strange remark, but it hit me so hard my face instantly flushed. I replied stiffly and formally, "No, I do not. I am not familiar with this." There was a roaring sound in my ear and my face was hot. "So your parents see you, then. Here? In the clinic?"

"Yes. My mother comes every other day. She tells me to eat."

"Aah. This is good."

Michael turned to look at me. His eyes were dull and his face waxy, like a candle, and I sensed that I had somehow added to his great sadness, even though he was too tired to remonstrate with me.

153

"Perhaps it would help matters if I met your parents. Would you like this? For me to meet them?"

I will never forget the way his eyes widened in alarm. "No. No," he stuttered. "Absolutely not." I was taken aback by this sudden burst of passion, the first real inflection in his voice.

"I won't if you don't want me to," I said, fanning myself with the poetry book. "But why?"

"My mother will take you from me. She'll steal my religion."

What a strange remark. And wrong. He should be welcoming her into our Buddhist faith. It was part of his religious duty, to lead others to the Cluster of Jewels Mandala. But I decided—as difficult as it was for me—that the situation called for sensitivity on my part and I should be careful with my tongue. He was very unstable and it was unwise for me to add any pressure.

"No one can 'steal' your religion if it is built on true faith," I said carefully. "And I will not see your mother, Michael, if this is your wish. This I promise. But perhaps she is not as bad as you say. It's very hot in here. Would you mind if I open the window?"

He did not answer, so I went to the window. It was bolted shut. I sat down again, sweat trickling down my back.

"And your father?" I asked.

"Dad's very good at crossword puzzles. Period."

"I see."

I looked around the room, at a loss for words, until I saw the altar again, including the freshly cut greens in the vase. "You say you have trouble praying, but I notice your altar is set up properly."

"I pray. But sometimes I am too tired to sit up. I don't have the energy. So I pray lying down in my bed."

"Hmm. It is, of course, better to kneel in front of the altar in proper respect and appreciation. But do not be concerned with this. All prayers, even if said half unconscious, are heard by the Buddha." Michael shifted his weight, sat up slightly, and I had the distinct impression he was relieved to hear this news.

The sun was dropping when we began our evening prayers, a

passing into that strange winter quiet that lies between light and dark. My prayers had been rather uninspired as of late, but this prayer with Michael, both of us on our knees at the end of the day, was a thing of rare beauty. I was carried downriver by the rhythmic chant of his sincere prayer and the incense smoke curling to the ceiling; by the resonating thud of the padded wood hitting the copper gong and the fading light filtering in through the blinds. All these sensations swirled together and my own tense preoccupations of this last month washed away from me, as if I were standing under a waterfall. The heat that had been steadily pressing in on me finally ratcheted down. And then I began to breathe clearly, not through my nose but through the very pores of my skin, soaking up the odors of a slightly rotting pear on the altar, the robust eucalyptus in the vase, the perfumed incense.

Prayers completed, we said our goodbyes. Michael awkwardly leaned forward and hugged me in the Western way, and then shyly stepped back into his room. The woman at the reception desk called a car service and I waited outside for the taxi so I could get out of the clinic's unbearable heat.

While I waited, a black Mercedes pulled into the driveway and rolled in one motion directly into a parking spot. The sun was in its final descent, and the last ice-orange rays of the day filtered slowly through the spindly tree branches stripped of all leaves. A little woman emerged from the Mercedes, slammed shut the door, and marched briskly toward the clinic with two large paper bags from the Whole Foods store, her leather boots crunching the gravel underfoot.

I sucked in my breath, stunned as I was by the karmic wave that had unexpectedly just crashed over my feet. The woman marching across the gravel was Michael's mother, this I knew instantly, and, in accordance with his wishes, I stepped behind into the shadow of a pillar, so she would not see me.

Mrs. Bernadine Horovitz, *The New York Times* fashion editor, sailed right past without ever casting a glance in my direction, and from the interior of the clinic I soon heard her loud and nasal voice aggressively questioning the nurse about her son's condition.

My taxi arrived and we drove off.

I rolled down the window. All the way.

There was such unbearable heat.

The next communication from Japan was from Sensei. Besides the usual questions about the New York temple's status, his long letter expressed his concern that I was too alone and starting to act a little strange. He had formed this impression when he and Kashimoto passed through New York. He warned me that losing my sense of humor was the first sign I was becoming peculiar. He had seen this in me before and urged me to overcome my natural inclination to isolate myself from others.

I was both irritated and slightly amused by his letter. Now that he was the head of the International Division, Reverend Fukuyama seemed to be broadening his canon of religious literature, a bit pretentiously, I thought. In that letter, for example, Sensei quoted the Western religious philosopher William James, rather than our standard Buddhist texts. "There can be no doubt that as a matter of fact a religious life, exclusively pursued, does tend to make the person exceptional and eccentric." I did not make an issue of this affectation my old mentor had adopted, but I wrote simply in return, *You are right. People too alone, whether religious or not, do begin to act peculiar. But rest assured, in my case Miss Jennifer provides friendship and companionship. Of a sort.*

The previous night in the apartment I had decided to finish off the last of my precious bottle of Juyondai sake, and, not wanting to drink alone, I asked Miss Jennifer to not run off immediately after supper, but to share some cups of sake with me around the kitchen table.

We started, naturally enough, talking about our mutual love of poetry. I can't remember why, but after she told me about the fourteenth-century Italian poet Petrarch and his muse, we somehow wound up discussing the principle of Chudo, the Buddhist belief known as the Middle Way. I described Chudo, in my stiff English, as a "man walking with one foot in the spiritual world, one foot firmly on earth. It's the ability to see, at the same moment, both the spiritual world and the terrestrial world."

Her perplexed expressions prompted an example. "The most famous poem of the Buddhist poet-priest Kobayashi Issa goes:

> *The world of dew,*
> *Is the world of dew,*
> *And yet,*
> *And yet . . ."*

Miss Jennifer looked puzzled and said, "I don't get it. Sorry. Maybe it's the translation?" She looked embarrassed by her shortcoming, so I again tried to make her understand the elegance of the great Issa's writing.

"Issa wrote this poem in 1816, a year after his child, a two-year-old girl, died from smallpox. So he was saying in this poem, *I know this world is an illusion, and nothing here is more permanent than dew, and yet I am a human being who has just lost his beloved daughter. How can I not grieve for her?* So it is a beautiful poem, perfectly expressing the Middle Way, the spiritual world and the terrestrial world existing side by side, in just four lines."

I could see, in the way she pondered her cigarette ash at the windowsill, that Issa's story, the death of his daughter, touched her deeply. It perhaps made her think about her own loss, and I was greatly encouraged knowing she grasped this most Japanese of poems. Perhaps it was the story of Issa and his daughter that led her to ask the next question. "What's up with your family, Reverend Oda? You never talk about them. I gather you're not married. But what about your parents? Any siblings?"

"I am second oldest. There were four of us. Three boys and a girl. It was my parents' greatest pride that I became a Priest."

Through the gloom of the apartment I saw the tip of her cigarette glow brighter. I used this pause to pour myself more sake, waiting for her to press on with her personal questioning. My hands shook slightly. But she did not press on. Indeed, her next question, when it came, was totally unexpected.

"How'd you like to meet *my* family? At Thanksgiving."

𝒥t was Miss Jennifer's blond-haired sister who opened the door and urged me to step into the wood-paneled hall of the Brooklyn Heights home. "Reverend Oda's here!" she bellowed. She was the pretty younger sister, Sadie, I had met on Castor Street. I bowed deeply and expressed my sincere appreciation for the invitation. Miss Jennifer and her entire family responded to Sadie's cry by popping out of closed doors and swarming around me like over-eager puppies welcoming a newcomer to the pack. They shook my hand and helped me out of my coat and took the bottle of Takaisami sake from Tottori Prefecture from my hand, while profusely thanking me for the gift.

"You're just as handsome as Jennifer said you were," said Mrs. Meli, an elegant woman with silver hair. "Such lovely eyes." She clutched my hand and I blushed a deep red. Mr. Meli, tanned and in a black sweater, slapped me on the back and said, "You're all they've been talking about this morning, Reverend Oda. So get used to it. Enjoy it. The women will be all over you today."

"Hey, Reverend Oda. I'm Jack. Jennifer's favorite brother."

Another hand was thrust between the others, demanding to be shaken, and it was attached to yet another white-toothed and square-jawed sibling who could have modeled clothing. "He lies. That's me. I'm the favorite brother. Steve."

"What can we get you to drink? Scotch? Is it too early for scotch? Or maybe a beer?"

I had been five months in America when Miss Jennifer asked me to celebrate the American festival of Thanksgiving with her family. I of course agreed and then promptly went on Japanese Google, after she left the flat, to learn what this Thanksgiving was about. The tale touched me, unexpectedly, how the starving Euro-pean Pilgrims and ninety Wampanoag Indians stopped their war and sat down in peace to share their food. You could not find an American holiday more steeped in Buddhist principles—simply, a deep appreciation of life—so I was quite curious to experience this American national holiday.

"Sorry about the family," Miss Jennifer said, sliding her hand under my arm and walking with me into the living room. "They can be a bit overwhelming."

"No. No. They make me feel welcome. I am most grateful."

Mrs. Meli's piping voice rose above the general din; Miss Jen-nifer, with a look of regret, dutifully disappeared into the kitchen with a few of the other women. There were a dozen people already standing in the front living room, with more coming in behind me. The brother Jack pulled me to his side and asked me about sumo wrestling, which he enjoyed watching on YouTube. "What the heck do they eat to get those bodies?"

There was loud chatter, amber liquids splashed on ice, napkins and little silver trays of deep-fried eggplant sticks passed about. I clutched my too-strong scotch drink and was shuffled around between Miss Jennifer's siblings and in-laws and aunts and uncles and childhood friends, each engaging me in their circle of chat. The dining room table next door was banquet-sized and set for thirty people, with a lace tablecloth and sparkling crystal glasses and silver candlesticks and a paper turkey wearing a Pilgrim hat, an American version of origami. The smell of turkey skin and sweet onions, crackling in the oven, filled the house.

Near the foyer entrance, her older brother, Steve, tried unsuc-cessfully to engage me in a conversation about cars, which I knew nothing about, so we quickly switched to talking about his sister.

"Poor kid," he said.

"I am sorry. I don't understand."

"You know about Jimmy, don't you? Her fiancé?"

"*Ahso.* Yes."

"She's still waiting for him to walk through the door. It's been ten years. She's halfheartedly dated some bozos since the accident, but they never last long and it always ends the same way. I think she only goes out with them to keep my parents off her back. Jimmy was her soul mate. Her great love."

"Hmmm. This is very unfortunate."

"Sure is. But me? The next morning I have forgotten the woman's name and am on to the next. But maybe I shouldn't be telling a priest that."

The whiskey had gone to my head by the time the dinner gong was finally struck. Two turkeys the size of small pigs—"organic free-range," I was told—were strategically positioned at either end of the long table. I had never seen so much food. Between the bird carcasses stood bowls of homemade cranberry sauce, Brussels sprouts smothered with bacon, oven-roasted onions and carrots and squash, two different types of potatoes—one with yellow flesh, the other orange—various salads, gravy boats, and bowls of bread stuffing that Mrs. Meli told me were made with beer and cut-up turkey gizzards. The abundance—it was so excessive, so American.

There was lots of chatter and scraping of chairs as people settled behind their name cards, but at the sound of a knife banging against crystal the room fell into a hush. Mr. Meli said a few words of thanks and appreciation for the bounty before us, and asked us to pray for those in the world less fortunate, including American soldiers fighting wars in other parts of the world. Then he said a short Christian prayer before asking me to add a Buddhist benediction, which I did.

We were ordered to "dig in," which was the appropriate term, considering the food was heaped like manure piles before us. There was great commotion and clatter during the reaching for plates. The dinner was quite delicious and I quite forgot my sense of moderation and ate far too much.

At one point I looked down the long table and saw a pearl string of raw American beauty, power, and wealth stretched out before me—middle-aged men wearing bright cashmere sweaters and women with tinted hair and diamond watches and the young bodies of Ivy League swimmers and those white, white teeth and the elderly with their imperfections of age removed by the surgeon's knife. They talked about energy puts and the Democratic senator from New York and the IRS closing an accounting loophole in the oil industry's asset depreciation schedule and the drug war raging along the U.S.-Mexican border and about the best defensive stocks to buy during a recession and the latest spy novel to hit *The New York Times* bestseller list. I could not have felt more strange and alien, despite their warm welcome and acceptance of my presence. We spoke such different languages.

Miss Jennifer sat opposite me at the banquet, but the way we were seated it was actually difficult to talk over and down the divide of the boisterous table, not least because her blond-haired brother, Steve, sat to my left bristling with a lawyer's certitude as he lectured me on the most efficient tax shelters. Meanwhile, a fine-boned woman in a white dress, a cousin from New Hampshire, sat to my right and talked far too much about her three-hundred-acre horse farm in New England. So Jennifer and I had little chance to talk directly with each other. But when I looked down this table of America's blessed, so energetically pursuing their appetites, I heard Miss Jennifer's brother Jack across the table sneeringly say, "Oh, my God, Jennifer. You're just too weird. That wouldn't even occur to me. Or most other normal people."

I looked over at my assistant. Her face was mottled red and I could see she was cringing inside, as her brother and his wife laughed at her Buddhism and Italian literature and Ashtanga yoga and tattoos and perverse interests in psychology and voracious hunger for all things below the surface of the material life. In those rapidly blinking eyes and lowered chin, her head reeling back from her brother's attack, I saw that my American assistant felt just as strange and alien as I did, even in the bosom of her own family.

This insight touched me. Determined that Miss Jennifer not see the strong feelings in my face, I lowered my head and reached for a plain biscuit to eat with my tea, but this apparently was unacceptable to the Meli cousin sitting next to me, for she pushed a thick wedge of black cake in my direction.

"You've got to try this. It's 'Death by Chocolate.'"

"I see. How interesting."

At the end of November, the Brooklyn plan examiner granted us an exemption from his department's bureaucratic error and the New York Temple Fund was issued a new "common-use" variance. When I heard the news I fell to my knees before the Stupa of Worship and gave prayerful thanks. Mr. Symes made sure the construction crew went immediately back to work, while I emailed Reverend Fukuyama the good news. He wrote back, simply, *I have always been able to rely on you, Seido.*

From then on I visited the temple site once or twice a week, watching with considerable satisfaction from the sidelines as the cement mixers backed into Nicolai Place and sent rivers of slurry down the chute and into the hole. We were protected by the *shoten zenjin,* the guardians of Buddhism. The foundation set just a week before the weather turned intensely bitter and the ground froze rock-hard.

It was a Friday night in mid-December when, during one of these trips to the construction site, I rang Miss Jennifer on my cell phone. It was five o'clock and already dark. I had several signed documents in my briefcase, which I had to turn over to her as the secretary of the New York Temple Fund, and I knew, vaguely, that she lived close by the temple site. So I offered to drop the papers off before I went home, saving her an unnecessary trip to Little Calabria. "I'm just on the other side of Atlantic Avenue," she said. "On Dean Street."

New Yorkers rushed home in heavy overcoats as a winter chill moved in from the north. Montague Street bustled with Christmas shoppers. Windows were filled with handmade candles smelling of apple and cinnamon, Christmas cakes at the Polish bakery, booksellers offering discounts on the latest bestsellers in business and politics. A lumpy-looking Santa Claus stood next to a kettle in front of Citibank, listlessly ringing his bell.

Atlantic Avenue was bumper-to-bumper with rush-hour traffic, but the evening quieted down again in the residential streets on the other side of the urban artery. The windows in the brownstone and brick houses of Dean Street beckoned with warm light. The decorated Christmas trees standing in the bay windows looked to me like elaborately spun candies. The first hint of snow started to come down, very fine, as if a frail old woman high above were combing out dandruff with a fine-toothed comb. My breath appeared white in the streetlamp's orb of light.

Miss Jennifer lived in the garden apartment of a brick building and she answered the gated door under the steps, wearing a well-worn apron and holding a wooden spoon. She wore old-lady slippers, blue and hairy, and her spiky-haired style was even more unruly than normal. But perhaps I had become accustomed to her look, for I thought she looked very pretty and at peace with herself that night, in a white-toothed and fit American way.

"Are you hungry?" she asked. "I was just making dinner."

"Oh, excuse me. So sorry to interrupt. I just wanted to drop off papers. Please do not put yourself out."

"It's up to you. But come in for a moment, please. It's cold with the door open."

The flat smelled of stewing tomatoes laced with some other briny and feminine sea smell that was vaguely familiar. The cream walls of the entry hall were hung with gold-framed lithographs and etchings, which I guessed were Italian literary scenes. In one, a handsome young man recited poetry to a beautiful woman on a balcony, as an elderly and beaked-nosed husband peered out from behind a tree.

A Venetian carnival mask hung from the roof beam at the entrance of the L-shaped living room and I had to duck to pass under it. The room was packed floor to ceiling with books, each shelf stacked two or three layers deep with heavyweight hard-covers, airport paperbacks, and large antiquarian folios of major literary works. It was, in its Western way, my fantasy room. A Persian cat, clean and friendly, jumped forward and brushed up against my leg, purring. The couch against the wall had lion's-claw feet. Zebra-skin cushions were thrown across the couch, a rust-colored Indian blanket folded over its arm.

"You have very nice home," I said, removing the temple papers from my briefcase.

She took the folder, smiled, and said, "Are you sure I can't convince you to stay for dinner? It'll be ready in twenty minutes. It's squid, stewed in its own ink, which is a Sicilian method of cooking calamari."

Squid was in fact my favorite seafood, a great luxury in the mountains of Fukushima, and I stuttered, "Per ... perhaps, if I am not an inconvenience. You must tell me the truth."

"Please. It's nothing. I made too much and was going to bring you some anyway."

A small dining room table was quickly set for two under the basement window that looked out at people's ankles as they rushed down Dean Street. Miss Jennifer talked gaily from the behind the kitchen counter, asking me if I wanted a drink. I suggested, if she had not done so already, that perhaps we could say evening prayers first.

"Yes. Of course." She put down her spoon, lowered the gas flame under the pot, and led me down the dark hallway, past her study and bathroom, to the bedroom in the back of the apartment.

The bedroom had French doors that opened out onto a patio garden and a yew tree. It was nighttime, but I could see the outlines of the trees and bushes because she had strung seasonal fairy lights around her walled garden. Her altar commanded the wall to the right, away from her pointed feet, and the stupa I had made for her dead fiancé stood flat against the brick.

The room contained a wood-framed bed, like a sleigh, very

high. Directly at the foot of her bed the wall was hung with family photos and more bookshelves. The recessed walls in an alcove to the left were devoted to a young and handsome man, covered in framed photographs, personal letters, and sports medals that hung from colorful ribbons. Lively but odd artifacts, like a framed Chinese take-out menu or airline tickets to France, were reminders of their intimate moments together. I tried not to appear too curious.

We said our prayers together, vigorously, and read a few pages from *The Eternal Teachings*. When I shut the book, I asked Miss Jennifer if those were pictures of her fiancé hanging on the wall.

"Yes. That one was taken in the lobby of his office building. He was in advertising. Just starting."

She did not speak as I scanned the brick shrine, stopping on a neatly framed letter. While I did not wish to invade her privacy, I saw he had closed his letter with a few lines of his own poetry.

"Your fiancé was a poet?"

"Only privately. He 'scribbled.' That's what he called it."

"He seems like a very fine and decent man," I said carefully. "Is very sad you experience this great loss. But, Miss Jennifer, there are many attachments in life that can cause us suffering. It is not just material attachments. It is also possible to become too attached to the dead."

She stiffened. I could feel her cold fury rolling toward me in the room's faded light. "Dinner must be ready," she said, turning to head back to the front of the apartment. "Come on. You must be starved. I am."

Miss Jennifer brought me a porcelain plate covered in a generous portion of Italian rice with mushrooms, on which she ladled the squid. We sat under the window and it was as if the tense moment in the bedroom had never occurred. She poured wine, lightly adding she would serve salad on another plate, after the main course, which was the Italian way of doing things.

Our heads down, eating the squid and rice, I said, "I am thinking of the dish you serve. Is very good. My favorite dish in Japan is *ika meshi,* squid stuffed with ginger-flavored rice, which is, if you don't mind me saying so, a little more refined than this rice. In many ways my dish in Japan is very different from this, almost unrecognizable in taste. But the core ingredients, between what we eat here tonight and what we eat over there, are identical. Not close but in essence the very same."

She stared at me for several moments. "I don't mean any disrespect, Reverend Oda, but you really need to get out more often."

"My superior at Head Temple gives me same advice."

Chapter Eleven

From the Canadian north and the Atlantic to the east came a cutting wind that whipped through clothing and settled into bone joints. For a few days, the two fronts met over Brooklyn, and a waterfall of white cascaded down upon us, punctuated by claps of rare snow-thunder. The sidewalks were covered in a thick brown slush during the warmer parts of the day and on a few occasions ice water poured over the tops of my boots when I stepped off the curb. The winds began to roar again toward evening, temperatures plummeted, and everything on the ground again turned to solid ice.

It was unusual, Miss Jennifer told me, for winter to arrive so soon and with such bitter ferocity. Long icicles threatened and dripped from above the doorways of the brownstones on First and Second Streets. Few people went out in the subzero temperatures unless it was absolutely necessary. Tired of the confines of my room, however, I sometimes dashed to a diner a few blocks south on Cortina Street. It was so cold and windy the skin on my shaved head shriveled and rippled the minute I stepped outdoors. Once inside the warm restaurant I ordered minestrone soup and hot coffee, and watched the world pass through the steamed windows. A copy of *The Eternal Teachings* lay unopened next to me on the table. With each spoon of soup more snow fell, while human bundles in caps and scarves and down jackets scuttled past the diner window.

Even the subway tunnel signals seized that winter. I woke up one morning to find trains lined up outside the studio. That evening, irate commuters with dripping noses barked into extended microphones on the news, furious at the Metropolitan Transportation Authority.

My landlord's shop always managed to carry fresh root vegetables, greens, and winter melons. Every day Miss Jennifer loyally fought her way through the bad weather, never complaining, showing up as promised with more supplies and precooked dinners in Tupperware. Sometimes she bought Italian sausages from D'Amato's across the street, which she fried up and served with crusty bread, a hearty meal that kept us warm.

The Americans, I found, heated their apartments to an excessively high temperature. All winter long my studio was filled by a cacophony of clanking radiators and steam. The plant I had bought in the fall, to cheer up the flat, started sprouting wildly in the middle of winter. Other signs of life unexpectedly popped up in this torrid heat. I was setting the table with soup bowls when Miss Jennifer brought a pitcher of water to the table. We both reached across the Formica at the same moment, and the backs of our hands brushed roughly against each other.

Instantly, I experienced a powerful stiffening inside my pants. I was ashamed, and a red-cheeked flush spread hotly across my face. I had not been this close to a woman in a long time and I was unprepared for this pounding of blood that rose so rapidly to the surface. Miss Jennifer smiled at me, but I did not know if this meant she had seen my involuntary reaction or whether this smile was just vaguely friendly. A moment later she had turned her back to pop brown bread into the toaster.

It was a bright and sunny day on Christmas Eve. The people of Brooklyn rushed about making last-minute holiday purchases. They lined up at the butcher across the street, waiting to pick up their preordered Christmas roasts. D'Amato, his pin-striped apron tied on over a heavy wool sweater, brought a metal tray of cooked turkey and ham out on the street. He walked down the line that snaked from his shop door and ran halfway down the block, handing to the patiently waiting customers slices of meat at the end of his round-headed knife.

The owner of the nearby liquor store, hoping to lure the butcher's customers to his own shop, also came out with plastic cups of hot, spiced wine. They gratefully held the steaming cups of warm wine in their gloved hands, and it put them in a festive mood, despite the cold. They laughed, chatted, and stamped their feet as they patiently inched forward into the butcher shop, new customers just as quickly adding themselves to the back of the line.

By late afternoon the last-minute shopping had wound down, and the Brooklyn families hurried back to their homes. The weak and orange sun set behind the aged chestnut tree on First Street, and the air was filled with the rat-tat-tat of metal shutters coming down over the glass fronts of the hardware store, the baker, the Laundromat.

Cortina Street was soon black and thick with the night, only the odd car drifting down the ice-rutted street. I was about to turn from looking out the window, to warm up my leftover meal, when I saw neighborhood residents of all ages, dressed in heavy coats and scarves, drifting in a knot down a side street. They held flickering candles and sang songs about silent nights as they moved solemnly and gently through the neighborhood, wishing peace and goodwill to all. I pulled down the shades.

The next day all the bells of Brooklyn rang out.

Between Christmas and New Year's I went several times to see how the Nicolai Place construction site was faring in the harsh weather, and it was hard to imagine a future temple in this spot; holes and piles of rubble were buried under snowdrifts encased in slabs of ice. Even the scaffolding was covered in a frozen crust. A skeletal crew performed only the most superficial tasks, and, from the looks of it, spent most of their time drinking coffee inside the trailer.

When the weather thawed a little, I agreed to meet Miss Laura at Café Sorrento across the way on Cortina Street. She was following my study and guidance to the letter but wanted a bit of extra attention.

It was another cold but sunny day. Miss Laura wore sunglasses and a silk scarf over her head and looked, I admit, like a movie star. The other men in the café gawked and stared, but she was oblivious to their hungry looks. She talked in such a way that it was not necessary for me to speak, but simply required me to nod my head occasionally, so she had the impression I was listening. I was grateful for this. I had little energy to do more. Perhaps I was a little depressed.

She talked on and on about herself: how she treated herself to a little gift for every week she lived up to her strict prayer and study schedule, and this was why she wore a new scarf. Did I like it? She talked about her work, how she had a new position at the United Health Clinic off Atlantic Avenue, which required her to study new physiotherapy techniques for stroke victims.

When enough time had passed for me to make an excuse and slip away, I begged my apologies, saying I must return to duties in the flat. She paused for a moment and then cheerfully said she would leave with me.

As we left the café, old Mrs. Colonese was making her unsteady way down the icy pavement. One hand was grazing along the wall to steady herself, while the other hand gripped a heavy sack full of shopping. The old woman fell just as we were about to cross the street, hitting the sidewalk with such force we heard an ugly slap and the sound of glass jars shattering.

The woman screamed horribly and rolled on her back. In that instant, her son, serving customers at the shop across the street, saw it was his own mother down on the ice. He bolted across the street traffic, forcing cars to slam on their brakes. Falling on his knees in the slush, my landlord moaned and begged his mother to tell him where it hurt. He carried on in such a way it was impossible to tell whether it was Mr. Giuseppe or the injured woman who was moaning loudest.

By now curious onlookers had gathered excitedly around the

fallen woman and I could no longer see what was happening on the ground. A man broke off from the crowd to call an ambulance from his cell phone. I turned to Miss Laura, but she was gone. Without saying much—just a hand here and there in the small of a back—I watched her make the crowd part. She took off her own coat and draped it over Mrs. Colonese, just as Mr. Giuseppe barked, "Get away from my mother, woman! What do you know about this?"

But Miss Laura placed her scarf under the woman's head and calmly responded, "I work in a hospital. I know what I'm doing. Now, please, act like a man." And with that she turned her back on Mr. Giuseppe and held Mrs. Colonese's arthritic hand, cooing soft assurances, while ever so delicately examining the knee that was pointing in an odd direction and looking increasingly red and angry.

The ambulance came and the old woman was hoisted on a gurney and packed into the back of the vehicle. But she would not stop gripping Miss Laura's hand, so the young woman had to jump into the back of the ambulance alongside Mr. Giuseppe, and together they raced off to the emergency room at the Brooklyn Hospital Center on DeKalb Avenue. What strikes me now, looking back, is that Miss Laura had done all this while I remained frozen in place on the sidewalk, my mouth gaping like a gaffed fish. I lowered my head, consumed by my red-faced shame.

A day later, descending the stairs, I found Mr. Giuseppe in our building's front hall taking a moment away from his customers in the store. He wiped his eyes with a white linen handkerchief. I stopped when I realized he was crying, not sure what to do, but as I shifted my weight the wooden step creaked. Mr. Giuseppe looked up.

"*Mi scusi*. Don't mind me. Come down. Please."

And I thought to myself:

> *Such loneliness.*
> *Such suffering.*
> *I cannot bear it.*

The year came to a close. Mr. & Mrs. Symes took down the red velvet rope stretched across their grand living room and invited us—the entire Buddhist community—into their home to celebrate the new year. It was a joyous event. Close to seventy Believers showed up on New Year's Eve, including the regulars: Miss Laura, Michael, Mrs. Graham and her daughter, the men's choir, and, of course, the fellow in the front row who invariably fell asleep. We all fit comfortably into the living room, with our shoes off, kneeling on the platinum rug. I was relieved to discover the nude portrait of the Symeses was hanging in the apartment's other living room. Miss Jennifer arranged for a temporary altar to be set up against the living room's far wall; there were too many in attendance that day for us all to fit comfortably into the Symeses' formal prayer room.

Outside the large windows of the apartment, the man-made mountains of Manhattan soared, apartments tidily stacked like yellow-paned building blocks against the black backdrop of the night. I led the prayers and in this way the Buddhist community of New York ushered in the new year. The lecture I gave was on the Buddhist importance of the New Year's festival, how it was traditionally a time to get one's house in order and that many Japanese businessmen used this point in the calendar to settle their outstanding debts so they could start the next year fresh and with a clean slate.

"This is a good practice for America, too," I said. "If any of you suffer from too much debt, reflect deeply and pray and determine to settle your karmic obligations, so you can start the year like a newborn child." There were some older women in the room, housewives who had come in from New Jersey, and to them I said, "We all must do our duties. Clean the home. Clear away cobwebs and mend old shirts and in all ways clean away anything that is not worthy of entering into the new year. This is the time for us all to do the unpleasant tasks of life we put off, to once and for all expiate the old karma, so we can renew ourselves and enter the next phase of lunar months with a genuinely pure outlook and spirit."

A young man cried out, "But what if you can't find the means to pay off your debts? What do you do?" I told him the story of the time the great poet-priest Kobayashi Issa was drowning in debt. "Unable to pay off his obligations, on the verge of bankruptcy one dark New Year's Eve, he wrote:

> *Trusting to Buddha,*
> *Good and bad,*
> *I bid farewell*
> *To the departing year.*"

Wanting to make sure the meaning of this poem was clear, I added, "Issa wrote this haiku in a spirit similar to the Christian prayer, 'Let thy will be done.' The poem is prayer in its own right, for Issa is saying, *I have no power here and so I surrender all to the Buddha, whatever happens.* If you are in a similar financial predicament, then, in your prayer and attitude, I urge you to do as Issa did. Turn your life over to the Buddha."

I think, on this cold New Year's night, my lecture hit the proper note with the New York community, for after the prayer there was a palpable lightness in the air, despite the darkness in the world outside. We shared the traditional Japanese fare for the new year, toasting the coming year with sake poured into paper cups and nibbling on *mochi* cakes, and there was a pleasant hum of hope and conversation in the room. I went home and had *ozoni*, a traditional New Year's soup I ordered from a Japanese restaurant.

Unfortunately, this feeling of renewal and goodwill did not even last to the first Oko in January. In those bitter days of winter just a handful of the most dedicated Believers showed up at the study-lectures in the Manhattan hotel. The severe weather undoubtedly had much to do with this reduced appetite for the Tranquil Light, for some had to commute from as far away as Summit, New Jersey, or Darien, Connecticut.

Still, it was rather disheartening, not least because the American Believers started to complain about my lecture style. Sister Marie was a very tenacious woman, it turns out. She continued to attend the Okos even after our confrontation in her home, and, indeed, even after I had more occasions to publicly correct her practice. She was dogged, kept on coming back for more, and I decided I would never be rid of her. But that January Sister Marie sent me a rambling letter notifying me she would no longer attend my study meetings. It wasn't because I had corrected her practice; it was because my Oko lectures were too "dead" and "technical," she wrote in her spidery script: *Your lectures just plain don't make sense. They're gibberish. Say what you will about Eddie Dolan, him I can at least understand.*

This did not upset me terribly. I told myself the woman was half-mad and her comments were not worthy of further reflection. But within days of Sister Marie's missive, Mrs. Graham and another Believer mirrored the Haitian woman's criticism, almost to the letter and independently of each other.

Mrs. Graham's comments unsettled me the most. She came up to me after the Oko, eyebrows arched, and pointedly asked what the next lecture was going to be about. I told her it would be about the esoteric proof found in the *Lotus Sutra, The Eternal Teachings,* and the seminal thirteenth-century Buddhist text *The Golden Bough Teachings*—an outline of the doctrinal evidence establishing the Simultaneity Cause and Effect Law. We stared at each other for a few moments before she said, "With all due respect, Reverend Oda, your lectures seem to be more technical than spiritual. They are not exactly *enlightening*."

I bristled inside but managed to say, "I teach American Believers what they need to hear, Mrs. Graham, not what they want to hear. This is the duty of the Priest. I am sorry, but I cannot bend the Eternal Teachings simply to accommodate current tastes. Or the capacity of the people to listen. The teachings are eternal."

She peered at me over her bifocals. "Eternal? Really? Please don't think me disrespectful, Reverend Oda, but I have been listening to your lectures for several months now and I have the distinct impression that half of what you are preaching is not eternal at all, but empty dogma handed unquestioningly down through the ages by successive generations of Buddhist Priests. I am just an ignorant American woman, of course, but I suspect the doctrine you preach, and the specific practices you make us follow, are jammed with Japanese-specific cultural ritual. It's hard to tell where the superficial practice ends and the profound practice begins. Is it really necessary to light *three* sticks of a specific type of leaf incense made from the slopes of Mount Nagata to become enlightened? Why not some other incense? And what's this rigid obsession about kneeling during prayer? Isn't it possible a Believer could have a suitably humble attitude while sitting in a chair? Tell me, have you ever honestly asked yourself what part of the Headwater Sect's doctrine is genuinely the Buddha's path to enlightenment and what part of this Buddhist practice is just Japanese cultural habits and biases masquerading as something profound?"

It was clear she had been saving this speech up for some time. Perhaps she had even rehearsed it. In either case, I would not give her the satisfaction of knowing I was shaken to the core by the attack. I took a deep breath and replied stiffly, "I must repeat, Mrs. Graham, the Eternal Teachings are the Eternal Teachings." I snapped shut my briefcase. "Now, if you will excuse me, please, I have appointments and must leave."

But how Mrs. Graham's comments tormented me! I couldn't get them out of my head. I found myself pacing back and forth across the floor of my flat, furiously spouting counterarguments I wish I had said at the time, such as how Believers had to be humble and surrender the arrogance of their small egos if they wanted to attain enlightenment. I was livid. Such impertinence, to talk with an ordained Priest in this way.

A few evenings later, when I was a little calmer, I asked Miss Jennifer to shave my head. It had been several weeks since I had a haircut and I was looking untidy. "Oh. Are you sure?" she asked, as I handed her the electric clippers. "I don't want to hurt you. What if I knick your ears?"

I pulled a dining room chair onto the floor of the kitchen, sat down, and wrapped a towel around my shoulders. I took her hands and said, "It is very easy. First get the feel of my head." I closed my eyes as she ran her hands over the bumps of my cranium. "When you are ready," I said sleepily, "run the razor from one end of the head to the other, in a row, like an American mowing his lawn."

The feel of that rough stubble of hair reduced to the smooth skin of a plum, the firmness of her grip on my head, it was all greatly soothing. I was in a trance when she turned off the humming clippers.

"All done. That was actually kind of fun."

I opened my eyes. "I must ask you a question, Jennifer." It was, we both realized, the first time I had addressed her in this informal manner. "I hear much criticism of my Oko lectures. It is my priestly obligation to reflect on such comments if they are true. Do you think my lectures are stiff and boring and shallow? Is this your opinion as well?"

There was a pause as I heard her, behind me, putting the clippers away in their case. "I don't want to overstep the boundaries here," she said cautiously. "Do you want a straight answer?"

I paused. "Oh, I see. Thank you. This is clear enough."

Her remark stung, but I did not show how much.

More disturbing still: I found myself revisiting the feel of her strong fingers kneading my head. I tried to put such thoughts out of my mind, but the memory imprint of her touch stayed with me.

That Sunday, Jennifer did not run off as usual after she made my lunch. It had started to snow hard and she decided to let the bad weather pass before venturing outside again. At my invitation, she settled into the armchair opposite me to read from the heavy book she carried around in her oversized bag. I spent the day working diligently on my next lecture, four volumes of *The Sacred Writings* stacked at my elbow on the Formica table, the critical comments on my lecturing style spurring me on to do better.

"Seido-san, listen to this."

I looked up.

"I've been wondering why you've been able to help Michael in ways the psychiatrists haven't. It's kind of strange when you think about it. You hardly even know what's going on around you half the time."

"Hmmm. Thank you."

She licked her lips nervously. "That didn't come out right."

"It is all right. I understand."

"Well, this psychiatrist I am reading has a plausible explanation as to why you're so effective."

She looked up from the book and I put down my pen to indicate she had my undivided attention. I am not sure I understood everything she was trying to tell me that afternoon, but according to this theory she was studying, none of us had "masterless freedom." Such freedom was purely an illusion because "psychic factors," powerful inner voices, could seize us at any moment.

"Let me give you an example," she said. "Take the politician compelled to frequent cheap prostitutes, knowing full well that if he gets caught his career is finished. He knows it's crazy, it's totally dangerous, and yet a voice compels him to visit the lane full of prostitutes anyway. Or consider the suburban couple, normally conservative, who are in the mall one day and just go berserk, taking on a self-destructive amount of debt during an orgy of shopping. That, too, is an example of people getting seized by 'psychic voices.' This psychoanalytic theory I am studying argues that religion is in some cases a practical means to keep these destructive psychic forces at bay."

She was so excited by the ideas in her head she began to stutter. "What I mean is, by *choosing* the 'master' we wish to serve—for some, God, or in our case, the Buddha—we can sometimes withstand these destructive psychic voices demanding servitude and always threatening to overrun us."

My raised eyebrow and dubious expression made Jennifer laugh. Still, she pressed on, insisting that something like this had occurred with Michael. "You were very clear. You promised Michael all devils would become Buddhas, all his poisons, medicine, when he recited the *Lotus Sutra* at that makeshift altar."

"I said this?"

There was a pause.

"You're really kind of out there, you know. It's a little spooky."

I smiled. It was the best I could do. But in that moment another part of me, long ago withered, took over. I was never a very sexual man, and my experience, as I have already stated, was quite limited. But that evening, after green tea, I had an overwhelming need for intimacy, a jolt of feeling that would reassure me I was part of the human race. There Jennifer was, beautiful and with such fire in her eyes, so alive with life. Before I knew what I was doing I had crossed the room and was running my hand through her peculiar hair, quoting Bashō:

> *"Will you turn toward me?*
> *I am lonely too,*
> *This autumn evening."*

Jennifer looked up and soberly said, "I am not sure this is a good idea. That this is what I want."

I stiffened, withdrew my hand from her hair, mortified that I had so misread her again, and, worst of all, overstepped the proper boundaries of our relationship. But the frightened look on my face must have touched her, because Jennifer smiled, put down her book, and calmly took my hand.

I remember, to this day, how she kissed my rough and red knuckles before gently placing my hand on her heart, like it was a frightened bird beating its wings under the soft shirt. I understood, then, for the first time the Romantic poets' verb "to swoon," and in this overwhelming state of desire I disrobed Jennifer in the cramped rooms of the Cortina Street apartment. She reciprocated, but much more slowly, gently removing my clothes with a naturalness that made me tremble, before moving us over to the cot in the alcove.

Never before had I experienced anything like this. Jennifer, sensing my inexperience, guided us through the night. The places she put her fingers and tongue, my heart quickens and I blush just remembering it all. It hardly seemed possible, so powerful were the emotions and sensations that she produced out of thin air. I was even inexplicably taken by the tattoo high on her bottom cheek, a skin-etching of the Brooklyn Bridge linking two islands.

The next morning she woke up, tousle-haired and at ease. I was already awake and sitting upright in the armchair, quietly studying her as she slept. "Good morning," I said.

"Good morning."

She stretched, yawned, made a yowling sound. Then, as if suddenly remembering what had happened the night before, she smiled shyly. "Well, that was fun. But what time is it? I've got to get back to my apartment. The electrician is coming."

Jennifer disappeared into the bathroom and I made her a pot of tea. She hastily drank a cup when she came out, shrugged on her jeans, and left the apartment as I was sitting in my armchair, reading *The Eternal Teachings*. Before she bolted from the flat, she paused by my chair and lightly rested her cool hand on my face. I tilted my head, happily pressing my cheek against her palm.

When later that day I stepped out for the paper, I felt such elation I was secretly convinced Jennifer had pumped me full of drugs. The blue winter sky, the green shutters, the red overcoat on a schoolgirl—colors had never before looked so vibrant—and I walked down Cortina Street, bouncing up and down on the balls of my feet, happily humming ancient Shomyo to myself. I wanted more of Jennifer and began fantasizing about showing up at her apartment that evening. My mind filled with all manner of torrid fantasies, like a teenage boy, which is precisely the problem when middle-aged men finally discover the erotic life. It's not a pretty sight. Not at all.

But the river's current takes you where it takes you. Over the following days we continued as usual to perform our religious duties together, rather stiffly immediately following our night of intimacy. But the routine of work relaxed us, brought us back to ourselves, and one afternoon, back at the Cortina Street flat, our hands again touched inadvertently while reaching for a file. We shortly found ourselves hotly entwined in the alcove. I suppose we were both lonely.

I know it sounds trite, but our relationship unfolded naturally, like a lotus slowly opening. After working late in my apartment, we pushed the temple papers aside and concluded the workday with evening prayers. Then, sipping wine and preparing dinner in the narrow galley, our conversation flitted lightly between poetry and the latest gossip about the Believers and back again. After dinner Jennifer insisted we take a short, crisp walk around the neighborhood, for our digestion, she said. We retired then to the alcove, to read under the bedside lamp, until my hand timidly reached out for more of that pleasant drug I had recently discovered.

I will always think of those moments with Jennifer as some of the happiest of my life. One evening, when she passed me a bowl of steaming spinach across the Formica table, I instantly recalled a long-ago life—a similar moment of contentment I must have once felt around the family table in Katsurao. It was as if a genetic imprint of domesticity had been rediscovered, and in that moment this faint hearkening back to a past home restored me to myself. Perhaps this was what I most fell in love with. That Jennifer somehow reconnected me to my past.

When I stayed at Jennifer's flat, we usually dined at our favorite Syrian restaurant on Atlantic Avenue before returning to her sleigh bed, where we reclined on high like an emperor and queen on a celestial throne. When I became too amorously eager, Jennifer would whisper, "Slow down, acolyte," and the comment, the sheer upside-downness of it all, made me laugh. From those blissful nights, I most remember the smell of Jennifer's pajamas, a heady mix of forest moss and lilac, which came from the scented bar of soap she kept in her drawer of undergarments.

Of course, there were other signs, too. One evening, after falling asleep in her apartment, I woke up with a jolt in the small hours of the morning. The flat was pitch-black. The shrine to Jennifer's late fiancé glowed against the brick and the drapes appeared to be moving. The terror I felt is hard to describe. I was convinced someone was standing behind the curtain, an intruder who had broken into the garden flat and was about to set the room on fire. Just as I was about to cry out, Jennifer rolled over and nuzzled me. Her touch, her warmth, it brought me back to myself and I slowly fell back asleep.

This bliss, my bliss, had to self-correct. The mist of illusion had to be cleared. Looking back, I now see it was the confusing mix-and-mash of temple work and bedroom intimacy that ultimately created the rupture in our domestic arrangement. The break happened at the apartment in Little Calabria. What started out as a mild exchange of ideas—the philosophical and spiritual differences between East and West—gradually increased in virulence until Jennifer and I found ourselves on a very personal, very charged plane.

Jennifer lit a cigarette and poured herself tea. I sat down to read *The Eternal Teachings*. "I might be out of line," she said, "but what I am about to say now is out of the deepest respect for your abilities as a priest."

I closed my book and returned her look with my own steady gaze.

"Who are you? Look, I know you have a real understanding of Buddhism and the world we live in, knowledge I am sure you are just *dying* to share with us. But the fact is you're just not good at communicating your understanding of Buddhism. It's not just the language barrier. Everything you say and do gives the impression you're secretly sneering at us, like you think Americans are not really smart enough to understand Buddhism, that only the Japanese are sensitive enough to really get the subtle depths of this faith. It's really incredibly insulting. And, when you think about it, it actually slanders the teachings. It makes a mockery of the whole premise that we all have a Buddha nature."

I was stunned, particularly when Jennifer then began telling me she had seen another side of me, late at night, when I looked out the window at the passing subway trains. "I see it, then, in your face—the suffering," she said. "It makes me wonder if you're holding on to something that's somehow undermining your abilities as a priest."

This was too much. I held up my hand. "Do not continue. Please. It is clear you know very little about me."

Jennifer licked her lips. "You're right. I know almost nothing about you. But that's my point. You won't let me know you. And it's not just me, it's all the Believers in New York. There is just something about you cut off and buried in ice that is totally inaccessible to the rest of us."

"Out of self-protection a Priest must remain aloof, otherwise he will be consumed by the Believers' neediness. You know nothing about my inner life or what I do and do not care about."

"We're going 'round and 'round in circles here. That's my point exactly, Seido-san. I know *nothing* about you. The Believers *know nothing* about you . . . ."

"The Believers must feel my sincerity. In this way, there is transmission, between teacher and disciple."

"How can we feel it? You're totally inscrutable. It's probably a Japanese thing, but while in the West, you have to express yourself clearly. Tell us what you are thinking and feeling. That's just how it works here. I hate to say it, but until you understand this, I doubt you're going to make headway in America."

This was all infuriating and I wasn't about to let her have the last word. "Who I am, personally, is immaterial," I said, with, I admit, a certain amount of Head Temple imperiousness. "I am unimportant. Of no significance whatsoever. But the teachings I convey, the robes I wear, they are everything. I represent the priesthood, the protectors of the law. These are the only things you and the Believers should know and concern yourselves with."

She ran her hands through her hair and sighed. "Oh, I don't know. Maybe this was all a big mistake. There are moments when I feel close to you, but most of the time you just seem like this cold and distant mountain. I could just wring your neck."

I smiled stiffly and made some comment about how, at that moment, I would also like to override my pacifist Buddhist training and thump her on the head. This remark seemed to change the atmosphere in the room. We both laughed, a little nervously, and the flare-up died as quickly as it started.

"I'm too blunt for my own good," Jennifer said, holding on to my arm. "But you know what? I don't have any regrets here. I believe wholeheartedly in what I just said." I took back my arm and fussed with papers on the desk. "I must think about your comments," I said. "But now, please, I want to be alone. It is really best you leave."

I don't think she expected me to push her away like that and for a moment she looked unsure. Then she silently collected her belongings. She brushed her lips across my cheek on the way out, gently saying, "Take care, Seido-san. Please know I do care for you. Very much."

I eased the door shut after her, but I could not shut out the thoughts that came to me when suddenly left alone in the apartment.

Why was I a Priest? How did I get here?

Not even Jennifer could I reach.

Chapter Twelve

Several days later I was pressured, against my natural inclination but in the interest of "community-building," to show my support for the men's choir so well represented among the Believers. Nothing seemed less enticing, but one Monday evening I dutifully dragged myself to the lobby of the riverside development, under the Manhattan Bridge, where the men were performing.

The all-male a cappella choir was dressed in black tails, white cotton gloves, and stood in two rows before the lobby's glass wall overlooking the East River. Across the water Manhattan was aglitter: headlamps soared up and down FDR Drive while a brightly lit leisure cruiser headed out to the New York Bay for a nighttime trawl up the coast.

Choir volunteers circled the building's lobby, handing out plastic cups of hot apple juice and wine. I impatiently looked at my watch, wondering when the concert would begin and I could return to the apartment. But just when I had had enough of this waiting and was about to leave, the lights dimmed, a hush fell, and the men slowly raised their voices until the lobby was filled with the skin-tingling harmony I so desperately wanted to achieve during prayer with the local Buddhist community.

When they sang Schubert's "Ave Maria," a Christian hymn, I found myself deeply moved. My skin prickled when they hit certain notes, and I had to wipe my eyes. This I did not expect. But there it was. After the concert, I got in line to congratulate the choirmaster and all the Believers who had participated in the concert. "This is precisely the one-voice I want the Believers to create during prayers," I told Mr. Doric. "Perhaps you can help with this."

The New York Temple Fund board member was standing beside Mr. Jonathan, a younger Believer and fellow choir member. The lawyer said, "I don't know. We can try. But this sort of harmony takes a lot of practice. We've been rehearsing ten hours a day for this concert. None of us have done anything else this weekend. Have we, Johnny?"

"Not a single thing. All choir and no play."

A few weeks later I was reviewing the New York Temple Fund accounts, in my position as chairman. Mr. Doric, a high-priced New York corporate attorney, worked entirely pro bono for the temple while passing on the costs of the temple's basic legal filings. This low-level legal work was executed by the Believer Mr. Jonathan, who was a young paralegal launching his own business at the time. That day I noticed Mr. Jonathan's monthly bill to the temple was for $3,900, most of the itemized hours booked on February 13 and 14.

I picked up the phone and called Mr. Doric. I was embarrassed by what I had to say and stuttered, "I believe you told me choir members were in rehearsal the weekend leading up to the performance on the fifteenth? Is it possible Mr. Jonathan did fourteen hours of legal work for the temple that Saturday and Sunday? This is what his bill claims."

There was silence. "I'll look into it," the lawyer finally said.

Mr. Doric confronted his young friend, who eventually confessed he was struggling financially and had, as a result, inflated the hours he charged the temple. Mr. Doric was enraged by this discovery and, to his credit, apologized profusely to the New York Temple Fund board before writing a personal check to cover the sums falsely charged by his young friend over several months.

At the next Oko the two men got into an argument in the hotel ballroom. I tried to intervene by discreetly guiding them out into the corridor and away from the other curious Believers. But my intervention seemed to inflame the situation, so much so Mr. Jonathan finally turned on me.

"Have you never made a mistake?" he said. "Who hasn't padded their expense account? Or their billable hours? It's human nature. Even a priest as out of it as you should be able to understand that!"

This was too much for Mr. Doric and, in a fit of rage, he swung wildly at the young man. Mr. Jonathan easily sidestepped the attack, however, and felled the older lawyer with a hard counterpunch to his stomach.

As Mr. Doric groaned and staggered back with the force of Mr. Jonathan's fist, he knocked me into the large basin housing a junglelike arrangement of plastic plants positioned in the corner of the hotel's hall. I fell backward, disappeared into the ceramic pot, my legs and tangled robes flailing in the air. By the time I had extricated myself from this upside-down position in the plastic foliage, several Believers—including a few of our more robust women—had Mr. Jonathan by the arms and were frog-marching him downstairs to the lobby, where he was shoved out onto the street. I never informed the Head Temple of this humiliating altercation in any of the updates I sent back to Reverend Fukuyama. At the time, I did not believe an omission was a serious offense.

The morning that followed this eventful Oko, I stood up from my bed as usual, but a profound weariness made me return to my cot. For several hours I lay stretched out on the narrow bed as my downstairs neighbor ran her washing machine. I think I slept a little, moving between this world and the next. A muffled samba from a TV came through the wall. My hands were tucked under my armpits as I lay on my side, staring at the brick wall.

A fly settled on my knuckle.

I twitched. It flew away and came back.

Rubbing its palms.

Michael made steady progress those winter months, stabilized by medication and prayers, and he was granted the privilege of leaving the clinic for the day. He called, hesitantly asking if he could visit me in Brooklyn so we could say prayers together. I reluctantly agreed. I really did not want any Believers in my flat, but I also knew that I owed Michael of all people this one concession. There was no temple yet in which he could seek refuge.

On the day he was scheduled to visit my apartment I spent the morning at my kitchen table, listlessly holding *The Eternal Teachings* in my lap and nervously sipping tea. When the doorbell rang, I jumped up.

Michael stood quiet in the doorway, dressed in jeans and a heavy coat, holding a white plastic bag. The nineteenth-century courtesan whom I had seen on past occasions was gone, and standing in front of me was a man. Michael looked me in the eye and smiled. He was so much more solid than on those awful West Village nights when he was manically conversing with the Buddha.

In the plastic bag were offerings he had brought to Brooklyn: a $200 check in an envelope, a dozen kiwis, and a bottle of fine sake, all of which I displayed on the altar's offering plate. To break the ice, I thought it wise we pray immediately and invited him to kneel with me before the altar. We incanted the *Lotus Sutra* for a half hour and were both quite invigorated when I finally hit the closing bell and extinguished the candle.

"Would you like tea?"

"Yes, please. If it is not too much trouble." He packed away his *juzu* beads in a leather prayer pouch and I gestured for him to take a seat at the table. As I warmed the teapot with kettle steam and shook out the green tea leaves, I asked Michael how things were at the clinic, and he told me about his group therapy sessions and his psychiatrist, all in such a matter-of-fact way that I soon found myself relaxing. He was clearly much better.

"I was pretty crazy the first time you came to the clinic. But you helped me a lot. By setting up the altar."

"I am pleased by this. I was afraid of saying the wrong thing— which of course I did. I am not a very skilled Priest in such matters."

"It's not your fault, Reverend Oda. Seriously, when I'm flipping out, everything spooks me. I'm just terrified of everyone and everything. I can't help it."

I poured the tea and we both sipped noisily from our cups.

"May I ask why you did not visit your parents today?"

Michael looked down. "That's difficult to answer."

"I do not mean to pry."

"No. No. I want to tell you. It's just very difficult to explain." Michael crossed his legs, and I could feel his foot jiggling under the table. "Whenever I am around my parents, particularly my mother—how can I explain it?" He looked away and talked in that disjointed way that sometimes made it difficult for me to follow the thread of his conversation. "I am an amoeba, under a microscope, just after its protective membranes have burst. My personality leaks out of me. I shrivel up and become nothing. Just disappear."

I looked down. "I see."

"Part of me knows my parents are good people, while part of me thinks they are out to destroy me."

The young man looked out the window to watch the subway rattle past. I studied his profile. I had the idea, at that moment, to tell him I bumped into his mother before I knew they were related. How we innocently met at the Waldorf dinner and the Brooks fashion show. But at that moment Michael continued with his story and, such was the extraordinary nature of his confession, I was swept away from my intent.

"That day when I went off the deep end, Mom came to my apartment and told me I was a pig and had to clean my room more often. I was sitting in a chair, drinking a Coke. Mom was wearing this thick mascara, giving her this heavy-lidded appearance, and I kept fixating on how much she looked like a lizard. When she opened her mouth next, this long, slithering tongue shot out of her face and started lashing the air."

I quietly turned and turned the cup of tea in my hands.

"When I am really flipping out I think that everyone is running back to tell her what I am doing, where I am going, and what I am thinking. Even taxi drivers. I can't help it." Michael smiled and gently shrugged his shoulders. "I'm paranoid. Always will be. It's just something I've got to live with."

"I see. This is very helpful for me to know. To understand."

"And sometimes I hear voices. But you know that."

"I do. Yes."

"I guess he wasn't the Buddha."

"No. Probably not."

"Only prayer is louder than the voices. The prayer, it seems to calm them down. The voices fade away when the *Lotus Sutra* is on my lips."

How long had I wondered what goes on in an unbalanced mind? The Buddhist gods had sent Michael to me, as some form of guide meant to lead me to a deeper understanding. More than that, talking with him that winter morning, I suddenly had a firm belief that my true purpose for being in America this last year was to save this young man from a terrible end.

Over the subsequent weeks, Michael's recovery progressed so well he was allowed to return to his Greenwich Village apartment, where I visited him in early March. We were initially a bit shy with each other, but in due course he made another one of his startling confessions: "It was in the darkest point of the night that the Buddha extended his hand and pulled me to safety, but he was not alone. Around him were all the lesser Buddhas and gods, summoned to protect me."

I was stunned because this unusual language he used to describe his vision was almost identical to how Buddhist scriptures thousands of years old described the Great Blessings. It was a mystery to me that the spirit of the finest Buddhist poet-priests and sutra writers was alive and well in this unlikely American, and I grappled, in my awkward manner, for an appropriate response.

"I have never been a parent," I said. "But I can imagine your accomplishments have made your parents very proud."

"I still don't feel strong enough to go back to school."

"No, perhaps not. Yet you have already fought like a samurai."

My phrase was so formal and unsatisfactory that I stopped talking, but when I glanced across the room and saw that my comment had pleased Michael, I blurted out, "You remind me of my brother, Onii-san. Your natural wisdom and strength. You remind me of him. I cannot help it."

As soon as this remark erupted from me, so unexpected, I was seized by a terrible fear: It was much more personal than I had intended it to be. I felt I had overstepped the proper boundaries of behavior; it was a visceral sense that a crack had just opened up and I was, from this point on, in serious danger. I tensely turned my cup around and around. A train shot by.

When Michael finally turned his head back in my direction, however, there was a kind and forgiving smile in the corner of his mouth. "That is the nicest thing anyone has ever said to me," he said, and, on that note, we both gratefully turned our attention back to our coffees.

"Do you have plans to go back to school?"

"Mom is paying me to do some chores for her, but I think I am going to take a course, on an audit basis, to see how things go. Maybe ease my way back into NYU that way."

"This seems wise."

Michael put down his mug and offered up another one of his mercurial remarks, part poetic insight, part unintelligible word-jumble. Either way, what he said next left a deep impression on me, for he spoke a language that I understood. "Mental stability is found in constant and steady effort, like running water, not in the fireworks of bliss. Prayer, for me, is water. Not fire." It was an image that has forever since stayed with me.

While Michael's steady improvement and our deepening connection was something solid to cling to, the rest of my life was fast disappearing into the churning abyss. When I came downstairs a few mornings later, to purchase tea, I found the steel grille of the vegetable store shuttered down and locked.

Mr. Giuseppe was normally up very early unpacking boxes of

vegetables and fruit, and at this time of day the shop was invariably open, whatever the weather. That morning, however, a piece of paper was taped to the shop's metal shutter, stating, in handwriting that looked like that of child: *Death in family. Closed rest of week.*

I did not have the strength to visit my landlord and express my condolences by myself, and Jennifer was not available, so I asked Miss Laura, who had so helped Mrs. Colonese after her fall, to accompany me to the house of mourning on Sant'Andrea Avenue.

The Old Rectory foyer was full of Colonese relatives and friends when we arrived, all very somber and dark and wearing black armbands. Cards and letters of condolence were stacked on a side table. A phone was ringing inside and someone picked up.

The old woman was laid out in the living room in full Italian style. The casket was open and she looked to me like a marzipan figurine from the bakery, dressed in a powder-blue dress. The room was filled almost to bursting with wreaths and flowers. The dead woman's favorite pair of Sunday gloves, a colorful plate from her kitchen, a dried and preserved leaf from her village in Calabria—such mementos imbued with personal importance were on a side table that stood near the head of the casket.

Three elderly women in black stood in a chorus to the side of the room, beating their breasts with clenched fists, lamenting and wailing. I was shocked by this theatrical carrying-on. Miss Laura whispered, "Professional mourners. It's a funeral tradition from the old country. Back in Italy. It's a sign of wealth."

At the foot of the coffin a black-and-white photograph of Mrs. Colonese was framed in flowers and propped up on an easel. The photo was taken when she was younger, and she looked out at us, coyly, through cat's-eye glasses on a chain around her neck. She looked young, full of life.

White-haired and elderly cousins, aunts, and uncles sat in chairs close around the coffin, like village elders, while the rest of us mourners stood respectfully back from the dressed corpse. The low hum of death-talk served as white noise in the background, while children fidgeted around the long side table set with food. Foil pans, one lined up after the other, were filled with different pastas and meat dishes, but even as I watched, neighbors and friends brought in more plastic-wrapped platters so that the air was warm with the smell of mothballs and meat sauce.

Mr. Giuseppe stood toward the back, near the marble fireplace. His transformation was shocking. Always thin, he now looked gaunt, almost sick. The grieving son constantly dabbed his eyes with a white linen handkerchief, leaning first to speak to the president of the Italian Social Club to his left, then toward Monsignor Trebaldi, the local Catholic priest, to his right. They pressed in on my landlord like black bookends, as Mr. Giuseppe told them his favorite stories about his mother and openly wept.

So this is mourning, I thought.

We took our place in the receiving line behind the butcher D'Amato and his wife; he was carrying a roasted leg of lamb under an arm. When it was our turn to express our condolences, Miss Laura was first to speak to Mr. Giuseppe and whatever she said made my landlord weep harder. His shoulders shook. Too soon it was my turn to express my condolences, and the Catholic monsignor peered down his long nose at me as Mr. Giuseppe shook my hand in both of his and said, "Thank you, Reverend Oda. Thank you. God bless."

A framed notice near the coffin stated that at three-thirty p.m. mourners were to accompany Mrs. Colonese on her final journey to the cemetery, in a procession behind Monsignor Trebaldi. I whispered to Miss Laura that I would have to leave, as I could not participate in a Catholic religious service. She reassuringly patted my arm and told me that was fine, but she would stay, out of respect.

Back in my apartment, I heard sad-sounding trumpets coming from the street below. I went to the staircase window. Monsignor Trebaldi and two altar boys in black dresses and white lace led the procession down Cortina Street, incanting their Latin prayers and swinging a silver thurible that was spilling incense smoke into the coming night. The low-hanging clouds and fading light had turned the air dark, and shopkeepers along the way came out to stand behind the ice heaps and snow-crusted cars, their hats off, whispering their final goodbyes to their Brooklyn neighbor.

So Mrs. Colonese's coffin floated down the icy street, hovering in the air, held up by Mr. Giuseppe and strapping cousins from Long Island and New Jersey. They were followed by a small brass band and the three breast-beating professional mourners, while the dead woman's family and friends, one or two holding a white lily or a wreath, silently brought up the rear on Mamma Colonese's final walk down Cortina Street.

I turned away and entered the old woman in the Calendar of the Dead, a log I kept under the altar in which I recorded death dates, a priestly technique to ensure Buddhist ritual prayers for the dead were accurately performed on key anniversaries. I then took out my brushes to write Mrs. Colonese's memorial totem, propping up the completed wooden stupa next to the altar. I had promised Mr. Giuseppe that I would say Buddhist prayers for his mother, and, as arranged, Jennifer and Miss Laura appeared at my door at eight o'clock to join me in the woman's Buddhist memorial service.

Jennifer and I had been keeping a distance from each other since our argument, each waiting for the other to make the first overture, but, to her credit, she never allowed these personal issues to interfere with our religious obligations. She was always proper, always had a composed, nunlike discipline about her, and for this reason alone, let alone her other admirable qualities, she always had my deepest respect.

That night Jennifer removed her boots in the threshold of the apartment door, and, alongside Miss Laura, wordlessly followed me to the other side of the horseshoe-shaped studio flat. We knelt before the Cluster of Jewels Mandala to perform the Ceremony of the Dead, and as we prayed for Mrs. Colonese and her son, I once again heard that strange extra voice, that eerie presence distinctly joining our incantations on 429 Cortina Street.

I cannot describe it. The terror that seized me that night.
Who does this voice belong to?
What does it want?

And so we come to the event that changed my life. It is impossible to know, when tensions mount between competing tectonic plates, what final tipping point creates the quake's cataclysmic fissure ripping through the earth's crust, sending whatever was molten and down below spewing up to the surface. In my case it wasn't one thing, but a series of pressures bearing in on me from different places. Mrs. Graham openly challenging the rigid rules that had guided my Japanese life for so long; the coarse brawl at the Oko; Jennifer personally attacking my reserved nature and insisting I was "hiding something"; the act of watching Mrs. Colonese's body carried through the Brooklyn streets while her son openly and unabashedly mourned his great loss—they all, possibly, contributed to the final pressure point that cracked my composed front.

It occurred the night of Mrs. Colonese's funeral, when I tossed and turned in bed until the small hours, until, giving up, I switched on the bedside lamp. I swung my feet onto the cold floor. My ankles were beaded with perspiration and glistened in the lamplight. The alarm clock glowed 2:35 a.m.

My chest pounded hard like a prayer drum: *Get up! Get up! Get up!*

I shrugged on pants and a flannel shirt, found heavy socks and boots, a thick sweater, scarf, and coat, and then let myself out into the hallway smelling of rotting turnips. The cold outside hit my face like a slap and the same powerful force that compelled me to get up now compelled me to walk and walk and walk through the streets of Brooklyn. The city's orange light spread into the skies, creating New York's surreal nighttime, a place both black and aglow. And the stars, hidden behind this black-orange blanket of night, were nothing more than an earthly string of bare bulbs strung around a leafless tree on Fourth Street.

At some point I stopped before the shuttered shop-front of Miranda's Patisserie, totally spent by the compulsive walking. The softly lit store window illuminated a china cake plate and jars of handmade jam. Dew crept up the glass.

A terrible noise filled the night.

I slowly turned my head in its direction.

Rotating lights and night-shattering blares rose from the far end of Cortina Street, as fire engines rushed to a blaze in deepest Brooklyn. Over the ragged roofs of the borough I saw the rise of the night's crackling flames, a family home crumbling into white ash and fiery ember. Purple and black clouds covered the heavens, and in the folds and puffs of the cloud swirl, a face began to take shape.

The next thing I remember I was back in my own bed. Brooklyn was already clattering with commercial noise. I rose from the cot, dressed to get the paper, determined to keep the thoughts at bay by staying active. But an image of that massive crack in the west wall of the Head Temple's Pilgrims Dormitory, the fissure that appeared during the earthquake and signaled the entire edifice was about to come tumbling down, was continuously forcing its way into my head.

I vaguely recall emerging from my apartment and standing stock-still on the Cortina Street pavement, looking up at the sky. Purple and black clouds covered the heavens, just like the previous night, but this time, in the folds and puffs of the cloud swirl, my father's stern face took shape.

Giuseppe Colonese, with his black armband, wished me a good morning. I do not know if I returned his greeting. I think not. I walked with my head down as a clammy sweat gathered on my forehead. When I looked up again I found I had, in my dazed state, wandered away from Castor Street. I was down by the abandoned docks instead. The sky was gray and black. Otousan glared at me from above. The ice had finally broken up; white tables flowed down from the Hudson River, bobbing about Upper New York Bay, the first signs that spring was approaching.

I slipped through a hole in the fence and found myself standing at the very edge of the rotted pier jutting out into the water. The impersonal steel high-rises of Manhattan stood cold and indifferent on the far side of the water. The heat inside me was unbearable and I remember how the bay's chop looked so cool and inviting, a mercurial shimmering of quicksilver at my feet, almost pleading with me to put out the flames.

I reached into my overcoat, pulled out my *juzu* beads, and knelt in prayer for what I believed would be the last time. My voice rang out with the sacred words of the *Lotus Sutra*, each syllable rolling crisply out across the water. Seagulls circled and cried overhead. Sparrows landed at my feet. They chirped, hopped toward me, hopped back, hopped toward me, until they were just inches away from where I knelt. And then a few brave birds fluttered up a few inches into the air before descending lightly on my knees and thighs.

I continued to pray with all my being. The pigeons arrived with heavy-beating wings. The Canadian geese honked loudly and circled above before landing next to the pier in a spray of water. They found the boat ramp and waddled up the cement slope before kneeling down at my feet. Even a peregrine falcon landed on the pier post and drooped its head, cocked it, probing me with its black eyes.

In the middle of the rhythmic incantation of the *Lotus Sutra* several hundred birds surrounded me, a great cooing and chirping and fluttering of wings so close I could touch them. Friends from the Four Corners Heavens, perhaps even from the slopes of Mount Nagata, had come to hear my troubles. My rational mind deduced that the suffering in my voice, as it rang out across the water, summoned the birds and they came to comfort a fellow animal in pain. But the Priest in me knew these birds were sent by the Buddha, manifestations of this infinite compassion.

For the birds landing at my feet brought as gifts a deep sense of security, which at first sat side by side with my great horrors. But then I was in a calm clearing, and the constant anxiety, my heavy companion for so long, lifted and lightly floated away, no more significant than a dust mote. For how could I possibly despair over the trifles of life when at the hour of my greatest need the Buddha had come to protect me, sending me both succor and comfort from the Four Corners of the World?

It is fact that a man of incorrigible cynicism died on the Brooklyn piers that day. The man that remained praying among the birds, thanking the Buddha from a depth he did not know he had, shook with one all-powerful emotion.

The privilege to be alive.

The immense privilege.

Chapter Thirteen

$\mathcal{J}$ do not know how long I was on my knees, but eventually I was ready to end my prayers and return to the mundane world of Brooklyn. I bowed to the Buddha one last time and carefully put away my beads. My feathered friends scattered when I stood, flying back to the Four Corners Heavens.

On my return to the flat I noticed, for the first time, an art supply store tucked to the side of Cohen's Tailors on Cortina Street. I must have walked past the shop hundreds of times before, but, blind to the Brooklyn in front of me, I never noticed it. I took its sudden appearance as an auspicious omen, and I quickly crossed the street and pushed open its door.

Somewhere in the bowels of the musty store a bell tinkled. A stooped man came from behind a screen and I spent the next forty minutes in his cheerfully cluttered store poring over drawers filled with fleck-filled rice paper and India ink. I finally emerged from the shop looking like Jennifer, my arms loaded down with bags full of teak frames, new brushes, fresh ink, watercolors, and a box knife.

It seemed to me, as I mounted my building's creaking stairs, that I was at last at 429 Cortina Street in a different life, and once inside the flat my heart filled with joy at the sight of my teapot, the Formica table, the cot in the alcove. They were suddenly very precious to me and I dropped my parcels and again gave prayerful thanks to the Cluster of Jewels Mandala for all that I had.

Over the next hours I worked tirelessly at my kitchen table painting Mother and Atsuko, Yuji, and Daiki, before neatly matting and framing my family in the handsome teak acquisitions. From Mr. Colonese downstairs I borrowed a hammer and nails and hung the paintings over my bed. But the biggest frame of all I saved for my father and that night I painted until the early hours of the morning finishing his portrait.

I awoke later in the day after a fine sleep. Otou-san had dried. After morning prayers and a shower I framed my father and put him in the center of the family. I gave Otou-san the place of honor over the head of my bed. He looked afraid and unsure.

He looked very much like me.

The paintings finally completed and hung, I very slowly conducted the Ceremony of the Dead for my family, each syllable pulled from the depths of my being and carefully enunciated. I had performed this ceremony many times before, but always while I myself was half-dead, never fully there.

Two days later, sitting in the armchair of my Brooklyn rooms, I randomly flipped to a page in *The Eternal Teachings*. The tea I brought to my lips halted midway and I brought the pages closer to the light to see if my eyes were perhaps playing tricks on me. But they were not. There, in formal characters on paper, in the eighth High Priest's own words, was the perfect description of what had happened to me on that Brooklyn pier that fateful day. When a caged bird sings his sorrow, the High Priest wrote, "birds flying in the skies are summoned by this voice of anguish. See them gather around the cage, lending assistance to the poor bird striving to escape his prison and find freedom." And so, too, he said, when we sincerely chant the *Lotus Sutra* with our mouth and heart, our Buddha nature, being summoned, will "invariably emerge" and free our mind of its many illusions. This I believe is what happened to me on that pier.

I closed the book. And picked up the phone.

Jennifer agreed to meet at Sant'Andrea Park. Near the bocce court.

"Thank you for seeing me," I said.

"Of course." She was cool as she lit a cigarette.

I clung to the wire fence. "I have been thinking much about what you said that night," I said. "It is very difficult for me to admit, but you are right. I have been very arrogant, very cold. Not just to you, but to all the Believers. I apologize." I turned and bowed in her direction, repeatedly. I was so filled with shame I could barely speak. "I apologize. Most sincerely."

She dropped her cigarette, put her hands around my neck, and kissed me. The emotion I felt, when I felt her lips pressed against mine, is too much to describe. But one apology is not enough to expiate deep karma. It is a process, earned by deeds. So, not long afterward, when we were quietly preparing dinner together in my flat, I said, "Jennifer, I have been thinking about you and your fiancé, and I just wanted to say, I know about holding on to the dead."

I then told her, as I washed the salad greens, the entire story of my family, of my father's mental illness, the fire, how our neighbor saw my brother burn to death. It was the first time in thirty years I had spoken of my family and the fire, and it came out so quietly and simply I wondered why I had buried it for so long. By the end of the story, Jennifer was weeping. This good woman put her arms around my neck, her lips against my ear, and once again uttered those words that had become so familiar. "You poor, poor man," she said.

"No, do not feel sorry for me. You see, my story is—I am alive.

"I know not how or why. But I am alive. We are both alive."

Spring came to America. A sultry, soft breeze blew in over the New York Harbor and we all came outside to bask in the weak but warming sun. We awoke one morning and it was there. The mango-scented trade winds of the Caribbean floated over Brooklyn's rooftops, gently nudging aside the winds that for too long had blown in hard from Canada's frozen tundra.

Little Calabria welcomed the new season with its own rites and festivals, a reawakening that gently unfolded under the budding elm and maple trees of Cortina Street. The old men emerged blinking from their social clubs, like bears coming out of hibernation, and unfolded clap chairs on the pavement to worshipfully face the sun. They puffed contentedly on their stubby cigars and talked among themselves in their local rasp, brushing away the cigar ash that dropped down cardigan fronts, a neck suddenly bent for a slurp of grappa-coffee from the cup balanced on an arthritic knee.

Women and children came out to scrub the colorful front-garden chapels, laying fresh gravel and flowers as offerings before the plaster statues of Saint Francis and Saint Lucy. A man from the social club tipped back on his curbside seat and yelled directions at the women scrubbing moss from the outdoor chapels, until one of the women in black turned and gave the old man such a rat-tat blast of dialect back, the hair on *my* neck stood on end. The other men laughed uproariously and the old fellow dismissively waved the woman away, but he never said another word after that.

The next day satin banners embroidered with red and gold tinsel appeared over Cortina Street, hanging from wires overhead. Blue NYPD barricades were erected, sealing off fifteen blocks of the street; soon beefy carpenters in fresh cotton T-shirts and jeans, with tools hanging from leather belt straps, were hauling and hammering and bolting together metal bars and planks of wood.

The pretty young girls wrapped their legs around the parking meters and swung gently back and forth, seductively calling out, but the carpenter apprentices, after a little back-and-forth tease, earnestly kept their heads down until a dance floor and stage was solidly standing in Sant'Andrea Park.

I, too, was drawn outside, to watch Brooklyn's spring roll in. It came in the form of caravans lined the length of Cortina Street. A middle-aged couple clapped back the shutters of their red-walled shooting gallery, revealing flashing lights and shelves filled with dolls and pandas. More such caravans opened shutters and the delicious smell of hot-candied almonds soon mingled in the air with the cigar smoke of the old men intent on playing their bocce.

The machinery and music were fired up, grease was slathered on joints of the bumper cars. I watched as the teacups began to whirl. Just after the sun slid behind the old maritime guesthouses of Fourth Street, the strings of colored lights along Cortina came on and a band of old men and their dented musical instruments took up positions on the park's stage, launching into a drunken polka.

The Little Calabrese Spring Festival had officially begun.

I took Jennifer by the arm and promenaded her up and down Cortina Street, like any other proud local man out with his woman. We ate the peppers-and-sausage fry-up from a booth, sipped Gallo wine from plastic cups, and walked like a regular couple through the fair. I unsuccessfully threw wooden loops at a radio, but Jennifer, fiendishly good at the shooting range, won a glass cake dish.

We found common ground in the bumper cars of Sant'Andrea Park. Jennifer was ruthless with the cocky young teenagers when their cars were temporarily wedged immobile, and several times we managed to viciously ram these tough Brooklyn teenagers, cackling fiendishly after each successful attack, until Jennifer and I were similarly smacked hard and fell about laughing helplessly.

By 10 p.m., night had dropped its curtain, and under the stage lights I watched a solitary old woman dancing energetically with herself, surrounded by aged couples working the wooden dance floor. She was wearing a peach-colored gown and a tinsel tiara, her mind obviously suffering the effects of old age, but she moved with great feeling and grace around the other couples, her arms held out to some imaginary prince.

Then, through the bandstand, a slow-moving wall of candles appeared in the night. With a short sharp movement of his baton, the bandleader cut the music short. The dancers froze in place, all but the lonely old lady, who continued to rocket around the floor with a beatific smile on her face, oblivious, swirling to her own music in time and space.

There were "ahhs" and "oohs" and excited chatter as the crowd surged forward, sweeping Jennifer and me, against our will, to the police barricade on Fourth Street. Over the noise she told me that the archdiocese removed the Black Madonna from the Cathedral Basilica of St. James every spring, to march the sacred statue through the streets of Brooklyn. The Madonna's face was pitch-black. She was originally white, according to legend, but the Catholic faithful had over the years burned millions of candles at the Madonna's feet, and as she helped lead each of the sinners to salvation, she absorbed the blackness of their sins into her own skin, through the rising smoke of the penitents' candles.

A row of altar boys in black robes and white lace smocks came into view, illuminating the warm Brooklyn night with their hands cupped around the orbs of the burning candles, their high voices washing over us. Then came lay dignitaries with purple satin sashes across their chests, including my landlord, who momentarily broke his solemn expression to smile and wave at us, loftily. We energetically waved back.

Priests carrying ornate crucifixes and gold candelabras were next to arrive, the two lead clerics swinging silver perforated canisters and filling the night air with a pungent, smoky incense. Then the bishop, the Black Madonna, and the baby Jesus finally turned the corner, unleashing a crescendo of ecstatic cries.

What struck me most was how slowly the Procession of the Black Madonna moved, like it was deliberately trying to slow down the pace of modern times. The doleful-looking Madonna was finally before us, with her blackened face, the Christ child cradled in her arms. The woman next to me had her head covered in black lace, and she made the sign of the cross and kissed the crucifix around her neck. As the procession slowly passed before us, swaying drunkenly with the Latin chants, members of the overexcited crowd surged forward to pin money to the cloth strips hanging from the undercarriage, or tried to kiss the Black Madonna's feet.

And then, like a mirage, the procession turned the corner and was gone. For a few moments I just stood there, silent, taking it all in. Then the dance band struck up its soft waltz where it had left off, and the crowd drifted back to its earthly pleasures, the pinging of the shooting gallery.

At the next study meeting I ordered that chairs be set up at all Okos going forward, so that the American Believers who didn't want to kneel no longer had to, and those that preferred to kneel had the option to do so. There were many sighs of relief, and when I saw an elderly and overweight woman lower herself with a contented sigh into a chair, her swollen legs bursting from her buckled shoes, I was deeply ashamed I had been so stubborn and arrogant about a thing of no importance at all.

It was during this April meeting, while I was explaining some technical feature of the priesthood—how the Priests prepare for debates, I think—that Harriet Symes cut the whole conversation short with her shattering voice.

"What's enlightenment? No one ever tells me."

I took one look at her pileup of orange hair and began a simplistic answer. But then I stopped. She deserved better from me. "Enlightenment is not a state of superhuman bliss, where one day the lights go on and, bing, one is enlightened," I answered, groping for the words in English. "We believe that the person who tries to become enlightened is at that moment enlightened, because the cause of enlightenment simultaneously contains the effect of enlightenment. A seed contains its flower. An oyster contains its pearl. What this means is, the person who simply and deeply enjoys prayer, who appreciates the rare good fortune of being born human, he is at that moment the Buddha. That is all enlightenment is."

"Oh," said Mrs. Symes, clearly disappointed. "But what good is that? Don't we become better people?"

What followed was an hour of questions and answers of great depth. I was amazed and humbled by the quality of the community's questions and I struggled, in my stumbling way, to do their seeking justice. I tried to explain we become enlightened as we are, fully engaged as humans in earthly existence, with parking tickets to pay and children to pick up from school and trips to the dentist, finally correcting the impression that all our problems disappeared once we are enlightened.

Furthermore, I explained that enlightenment was a clear-eyed absence of fear, not the absence of problems. Even an absolute beginner could become a Buddha with just one sincere syllable of prayer, but that Buddhahood was never constant. It came and went as we moved through the volatile swings of daily life, what we call Samsara, appearing only irregularly in our life so that we could not depend upon enlightenment all the time but must continually strive in its general direction. Yet the more we prayed, the more these precious moments were stored in our lives, creating a reservoir of peace and strength at the core of our being.

"Reverend Oda," said Mrs. Symes, rummaging in her purse for chewing gum. "I can't follow a word you're saying. It's like you're talking Swahili."

I took a deep breath and tried again. "We are trying to put into words what is unmentionable. As you can see, I am stumbling. I am a Priest of many failings. But I am trying."

I glanced down for a moment. When I looked up again, across the sea of heads, I said, "You are not alone with your confusion, Harriet. I am, for example, no stranger to anxiety, self-doubt, and great sadness. I am someone who is often afraid. But what a great blessing these fears are, because they bring me to my knees before the Cluster of Jewels Mandala. So in an essential way my fears *are* my enlightenment. It is an irony that nothing awakes hunger for the Buddha like suffering. Some inner anxiety, perhaps not a destructive amount, but a certain amount, is needed to live the religious life. Or else we are just pointlessly reading texts and rubbing our beads. It is in fact my fears that push me to practice this faith to its fullest. And when I do, my personal problems do not go away, but neither do they paralyze me. I bow at them courteously, like they are rather irritating and noisy relatives always demanding respect, before stepping past them to get on with the work at hand."

The American Believers laughed at this description, and when, at the end of the lecture, they lined up as usual to talk to me, our conversation flowed like the clear streams of Mount Nagata. So we found a path we could mutually tread, the American Believers and me.

When I visited Nicolai Place next, the plot was as busy as a Tokyo train station, with ditchdiggers and delivery trucks and workmen crawling over the property. Spring was having its effect here, too. The architect and site manager were standing next to the office trailer and grunted a hello when I arrived, but they also held up a hand, as if to say they would get to me when they finished the task of hoisting the temple's timber-framed roof.

Mr. Symes came into the site gray and tired-looking. Steel girders rose floor after floor from the pit in the ground and served as the temple's basic spine and bone structure. Men crawled around inside the steel frame, providing basic shape to the internal rooms as they assembled walls with much hammering and the repetitive thuds of the nail guns. But the real activity was overhead, where a whirring crane dangled a preassembled timber-frame roof, and was swinging it in to position over the half-completed building.

When I turned in Mr. Symes's direction again, I saw he had taken prayer beads out of his pocket and was offering up a prayer for the temple. I found this quite touching, and we stood, side by side, silently admiring the Treasure Tower that was emerging from the ground before us.

The roof was locked into position and the men on the scaffolding scampered across the timber and steel skeleton of the temple, performing the final steps of bolting the roof frame tight. The architect, important task completed, finally turned toward us, hard hat off, and shook our hands in formal welcome. He apologized in his singsong Finnish accent for not welcoming us earlier, but he needed to concentrate on the task at hand.

And then he politely asked my permission to temporarily set a small fir tree on the roof. I was perplexed. "A fir tree?" I asked.

He explained that in his home country, it was a tradition to erect a small evergreen tree on the roof of a new house. The fir tree is a symbol of longevity, like greens are on our Buddhist altars, a symbolic prayer that the house built would last for a long time and remain protected from fires and earthquakes and other calamities.

"The tree is good luck," the architect said, with not a little embarrassment, wiping away the band of sweat from inside his hard hat. "A superstition."

I consented. I could see no harm.

It was like this in America.

It is amazing to me, now looking back, how much attitudes changed that spring—most important mine. A week after we met at Nicolai Place, Mr. Symes called with a shaky voice. He asked me to come say evening prayers with him and his wife at their Park Avenue apartment. Clearly, something was upsetting him, but it was unclear to me what that might be or how I might help.

I found Mrs. Symes standing just behind the apartment's front door, fluttering nervously about with a finely embroidered handkerchief, her husband pale and angry at her side. Buffeted by the abrupt cooling of the construction market, his company's plummeting cash flow had required drastic action so he could hold on through the coming economic storm. Mr. Symes had been forced, in short, to fire eighty long-serving and decent workers that day, most of them family men or heads of households.

While we walked briskly down the apartment's corridor filled with lithographs of English aristocrats hunting with dogs and horses, Mr. Symes turned his head in my direction and said, "I have done so much for this faith. Why doesn't the Buddha give me a goddamn break?"

I was disheartened by this remark and was, in my old way, just about to say something sharp about his childish comment and superficial understanding, but I held my tongue. *This is the Buddha's business,* I thought. *Keep your nose out of his affairs.* So I did not respond to Mr. Symes's plaintive question, but silently led the couple to the Cluster of Jewels Mandala in their prayer room. They followed me meekly, fell to their knees, and the evening liturgy was slow and heavy, like prayers for the dead.

Somewhere in the middle of the recitation Mr. Symes's voice broke and he started to shake, like he had just been struck with a heavy stick. Harriet Symes and I continued to make our way through the *Lotus Sutra,* but Mr. Symes was unable to continue for some time, until, that is, his wife reached out and gently rested her hand on her husband's knee. Her touch seemed to revive him, and he found his voice again, came back in, his voice ringing out clear.

I rang the prayers' final bell. As we silently put away our prayer beads and liturgy books, Mr. Symes said, to no one in particular, "I don't think I have ever been this ashamed."

"If saving the company required such measures, there is little that can be said about such painful things," I said. "Reality has its own logic and force."

Mr. Symes looked down at the pouch of prayer beads in his hands and quietly said, "I fired half these men nine years ago. After we came out of that recession, I lured them back to the company with all sorts of promises. 'This time it will be different,' I said. I sold them hard, that after completing the painful restructuring that time around, their futures would be rock-solid with me—if they bet on the Symes Elevator Company again."

His wife was visibly upset and said, "I won't stand for this, Artie. This . . . this beating yourself up. You did the best you could for these men."

"Well, no, I didn't, Harriet. One of the guys heading out the door today said, 'Why didn't you just let us go last time? I could have retrained in a new career. Now I am too old to get a second chance at anything else.' There is no way to sugarcoat this. I hustled them. I sold these guys a 'secure future' and delivered something else, and they, not I, are now paying the price for my bullshit. That's the truth."

That day Mr. Symes saw his karma clearly by the Buddha's

Light. I was very proud of him. The three of us were silent, our heads bowed for some minutes, before I said, "Mr. Symes, when I first met you last year I secretly thought, *This man will never understand Buddhism. He is too shallow. Too stupid. He thinks Buddhism is all about the fall and rise of his elevator sales.* But today I am humbled by how you read the *Lotus Sutra,* not with your mind, but with your life. It is I who must now sincerely apologize to the Buddha, for so underestimating his devoted follower, Mr. Arthur—"

But I could not complete my sentence because the couple burst out laughing, so badly did I mangle, in Japanese fashion, the many *r*'s of his name. I did not take offense. I think I even smiled.

That Saturday I took Jennifer to Okinawa Spa, after we both had a long but pleasant day visiting a boisterous family of Believers in Bedford-Stuyvesant. The simple Japanese bath was located in a Williamsburg strip mall, sandwiched between an African American hair salon and a Hasidic day-care center. I had a word with the attendant and she took Jennifer by the hand and led her away into the women's section of the baths.

I went the other direction and squatted before the chrome floor taps with a brush, a bar of soap, and a yellow bucket at my side. I scrubbed myself raw over the next half hour. Cleansed, I made my way to the steaming, iron-rich tubs of hot water in the next room, easing in up to my chin as plump Japanese businessmen bobbed about the tub, buoyed by their swollen stomachs. I closed my eyes, sweat beaded my brow, and the water running ceaselessly through the tub taps called me back to Japan, called me back to the natural prayers of my beloved Kappa-gawa.

Afterward, I waited for Jennifer in the lobby. Her cheeks were glowing red when she emerged, and I could not help but smile, for she wore a deep contented look like a baby after its milk. She thanked the attendant profusely and left an American-sized tip and there was much bowing all around.

So we went out into the evening, cleansed, our skin tingling from the hot bath, and held hands in the parking lot.

"Was it a good experience?"

"Yes, Seido-san. Very good."

A spring moon stood over the city. "This evening reminds me of a haiku by Nishiyama Sōin:

> *No, no, not even cherry blooms,*
> *Can equal the moon tonight."*

Jennifer circled me with her arms. "You have a poem for every possible situation," she said, resting her head in the hollow of my collar.

"This is because all life is in haiku."

"*Hai*," she said sleepily.

In that moment, looking at the moon over this urban parking lot in Williamsburg, our arms wrapped tightly around each other like we were each other's life rafts, I was reminded of that poem I had written in my head so many months ago, on a dark night, looking out of my apartment window. Then I had composed:

> *Over Brooklyn*
> *The sliver moon of silver*
> *Reveals the jagged roof.*

But as I held Jennifer in that parking lot, it occurred to me that I was not like the solitary Bashō at all but much more like the people-loving Issa, and on the spot I rewrote my Brooklyn-moon poem to make it better reflect the person I had become.

> *Over Brooklyn*
> *The sliver moon of silver*
> *Reveals my neighbor's roof.*

Chapter Fourteen

Michael returned to his old life step by measured step, and I was immensely pleased by his progress, for I knew I had played an important role, however small, in saving him from a horrible fate. That April he joined a band called the Blowhard Bloggers, and he invited me to attend their debut performance. So I ventured out into Manhattan for the set he said would start at eleven p.m., fervently praying I would stay awake. It was well past my bedtime.

There was no danger of falling asleep. The band was playing at Charlie's Castaways in Greenwich Village. Half a dozen young men and women stood outside the club, smoking cigarettes and shivering in the cool spring night. It was dark and hot and crowded inside, with a few uncomfortable-looking garden chairs standing close by the bar's stage. I decided to sit there, up front, so Michael could clearly see I was in the audience.

By eleven o'clock the bar was packed with New York University students. Michael's four-man band climbed on the small stage. He looked shy and nervous, but when he saw me, he smiled quickly before turning his back and strapping on his saxophone. There was a screech of microphone feedback, guitars were twanged, and when they launched into their first song, I was almost blasted out of my chair.

It physically hurt. The noise. I immediately pushed my way through the crowd to the men's toilet, and tore off a few sheets of toilet paper. I rolled the paper into two tight wads and stuck them into both ears. I returned to my seat and sat stiffly erect with the toilet paper cones protruding from my head. Several indignant young people looked at me as if I were mad, but I didn't care, for in this way I managed to hear out the set.

Afterward, Michael and I stood outside enjoying some fresh air.

"Was most interesting," I said.

He mumbled something. When he saw the incomprehension on my face he leaned forward and gently pulled the paper plugs from my ears.

"Is new sound for me. I am a simple Buddhist Priest."

"You hated it. But you came for me. That's what counts."

I looked across the street.

"Yes. I am here. You are right. This is what counts."

"Yeah, I know." He lit a cigarette and smiled. "The Buddha told me you would come."

Ten days later Michael and I agreed to meet at his West Eleventh Street apartment, to say morning prayers together before I had my meeting with the temple's accountant in Murray Hill. When I stepped out onto the fifth floor of his building that morning, I found a white envelope with my name taped to the door of his studio. It contained the key to his flat. The note simply read, *Come in!*

I have trouble recalling what happened next. It remains a blur. I found Michael sitting cross-legged in lotus position in the middle of his studio, his upper torso slumped forward like a deflating balloon might slowly sink to the ground. I remember the sticky-footed flies, how they walked in quick spurts through the blood that had leaked into the wool carpet and created a crimson ring radiating out from his body. I remember trying to determine what the metallic lump, coated in syrupy blood, could possibly be. It was the box cutter he had used to cut his wrists after swallowing the OxyContin. The orange pharmacy vial had rolled across the floor.

Grief can turn people a little mad and I had an inappropriate thought in Michael's apartment that I rather liked the smell of death—it left a clean and metallic odor in the air, like gunpowder residue. But what struck me most about that scene on the floor of that Eleventh Street apartment was how Michael had meticulously surrounded himself with all the things he had loved while on earth—his prayer beads, a birthday card from his father, a pair of old jeans, his saxophone—before he took his life.

It was while I was talking to the 911 operator that I finally noticed the two envelopes neatly addressed in Michael's handwriting standing on the sideboard. One envelope was for his parents, the other, addressed to me. I hung up the phone, went to the sideboard, and pocketed my letter.

The police questioned me, the medical examiner removed Michael's body, and in due course I was allowed to make my way home. I remembered, while waiting for the F train, that Michael had told me at Charlie's Castaways the "Buddha" was speaking to him again, and I kept repeating to myself, *You should have seen the signs. You should have seen it coming.*

Standing at the edge of the subway platform, waiting for the train, I suddenly leaned over the side and became violently sick onto the tracks below. It was during this retching that I had a momentary sense I was not in New York at all, but leaning over the stone bridge in Katsurao, once again spewing my innards into the Kappa-gawa below.

Somehow I made it home. I dozed briefly, from the shock, and felt better when I woke again. Jennifer came by Cortina Street as soon as she heard the news. She was pale, concerned, stroked my face. She tried to contact Mrs. Horovitz on my behalf, but the woman was hysterical and unable to talk, according to her husband.

I made a stupa and together Jennifer and I performed Michael's memorial service, our fervent prayers guiding him into the next life. The studio was heavy with incense and the vibrations of our heartfelt prayer when, two hours later, I drew the service to an end. It was afterward that Jennifer spotted the unopened envelope in Michael's handwriting, standing against the salt-and-pepper shakers on my kitchen table, and she said, tersely, "You have to open it."

I slit open the flap of the envelope with a shaking hand. *Dear Reverend Oda,* Michael wrote. *My mother pays me to do odd jobs. I just pasted two years of her clips into a large scrapbook and came across her review of Peter Brooks' collection. You have known Mother all along. Things are as they are. The Buddha has made me understand this. Michael.*

I was numb at first. Then the thoughts rushed in.

What had I done? What had this stupid Priest done?

I handed the letter to Jennifer and she read it while I fussed in the kitchen, putting the kettle on for tea. "It's weirdly lucid and rational," she said. "But I still don't get it. What's he mean here?"

"I lied to him," I said, stacking and unstacking teacups. "He was so strange about his mother, so obsessed I never meet her, I never told him that I accidentally met her through the Symeses. Before I know they were related." I looked over at Jennifer. "But I never spoke with Mrs. Horovitz once I knew he wanted to keep us apart. This I did not do."

"Come on. This was not your fault. It's just one of those inexplicable tragedies. He was so ill it wouldn't have made any difference if you had told him. He had his own destiny unrelated to you."

I did not speak. Perhaps, like they do in America, I should have explained what an incompetent Priest feels like when he discovers he has unwittingly pushed his devout Believer to a terrible and untimely death. But America had not changed me that much and I reverted to my father's silent language.

"Something else would probably have made him go off the deep end, even if you had told him," Jennifer continued, following me from kitchen to living room. "You know that's true. He told you he was paranoid, always silently thinking people were running back to his mother to report what he was up to. I'm sorry, it's heartbreaking, but believing you are responsible for his death is, well, a bit self-important."

Of course she was right, and through her ministrations I eventually saw that blaming myself for Michael's death was, in its way, another example of my inflation.

And yet . . .

And yet . . .

I did not save my brother.

I did not save Michael.

I am not sure how long it was I sat staring out the back window, as the trains roared by, the muscles in my jaw rippling up and down the side of my head until I had a blinding headache and had to lie down. Jennifer pulled up a chair beside the cot. But for all her efforts she could not take away the ache that was my constant companion and due. For this was my karma and I alone had to suffer it.

I sent Jennifer home and in the resulting silence I took up my brush and painted Michael. I was compelled to do so. It was not a pretty portrait, but, as on that first night in his apartment, a vision of a young man in a white kimono fighting the night. I could not bear to hang this picture and stuck it in the folder in the back of my closet.

Perhaps one day I would have the strength to put it on my wall, but that day the best I could manage was a mental note to tell Reverend Fukuyama something he very much needed to know. When you force open a window long sealed shut, it's not just the smells of sweet blossoms that come to you, but all of life, including the fly-filled winds of the village latrine.

During the listless days that followed I repeatedly found myself picturing Michael the way he was when he came and visited me in my Brooklyn flat—warm, funny, open. I spent hours sitting in my armchair, staring out the back window, taking stock of my life and questioning my calling as a Priest.

But then Mr. Symes called. There was a structural problem at the temple, he said, and I was urgently needed down on Nicolai Place. He insisted he could not make the decisions that needed to be made. Only the Priest could. So I dressed and wearily made my way to the construction site, a duty I had put off since Michael's suicide.

The site was busy, but I paid little attention to the rising structure, and trudged with leaden feet to the office trailer in the back, where the architect and the general contractor were waiting for me. After the usual courtesies, I was informed that their normal supplier of compact air-conditioning coils, compressors, and ducts had just declared bankruptcy, and the larger units the building contractor had to bring in from an alternative supplier were forcing changes to the temple layout and construction. "We can't fit the equipment in without cutting down the acolyte's living quarters," said the architect. "The air-conditioning ducts have to run behind panels here. The bathroom and shower have to be cut out of the space over here. So, when all is done, there's just a tiny space left for a person to live in. It won't be very comfortable."

I looked down at the architectural drawings. Strictly maintaining the hierarchy and authority of the priesthood had always been very important to me, as it was to all Priests ordained at the Head Temple, but such concerns suddenly seemed immaterial. I tapped the blueprint.

"This larger room. This is the Chief Priest's office?"

"That's it. Prime spot facing the street."

"A content acolyte makes for a well-run temple. The Chief Priest has other places he can find privacy—his apartment upstairs, his consulting room, the library—and he certainly doesn't need a shower in his office. So switch the rooms around. A modest Chief Priest office with a pleasant view over the garden will hardly be the end of the world, but a proper studio will mean everything to the acolyte."

So it was settled. Then Jennifer called with more administration issues to be resolved, and what last summer seemed like an eternity, a year, suddenly in April seemed like no time at all.

There were the updated New York State 190, 192, and 197 religious incorporation articles that had to be filed, a press release that had to be written, and furniture purchases to be made for the upper floors of the temple. All this while maintaining the regular Oko lectures and the individual pastoral work that was expected. It was, in short, the forces of life that prodded me into putting one foot before the other, down the forest path.

One evening back at the flat I made myself green tea, sat in the armchair, and hunted for meaning in the stack of books at my elbow. I did not find the consoling wisdom I was looking for in *The Eternal Teachings,* but found it most unexpectedly in a Haikai by the fifteenth-century monk Yamazaki Sōkan, printed in a cracked and yellow Tokyo University paperback from my student days, a poem I think Michael would have very much enjoyed:

> *Even at the time*
> *When my father lay dying*
> *I still kept farting.*

The young Brazilian couple who were at my birthday party gave birth to a healthy baby girl. When there was a break in the April rains the couple requested I come out to Queens to bless their child and officiate at her Headwater Precepts Acceptance Ceremony, a Buddhist ritual roughly equivalent to a Christian baptism. I agreed, of course. It was my duty.

They lived in a tiny one-bedroom garden apartment in a low-income housing development in Queens, sandwiched between a garbage incinerator plant and a power station serving the Long Island Railroad. The row houses were all the color of *agedashi* tofu, with identical little windows. The Brazilian couple lived in the last house up against the railroad tracks and I made my way to the front door and knocked. Before I could say hello, the young father had thrown his arms around me and clapped me on the back and welcomed me with such warmth and feeling I found myself gasping for breath.

"Thank you, Reverend Oda. Bless you! You come to our home."

The Brazilian family did not express their pleasure over this auspicious day with the sort of quiet pride I was accustomed to in Japan. Their style, it must be said, involved much familial shrieking and pungent smells from the kitchen and an overwhelming pile of beribboned gifts.

But the glowing mother came to me, speaking softly in her lilting Brazilian accent, and held up, like an offering, her lace-covered baby. I peered down at the child. She looked like a snow monkey, with a pink silk headband around her tufted head. When my face suddenly loomed before her, the startled baby opened her eyes very wide, baffled by my existence. I was, I confess, unexpectedly touched by this and took her in my arms.

It almost seemed to defy the laws of physics that such a large family of Brazilian immigrants could actually fit inside the small apartment. But they did. And when it came time for the ceremony before the roughly made Buddhist altar in the front room, a deep and respectful hush fell across the warm flat. The father delicately held the three-month-old Angelina in his arms, while on the clap chairs behind us the white-haired grandparents and aunts and uncles, none of them Buddhists, wiped their eyes and trembled when we incanted the *Lotus Sutra* in Angelina's honor.

I intended to slip out after the ceremony, but the family would not allow it. Plump aunts and grandmothers grabbed me by the arms and pulled me out into the tiny garden, up against the railroad tracks and the chicken-wire fence festooned with pink balloons, making me sit down in the honored position at the head of the tinny table.

I celebrated Angelina's special day with her family for the next seven hours, as they brought out fried fish, yellow rice flecked with mysterious meat, and bowls heaped with greens and grains. The trains periodically thundered past, rattling the balloons and drowning out all conversation, but they never interrupted the joyous spirit of the day. I talked and talked while Angelina's uncle grilled the cheapest cuts of beef and pork over a jerry-rigged barrel, and the little girl's father poured me many glasses of a Brazilian drink.

I do not know what was in this *caipirinha,* but toward the end of the evening—when it was dark outside and the aunts had cardigans over their shoulders and one of the old men brought out a Portuguese mandolin—I found myself standing and swaying and robustly singing Buddhist Shomyo to my hosts. They all clapped and hooted their approval, all but Angelina, who, innately wise and surely destined for great things, was singularly unimpressed and fell asleep after a yawn or two.

In the end it was sincere Buddhists like this young family, trying to find their way through the harsh urban American landscape to a clearing they could call home, who made me stand up and walk my path. Whatever my small issues, whatever my preoccupations, these decent people deserved the honest services of the Priest. And that was what I tried to give them.

In early May I finally informed Sensei he needed to have my replacement in place by June 21, for that was when the temple would be completed, on time and miraculously under budget. Mr. Symes had successfully renegotiated the overpriced supply contracts the New York Temple Fund had agreed to when the construction industry was booming and materials were in short supply. When I understood what Mr. Symes had done, I was humbled, for he had done the impossible: he had made me look good in the eyes of the Head Temple's powerful administrators.

Sensei was immensely pleased by the news, of course, and we emailed each other back and forth over the preparations for the Buddha-Entry Ceremony consecrating the new temple. In the end we agreed that he would fly to New York with Reverends Kashimoto and Watanabe—plus my replacement if he was found in time—and together they would lead the New York temple's consecration rites.

While all these preparations were unfolding, Jennifer grew concerned that I had swung abruptly from an inert state of mourning to toiling away at an almost unsustainable pace. So one day she showed up at the flat with a picnic basket. "Get your jacket," she said in a tone that would not tolerate dissent. "You need a break. We're having lunch in Prospect Park."

That day we walked the paths that ran through the apple and pear orchard of the Brooklyn Botanical Garden. In the pale spring light, the black-barked trunks of the fruit trees held up a delicate weave of pink and white blossoms, giving the illusion they were wrapped in wedding dresses, as they passed a honey-scent perfume to us in the breeze.

A young Hasidic couple, walking a respectable distance apart from each other and followed by a chaperone, earnestly engaged in courtship talk as they walked past us. The young man wore a fur hat and a long black coat, with the tassels of a shawl hanging out from under his black vest. The bony girl was in baggy stockings and a head scarf. But for all their black and ominous appearance there was lightness in the gentle way they sneaked peeks at each other, in the murmur of their tentative talk, in the way the soft wind sprinkled pink-and-white confetti across their shoulders. As the haiku poets wrote, under cherry flowers, none are strangers.

Numerous Japanese and Korean families had already staked out neat blanket squares in the park's cherry orchard. I felt a pang of homesickness when I saw them, as the Cherry Blossom Festival was my favorite time of year back in Japan, but the ache passed as Jennifer and I unfolded our blanket under a tree and languidly ate our lunch.

Afterward, stretched out on the blanket, my head in Jennifer's lap as she read a book, I drank a bottle of beer and watched through the tree branches overhead puffs of clouds rolling across the blue sky. The cherry blossoms fluttered down upon my bare arms, the old tree giving me its blessings. As a lone petal fluttered down upon my face, a long-suppressed scene from my childhood lightly floated into view.

"I just remembered a Cherry Blossom Festival from when I was a boy."

Jennifer lowered her book and listened.

"It started late morning, when all of us villagers climbed up to the mountain cherry orchards on the Head Temple grounds, just past the main gate. Every family from Katsurao sought out their tree, according to long-established custom, and as we made our way with the other villagers up the Head Temple hill, my father carried Yuji on his back and sang an old song about spring. In the orchard, under the old Oda tree, my mother snapped the blanket and it fell into position.

"We knelt under the tree's dainty flower clusters. It smelled so good. Like honey. Blankets and banquets of specially prepared foods were laid out. There was much lively chatter around us— an adult played a flute, children were playing ball. At noon, the chanting priesthood came in an orderly fashion down from the Head Temple, as they did on this day every year, bearing gifts and blessings for us villagers. Prayer drums followed the procession.

"Our sister was not yet born. I was five years old. We three Oda boys were like little ants, the way we crawled over our father's back, as he lay stretched out across the blanket under the tree, just like I am now. Mother was laughing as we tugged at Father's arm, tried crawling underneath, into his armpit, desperately trying to lift him from his prone position.

" 'Get up, Otou-san, please,' cried Daiki. 'A monster ride. Please.'

"I remember how Father groaned, climbed up on all fours, and we all squealed with excitement. He stood and Daiki immediately hopped on his left foot and clutched his arm. Yuji and I both hopped on to his right foot, and similarly held on tight to his right arm. 'Oh, no,' mother cried. 'The monster is moving. The monster is moving.'

"Father lumbered, first lifting Daiki on his left foot. My older brother suddenly shot two feet off the ground. Father put that left foot down hard upon the earth, like a heavy-footed giant, and then lifted his right foot, sending Yuji and myself squealing up into the air.

"We did not at first see the seventy-seventh High Priest as he approached our blanket with his entourage. But then we heard Mother call my father's name, and our game came to an abrupt halt. We scrambled off Father's feet and bowed.

" 'What handsome and strong boys you have, Oda-san.'

"My father bowed again to the High Priest, but was unable to talk. 'They must give you the runaround,' the High Priest continued. 'They are as energetic as snow monkeys.'

"I did not like this and yelled, 'We are not snow monkeys!'

" 'Shush, boy,' Mother hissed. But the High Priest just laughed at my impertinence. 'Oh? I apologize. Then what animal are you? A mountain hawk-eagle, perhaps? A badger?'

" 'We are *ayu*. Clever and quick.'

"The High Priest and his entourage laughed. 'Well, come here, then, quick and clever *ayu*. Reverend Takahashi here has a basket of toys for you to pick from. And for you, parents, we have a few adult choices, too. Just small things from the Head Temple— incense, *juzu* beads, calligraphy. Please accept our small gifts and best wishes on this auspicious Cherry Blossom Day. I have prayed for you all.'

"An elderly monk came forward holding out the basket of toys and Daiki solemnly picked a small wooden train and thanked the priesthood. Tiny Yuji was so excited he almost couldn't choose, but when Mother finally warned him to pick or lose out, he greedily snatched a bag of marbles. The monk came then in my direction with the toys, but I shook my head, and walked over to the adult basket extended to my mother by another monk. I lifted from that tray the green-stone *juzu* prayer beads that had caught the sun and my eye.

"My mother tried to pry the beads loose from my five-year-old hands, but the High Priest spoke up. 'Let the boy have the beads.' My parents bowed and I grabbed the green-stone beads and ran off. I sat down in a clump of buttercup clover to play, mimicking the Priests I had seen by rubbing the beads together and mumbling a childish facsimile of their chants. The High Priest watched me quietly for some time before telling my father, 'This is an omen, Oda-san. Bring the boy to us when he is of age.'"

"What a lovely story," Jennifer said.

But I could not respond, for as I brought the bottle of beer to my lips, I found my hand trembling with the memory, for on that blossom-filled Brooklyn day I finally understood that it was not my father who had picked me to live, after all.

It was the Buddha.

During the May Oko I looked out into the large crowd and found myself locking eyes with Sister Marie and her auntie. The Haitian woman's eyes roved maniacally about, as I remembered them to do, while her auntie sat like a poisonous toad and glowered. I groaned inside when I spotted them, but Sister Marie came up to me afterward and extended her hand.

"Let's try again," she said.

I shook her hand. "Yes. Let us try again."

Word spread among the Buddhist community that their long-cherished dream of a New York temple was almost realized, as did rumors of a more welcoming atmosphere at the Manhattan Okos, and faces I had not seen for many months resurfaced at the study meetings that had again swollen to nearly two hundred Believers.

Mrs. Graham and I had to compose the temple's official public relations announcement and we met at the café of the Brooklyn Museum, where she was a board member, to write the official release and discuss its dissemination. We did so over tea and biscuits, and when our meeting ended, I headed alone to the turnstile exit.

For a few minutes I stood blinking on the museum's steps.

The sun was very bright and I was momentary blinded. I looked up and down the streets that were, on this Saturday afternoon, teeming with New Yorkers heading into Prospect Park.

My landlord, Mr. Giuseppe Colonese, was on the far side of Grand Army Plaza, tall and gaunt as usual, loping his way across the white stripes of the crosswalk. He was in a thick crowd of pedestrians, but even at a distance I could see this normally dour man was radiating joy, the way he bounced up and down on the balls of his feet. The crowd parted for a moment and I saw then that Mr. Giuseppe was not alone, but crossing the street with Miss Laura. They were holding hands. Miss Laura's blond hair glittered as it caught the spring sun, and at that moment this strange Believer gently smiled up at my landlord, the two of them looking as content as could be.

So unexpected, the many changes of that memorable spring.

Still, Michael's death was a pall that hung over all of us, and it was a very emotional meeting when I finally got together with Mrs. Horovitz. She and I met repeatedly over several days, the two of us talking almost nonstop as the grief-stricken woman tried to come to terms with her son's untimely death.

Our first meeting was at a Sixth Avenue diner. Mrs. Horovitz shuffled through the door, reduced to just an old woman in a black pantsuit. Where before *The New York Times* fashion editor had come across as wiry, powerful, and arrogant, she now looked like a badly beaten dog, wearing big black sunglasses to cover her face, as if hiding bruises from a severe beating.

She slumped into the booth opposite me, smiled weakly, and ordered a tea with lemon from the waitress. "He killed us," she said, twisting the gold bangles on her arm. "You should see his father. He's a wreck. Michael has turned us into the walking dead."

We went back and forth over the events, her guilt, my shame. A tea with milk arrived and Mrs. Horovitz wordlessly poured the milk into her mug and sipped the hot drink. I confessed my role in Michael's death, and she talked about her "terrible love" for Michael, her inability to just leave him be and find his way.

It was, in fact, the exact term he had used to describe her suffocating love, and I wondered if she had uttered those words when he was alive whether it would have made a difference. Or perhaps his karma and destiny were well beyond such small things. But untimely death is like that. It makes you go over a litany of "what ifs," endlessly, around and around in the head.

Late one afternoon at her apartment, after we were both talked out and incapable of uttering another syllable, we dropped our eyes and stared silently at our cold coffee cups on the pink marble table between us.

She finally looked up. "Can I pray with you? The Buddhist prayers?"

"Yes. Of course."

I was too moved to say more. Right then and there we knelt between the coffee table and the television set, facing east. I wrapped my own *juzu* beads around her trembling hands and held open the *Lotus Sutra* liturgy so she could read alongside me. I did a very slow and methodic evening prayer, as Mrs. Horovitz falteringly tried to follow the kanji beat.

At one point she had to stop, overwhelmed as she was by the emotion of the moment. "Buddhism meant more to him than anything else," she said after we finished. "I want it to become a part of me."

After that Mrs. Horovitz began practicing and studying diligently. I had the impression the woman was practicing Buddhism only to stay connected to her dead child. Michael was right: she did try to "steal" his religion. But I also knew the Buddha would eventually open her eyes to the futility of this sort of attachment. The oneness she was seeking was on a different plane, and it was not just with Michael, but with all sentient and insentient beings.

When I came home one evening—bone-weary from Mrs. Horovitz's emotional demands and the constant nag of knowing how I failed Michael—I found a brown paper bag leaning against my door. It contained fresh strawberries, basil, a half dozen portobello mushrooms. Written in my landlord's uneducated scrawl was a note that I still keep on my altar as an offering.

To most it would appear as a simple message from a simple man, but to me it was a communication from the Buddha's realm.

The note stated, simply, *You are blessing to 429 Cortina Street. I think you are priest who save many people. God bless.*

It was in such ways, once I had been stripped of all vestiges of arrogance, that the good people of America built me back up again. The day after I received this note I had a coffee at Café Sorrento, where the owner had, with the improving weather, set some chairs and tables out on the sidewalk.

I stirred the little brown cup, the sun on my face, and watched the young mothers in front of Helena's Laundromat smoke their long cigarettes and snap their Brooklyn dialect back and forth among themselves.

A refrigerator truck from New Jersey was double-parked in front of D'Amato's, entire rib cages of raw meat hoisted on the driver's shoulder and carried inside the shop. I stirred my coffee. D'Amato turned and nodded at me, like I was one of them, just one of the men of Brooklyn.

I paid my bill, walked a few blocks south, and stepped into the Cortina Street Bakery, where I had bought my Italian ice the previous summer. The girl with the magenta hair cracked her gum and, in her usual fashion, sharply asked me what I wanted. I jabbed my finger here and there and asked a dozen questions about the pastries and bread on the shelves. "Is it fresh?" I asked. "What's that called? Don't you have smaller one? It's too expensive."

Within minutes others in the store were recommending purchases to me, shouting out when to eat this or that, and the whole sweet-smelling bakery filled with our laughing banter. The sugar-dusted "horseshoe" was, I learned that day, eaten for "good fortune" in certain parts of southern Italy, and I very much liked the sound of that. It was that pastry I finally bought.

The children's voices in Sant'Andrea Park beckoned like birds in the forest around the Temple of Everlasting Prayer. An old man and woman rested on a park bench with their parcels, wheezing jokes as they watched the passersby, passing back and forth the intimate, earthy poetry of Brooklyn.

The tired woman finally dropped her white head on the shoulder of her husband's peacoat. "Come on," he said, squeezing her thigh. "Let's get this stuff home. You're tired." It was good advice and I decided to return home, too, in order to give thanks to the Buddha. But as I moved to leave the park, as I breathed in the air, the reality of where I stood finally hit me.

Brooklyn.

It was the Buddhaland.

Chapter Fifteen

$\mathcal{I}$n the bittersweet shadow of my imminent departure back to Japan, Jennifer and I strolled the Brooklyn Promenade facing the skyline of lower Manhattan, one mild summerlike evening in late May. The air was breezy and clear. We leaned against the promenade rail licking our ice-cream cones; dog walkers, joggers with baby strollers, and dancing line-skaters whizzed by behind us.

The boils and currents of the city harbor ran back and forth, swirling flotsam. A tugboat was fighting its way up the East River as a tired cargo ship stood in the Upper New York Bay, a great ring of rust around its midriff, treaded water like a man at the end of his life. The Statue of Liberty seemed to stand by the ship in its final hours, the light of her green torch illuminating the way, while the Staten Island Ferry pulled out from its Manhattan terminal, a modernist orange cube resolutely plowing through the gray-blue waters.

Manhattan stood across the harbor from us. On this strip of rock the thrusting ambitions of man rose straight up into the heavens, skyscrapers at hard angles. I had always thought, from my outpost on Mount Nagata, that great beauty could be the product only of nature. But these American skyscrapers—columns of shiny black mica, windows the color of tremolite—were redolent with something else. They spoke to me of man-made dreams made concrete and grounded in rock, of lives fully lived. They were the solid manifestations of soaring human spirit and a kind of service to a greater cause. Even the broken Manhattan skyline, where the towers had once stood, spoke to me of immense human suffering and even greater endurance. There was something unique about New York's mountain ridge of buildings—and now we had added, modestly, a Buddhist temple to its strange summit.

As the sky above us gradually slid from blush to an inky purple, lights came on and the columns of steel and glass sparkled, points of light breaking through the misty air of the harbor that separated the islands.

Yellow taxis returned to Manhattan across the Brooklyn Bridge, a pearl-string of bridge lights showing them the way. It was time for us to similarly head back home and we slowly walked through Brooklyn's gloaming, pausing on Nicolai Place so I could say a brief blessing over its sacred ground.

The temple was complete but for some outside security lights that had to be installed. There was parking space for six cars under a raked green-glass and iron cover. A short set of granite steps ran up to the temple's black-lacquered, double-fronted door, and the Hall of Worship on the ground floor was, during the day, illuminated by natural light pouring in through the bay windows. Tidy red brick led the eye farther up the side of the building, to the Chief Priest's personal dwelling on the top floor and the gray slate roof run with copper gutters, its bookend towers echoing the turrets on the nineteenth-century houses next door.

It was as stunning in its urban way as the Temple of Everlasting Prayer, and back in the flat that night I found myself holding a horsehair paintbrush, once again sliding into a trance. The rice paper began to fill with a waterfall on one side, a raging fire on the other, and between these two threatening panels a lone man walked steadfastly down a narrow path, forging his way through the elemental dangers on his way to the tranquil land where the New York temple stood.

My time in America had finally run out. Reverend Fukuyama was expected to arrive shortly for the Buddha-Entry Ceremony, and the temple still had to be properly prepared and purified. Jennifer and I loaded up the Honda with buckets, cloths, and cleanser, and we arrived in Brooklyn Heights with our sleeves rolled up. Every cornice in the temple was dusted, every shelf swabbed clean with fresh water. I worked up from the downstairs, Jennifer worked down from the top floors, and somewhere in the middle, we met.

The decision came to me as I scrubbed the downstairs toilet and remembered my mother, performing the very same job in the family *ryokan,* so many years ago. In that moment I finally decided to take the New York posting and name the temple Home of the Lotus, after my parents' inn. I climbed the temple stairs to tell Jennifer, and she instantly threw her arms around my neck, planting a thousand kisses on my face and neck and whispering, "My prayers came true."

I sent Sensei an email of deep thanks and appreciation for the privilege of the New York appointment, not a little worried that he would say it was too late, he had already appointed a Priest. His response, when it came, was unexpected: *You are a bit late seeing the light as usual, Seido-san, but nonetheless your decision is most welcome. I was always convinced you would make a first-rate Priest in America, if I could ever get you out of the Temple of Everlasting Prayer, where you were stuck and had long stopped growing. I have, in fact, a small confession—I never looked for a substitute. How did I know you would take the posting, you might ask? It is quite simple. You have never let me down. You have always been the Buddha's loyal servant.*

The Symeses drove to Brooklyn Heights in their chauffeured Town Car, bringing with them stoop-shouldered Bernadine Horovitz, a cloud of eye-watering perfume, and a gift basket filled with chocolates and whiskey. First to arrive for the Buddha-Entry Ceremony, the Symeses were determined to secure prime real estate at the front of the Hall of Worship. "We have to be up front because Artie's hearing is *farkakte,* even though he won't admit it," Harriet told Jennifer at the door. "*Oyyy.* These men. But what are you going to do?"

Mr. Symes spent some time positioning and repositioning his gift basket at the table set up for the Believers' offerings, and it took a hauling of purses this way and that before the three of them could finally settle into their front-row positions. "Oh, no, no, no, no," said Mrs. Horovitz. "That won't do. I need to be on the left."

The threesome was finally settled when the Believer who nodded off at every Oko arrived to claim his usual spot. The narcoleptic appeared, since the last meeting, to have gone through a rough patch, for his hair was wild and his face was covered in gray stubble. He wordlessly studied the Symeses occupying his front-row spot and there were some tense moments when we didn't know what would happen next. But the fellow simply dropped down on all fours and somehow squeezed himself in among them, and there the four sat, tightly packed together, each determined not to lose an inch of their hard-earned floor space.

The New York temple's doors were in this way officially opened for the Buddha-Entry Ceremony, and excited American Believers soon arrived in large numbers, not just to witness the consecration of their temple but to catch glimpses of the four Head Temple Priests who had arrived from Japan for the auspicious ceremony: Reverend Fukuyama and his aide, Reverend Watanabe; my old friend, Reverend Kashimoto; and the acolyte Reverend Ojisawa, who came to humbly ask if he could join me at the new American temple.

Mrs. Graham and her daughter found a spot on the floor without a fuss, while Miss Laura moved across the room waving at friends, blowing kisses, stepping over bodies and purses to reach two clap chairs still available in the far corner of the hall. Mr. Giuseppe Colonese, her fiancé, came later, scowling as usual and carrying Buddhist prayer beads in his workman's hand. He was the most recent member to join the temple; Miss Laura had insisted on a Buddhist wedding and he was studying with me in preparation for the happy occasion.

By 10:45 that morning the Hall of Worship at the temple was

packed with three hundred Believers from across the entire metropolitan area. The Hall of Worship was, much to my conster-
nation, starting to smell a bit like a livestock market, but the
excitement in the room was palpable and there was a collective
"aaah" followed by a reverential hush when young Reverend Ojisawa emerged, *Lotus Sutra* liturgy and sandalwood prayer beads
dangling from his fingers, threading his way through the crowd
to kneel down before the altar.

Jennifer left her position at the temple's front door as Reverend
Ojisawa banged the gong-bell and proceeded to lead the American Believers in warm-up prayer, keeping them in line through
the rhythmic beating of the prayer drum. Backed by Mr. Doric
and the practicing members of the male choir—including the
rehabilitated Mr. Jonathan—the young Priest soon had the Hall
of Worship resonating with harmonious Buddhist prayer.

The rest of us Priests were still in the dressing room just off
the Hall of Worship, a room that also contained built-in cupboards storing the temple's supply of candles, prayer books, and
juzu prayer beads. Reverend Watanabe stood before the changing bench and assisted Sensei as he tied on the white *kesa* and the
charcoal-gray ceremonial robes. It was Reverend Kashimoto who
looked out of the glass portico of the dressing room door, into the
Hall of Worship, just as Sister Marie and her aunt began to bark
the Buddhist prayers in their usual odd manner, rubbing their
prayer beads so violently between their palms it looked like they
might start a fire.

Reverend Kashimoto clicked his tongue in disapproval.

I looked over his shoulder to see what he was seeing, and spotted what were now familiar faces: the horn-rimmed eyeglasses of
a Westchester literature professor, the Afro hair of an IT consul-
tant from Queens, the treelike arms of a policeman from Staten
Island. Three large sisters from New Jersey sat on chairs and commanded the southeast corner like the Ten Demon Daughters of
Kishimojin. Meanwhile, an agitated Wall Street trader, whom we
suspected of having a drug problem, was a row behind my young

Brazilian family and a homeless couple who had recently moved into a Bronx shelter.

"They are so *henna hitotachi*," said Reverend Kashimoto, using Japanese slang to describe extremely weird people. "This is terrible, Seido-san. I had no idea it was this bad."

"I am sorry you say this, Reverend Kashimoto," I said, deliberately using priestly formalities to address my friend. "It is hard for even us Japanese Priests, with all our training, to understand enlightenment, so imagine how much harder it is for these Americans who do not even share our cultural way of thinking. It is a small miracle these Americans practice at all. But they do, every day, on their knees. And I know, firsthand, some of these 'bizarre people' you refer to are closer to the Buddha than you and I and much of the Head Temple priesthood. This is the truth. So you slander the Buddha when you slander these American Believers. It is, to my mind, a great privilege for us to pray in their presence."

Reverend Kashimoto stiffened for a moment but then smiled. "I apologize most sincerely, Reverend Oda. You are quite right. Forgive me. Thank you for the correction." From the back of the dressing room we heard Sensei cry, "So. We are ready. Let us begin the Buddha-Entry Ceremony!"

We threaded our way down a tiny path through the Believers' knees, through the hands clasped palm to palm and held up in worship. Sensing our arrival in the fading prayers behind him, Reverend Ojisawa banged the bell in closing, and humbly retreated just as we, the Senior Priests, arrived at the altar.

Reverend Fukuyama knelt before the Cluster of Jewels Mandala and led us through the consecration ceremony. It was, for me, a very moving experience, and at one moment—as I inhaled deeply between two phrases of the *Lotus Sutra*—I had this odd, spine-tingling sensation the Buddha was physically sucked into the temple with just one intake of breath, his presence suddenly filling every corner of the hall.

In closing, Reverend Fukuyama instructed me, the New York temple's incoming Chief Priest, to lead in one final recitation of the *Lotus Sutra,* not all of it but, according to long-established ritual, the rarely incanted Chapter 3. I led my American community of Believers in prayer, until a point when I became overwhelmed and had difficulty completing the liturgy. I felt the vibrations of the Believers' prayers through the wood floor, sensed the molecular shimmering in the air that made the delicate leaves of the *shikimi* vibrate and the surface tension of the water cup tremble. The incense before me rose to the heavens, and the voices behind me were fused in one holy and harmonious cry, weaving in and out just as we began the Parable of the Burning House.

It was as we collectively reached the parable's phrase "Though the fire is pressing upon them and pain and suffering are imminent, they do not mind or fear and have no impulse to escape" that I heard the Third Voice join us, a background hum like a powerful but finely pitched tuning fork.

Earlier in the year, when I had heard this otherworldly voice, it had induced in me a cold-sweat terror. But on this day I was not afraid, for I suddenly knew to whom this voice belonged. It was the voice of my dead—a chorus made of Onii-san and my siblings and Michael and my parents and the seventy-eighth High Priest and Uncle Aki and Mrs. Colonese and Old Reverend Tanaka and my ancestors since time immemorial—joyously reuniting with me in that holy place that exists somewhere in the in-between world.

It has been twenty years now since that day the temple officially opened. I sit today on the stone bench in my Brooklyn garden, with eyes half-closed, savoring the spring sun on my face. A cup of green tea is cradled in my lap, radiating soft heat, while a light breeze brings to me the faint sound of cars honking in the distance, a few wet ribbons of harbor air. It is a mystery that I, of all people, have found this patch of earth that all humanity seeks. But there it is.

I am home.

The wind turns, flutters this way and that, and brings the pungent smell of peppers blistering and blackening on a grill. It is my neighbor cooking over the wall. He belches. Loudly. It is the beer. He is rather fond of it.

This gastrointestinal symphony over the ivy-clad wall articulates rather well the mystery of it all, for it is still perplexing to me that this sanctuary I have found is in such a strange land. It is without dispute I remain Japanese in many ways, still capable of being highly irritated by aspects of America. But I think one of my Manhattan friends got it right when, after a day fishing the east branch of the Delaware River in upstate New York, my host poured me a glass of red wine and said, "Seido-san, the thing you need to know about America is that it is the land of second chances."

Perhaps this is why I am at home here. It does explain the inexplicable. But of course we are who we are, even when on faraway shores. I wish I could say America helped me discipline my mind and that I finally stopped concocting "fantasies out of nothing," as Sensei calls my habit of misreading people and events around me. I wish I could. But I can't. My grasp of reality remains as tenuous and illusive in Brooklyn as it was in Fukushima Prefecture, and it is a simple fact I made many more errors of judgment and perception in the years that followed my arrival in America. Some of those misreadings were more amusing than serious, but others were almost as damaging in their way as what transpired with Michael. But that is precisely the point of it all—the Light of Enlightenment comes to us as we are, not when we are in a state of human perfection.

Of all the Americans, it is Jennifer, in my opinion, who has the deepest understanding of this Buddhist truth. A year or two after the temple opened, we walked silently back down Hicks Street, on a hot and still summer evening. It was late on a Saturday night and we had just eaten at our favorite restaurant on Atlantic Avenue. The brownstones were aglow with warm window light and a handsome young couple came toward us down the elm-lined pavement, their arms wrapped tight around each other in a passionate embrace. They were so entwined, so oblivious of the world around them, I found myself catching my breath. Before I knew what I was saying, I blurted out, "Will you marry me, Jennifer? Will you do this?"

As soon as the words left my mouth, I smacked my hip with a clenched fist and internally railed against my stupidity. My marriage proposal did not contain one word about my deep love and respect for Jennifer, this good woman at my side, but reflected only my own emptiness and hollow hunger. But Jennifer was always much wiser than I was, and a few steps onward, her breath soft in the night, she said, "No, I am sorry, Seido. I don't love you that way."

Over the next year I asked Jennifer to marry me several more times, in more sincere ways than I had that night, but her response was always resolutely the same. She simply would not marry me, and I eventually came to grasp, however slowly, that in her heart she remained married to the fiancé who had died before their wedding.

The last time I asked Jennifer to marry me we were sitting in a café on Montague Street. She sighed, a little irritated. "Seido, please stop this. Really. I do love you, but not the way you want. You just have to accept that. You're not exactly husband material. I am sorry if I gave you the impression I was interested in you in this way."

I lowered my head. "This misunderstanding is my fault. This would not be the first time I have misread intentions. I am very sorry."

"Oh, please, don't be sorry. It's not a big deal. I'm a big girl. It was fun for a while, and the marriage offer is very flattering, but a husband is definitely not what I want from you."

I looked away, to hide the hurt, and softly said, "But then you must tell me what you do want."

This she did not expect, and she stuttered, "It . . . it is very difficult for me to ask. . . . You'll probably find it ridiculous."

Her hand was resting on the table. I put mine on hers, to

impress on her the seriousness of my next remark. "My debt to you is very great, Jennifer. It is my karmic duty to pay back what I can. Let me at least do this. If I can."

She took a deep breath and said, "I want to become an ordained nun. More than anything in this world. I can think of nothing else."

For a few minutes I did not speak.

The waitress brought us a plate of nuts to go with our glasses of wine as a man with two mastiffs on chains crossed from the other side of the street. When I trusted my voice to speak again, I said, "I will formally train you as a nun, Jennifer. It would be my great honor. There is no question you have the right attitude for the priesthood. You are already a lay nun of great skill and compassion."

And so our relationship that started as Priest and assistant, then morphed into that of man and woman, finally drifted over, entirely on its own accord, to Priest and acolyte. This brought new hurt. I won't pretend otherwise. But I see now it had to end this way. When Mr. Doric finally learned that Jennifer and I had history, had been lovers, in fact, he smacked his head in horror. "What were you thinking? As the temple lawyer I have to advise you, Jennifer could still sue you and the temple for sexual harassment. That's how things are in America. You are so lucky Jennifer is who she is. Another woman could have so easily destroyed you *and* the temple."

But this did not help me. Quite the opposite. For he was simply reminding me of Jennifer's decency and it did not stop the ache for things lost. But the heart finds its own way to heal. Heading out to get the Japanese paper one morning, I nonchalantly glanced into the Hall of Worship as Jennifer was cleaning the altar. She was softly humming an American folk song to herself, and wore a kerchief around her head, as my mother used to do while working, with yellow gloves pulled up to her elbows.

When I glanced into the prayer hall Jennifer was starting to dust under the altar vase, her knitted forehead in profile as she wholeheartedly devoted herself to the task. Her look instantly brought back the intense look of my brother Onii-san the day he lost the monster trout and was afterward trying to retie his fly, concentrating on threading the nylon through the eye of the hook. The focused look in Daiki's face that day—and the look in Jennifer's face at the altar—were absolutely identical, and I was instantly brought back in time, to that moment when long ago I stood by my brother in the spray of the Devil's Gate Gorge waterfall, that watery ladder joining heaven with earth.

When Jennifer put back the vase and moved on to dust the rest of the altar, she vaguely reminded me of my mother, so similarly earnest when she cleaned the inn's bathroom. This was when I finally had my eye-opening. I, like Jennifer, had always wanted something much deeper than romance. What I wanted from Jennifer was family life, a domestic routine that could bring me back to the family I lost. This was what I hungered for. It was all much bigger than just her and me.

When I finally understood this, the hurt I felt that Jennifer would never formally marry me, all this pain and disappointment, suddenly did not matter in the slightest. It was insignificant, just morning dew on a rock, for Jennifer was in truth connected to me in the deepest way one human can be connected to another. She was my spiritual family, my chosen family—whether we formally married or not.

This was the essential truth.

So here we are, Jennifer and I, two old friends and fellow servants of the Buddha, toiling side by side in the New York temple, until our dying days. It is through the steady accumulation of this insightful moment and a thousand others like it that the place of it all, America, has become my true home—that clearing in the forest I imagined the week immediately following my family's massacre.

This simple reality finally revealed itself to me only years after the Home of the Lotus Temple was officially consecrated. Reverend Ojisawa became my second, and a very good one at that, and on this particular spring afternoon we were cleaning out the temple basement, which had become cluttered with bric-a-brac. Ojisawa and I were alone in the temple, for his young wife had taken their baby out in the stroller for a walk along the promenade, while Acolyte Meli was traveling the world. I had sent her to Japan, for language immersion courses in Tokyo, to be followed by advanced Buddhist studies at the Head Temple, both of which she concluded brilliantly. Reverend Fukuyama had, as usual, called it just right. Jennifer did make a first-rate nun of the Headwater Sect.

It was sometime in the afternoon that I took a break from this rough basement work in the temple. My back had grown stiff from all the bending and Reverend Ojisawa told me to rest. He would finish up our dusty chore.

I gratefully went upstairs, made some tea, and wandered out into the small temple garden in the back. The stone bench stood as usual on the far side of the temple patio; behind the low slate wall, large rhododendron bushes were starting to bud. It was my great pleasure to come here in the afternoon, when a few shafts of sun filtered at just the right angle through the surrounding buildings and trees, columns of angled light descending into the temple garden to warm that slate wall and bench. So I took a seat in the light, the sun touching my face, holding a cup of tea in my hands, in the end little different than the old men of Little Calabria.

I sat like this and rested and listened to the trilling birds. But the birds in the trees of Brooklyn that afternoon were like voices from the beyond, summoning me to remember the past. Which I did, and still do, on this day, as I write these final lines on the very same stone bench, my neighbor over the wall grilling his peppers and belching his beer.

It is a great mystery. I am in many ways so unsatisfactory as a Priest that I sometimes think to give up like Otou-san or Michael would be so much easier. But the Buddha lives within me, forever reminding me the flight from Tokyo to New York takes fourteen hours, and if I travel just thirteen hours and stop short, I will never be able to admire the silver moon shining over Brooklyn.

And the more New York and its people prod me to stretch beyond my natural abilities, the more I catch glimpses of the Tranquil Light. I now believe enlightenment is a simple state: it is the ability to suffer what there is to suffer; it is the ability to enjoy what there is to enjoy. To understand that, truly, is enlightenment. And this is the way it should be, for the Buddha visits us only randomly and in the hours of our greatest need, often when we least expect it, teaching us, in this way, to stand alone and firm in this world.

One day I will meet Onii-san and Michael and the rest of my family in the Pure Land of Eagle Peak, and I will tell them that, finally making amends for my many failings as a son, a man, and a Priest. And while I sit on this stone temple bench thinking such thoughts, a yellow butterfly floats into the garden.

It flutters this way and that.

And then is gone.

Acknowledgments

Thank you for reading my novel. Your time is valuable, the distractions many. I am deeply grateful.

The writing between these two covers is purely an act of imagination and should in no way be taken seriously as a doctrinal explanation of Buddhism. The Headwater Sect is invented, and while some readers knowledgeable of Buddhism might spot some similarities with Nichiren Shoshu, the Buddhist sect founded in thirteenth-century Japan, please know these similarities are superficial and meaningless. I invented Reverend Oda's world by borrowing ideas and images from many Buddhist sects and sources—including Zen and Pure Land sects—and even, when so inspired, from the thirteenth-century German mystic Meister Eckhart, and the twenty-first-century American psychoanalyst James Hillman. I have, in short, created the sort of mangled spiritual mishmash that would greatly provoke Reverend Oda's ire. But that's my point. My novel should in no way be considered a serious religious work depicting a particular school of Buddhism. It is entirely a work of fiction.

Having said that, I did, in my usual style, borrow from important religious and psychological works while creating my imaginary world: *The Threefold Lotus Sutra*, translated by Bunno Kato, Yoshiro Tamura, and Kojiro Miyasaka; *The Lotus of the Wonderful Law*, by W. E. Soothill; *The Writings of Nichiren Daishonin*, by the Gosho Translation Committee of the Soka Gakkai; the lectures, writings and translations of Reverend Kando Tono at Myokanji; *River of Fire, River of Water*, by Taitetsu Unno; *Mysticism,*

241

Christian and Buddhist, by D. T. Suzuki; *Meister Eckhart: Selected Writings,* translated by Oliver Davies; *Buddha of Infinite Light: The Teachings of Shin Buddhism, the Japanese Way of Wisdom and Compassion,* by D. T. Suzuki; *The Way of Zen,* by Alan Watts; *A Flock of Fools: Ancient Buddhist Tales of Wisdom and Laughter from the One Hundred Parable Sutra,* translated and retold by Kazuaki Tanahashi and Peter Levitt; *Psychology and Religion: West and East (Vol. 11, The Collected Works),* by C. G. Jung, translated by R. F. C. Hull; *The Dream and the Underworld,* by James Hillman; *The Soul's Code: In Search of Character and Calling,* by James Hillman; *Marriage: Dead or Alive,* by Adolf Guggenbühl-Craig, translated by Murray Stein; *The Varieties of Religious Experience,* by William James.

The idea to write *Buddhaland Brooklyn* sprang from one of my favorite movies, *Amarcord,* the autobiographical film by the late Italian director Federico Fellini; and *The Year of My Life (Oraga Haru),* a slim volume of haiku and verse by the eighteenth-century Buddhist poet-priest Kobayashi Issa that was translated by Nobuyuki Yuasa. Both these works are nostalgic fictional memoirs condensing an entire life into a symbolic year progressing through the seasons, but intriguingly come from entirely different epochs, mediums, and cultures. During the rewriting phase, I found myself frequently inspired by Anthony Trollope's *The Chronicles of Barsetshire.* Other important literary sources that I leaned on: *The Classic Tradition of Haiku,* edited by Faubion Bowers; *The Autumn Wind: A Selection from the Poems Of Issa,* translated by Lewis Mackenzie; *Classic Haiku: An Anthology of Poems by Bashō and His Followers,* translated and annotated by Asataro Miyamori; *Breaking into Japanese Literature,* by Giles Murray; *The Norton Anthology of Poetry,* edited by Alexander W. Allison, Herbert Barrows, Caesar R. Blake, Arthur J. Carr, Arthur M. Eastman, and Hubert M. English, Jr.; and *Making Out in Japan,* by Todd and Erika Geers. To this short list add an untold number of websites that brought far-flung information to my fingertips. Too numerous to list, they allowed me to describe everything from the mountain birds of Japan to the toilet slipper etiquette of a *ryokan*.

Deepest thanks are due Reverend Kando Tono, an unassuming Buddhist priest in New York who has, under very difficult circumstances, devoted his life to teaching Nichiren Shoshu doctrine to Americans. I am also very grateful to my lifelong friends Lizanne Merrill and her husband, Samy Brahimy, who is not just the brother I chose but was also my *consiglieri* on all things Brooklyn. Sincere and special thanks to Kozue Watanabe, who kindly read my work with a keen Japanese eye.

This book is dedicated with great love and respect to my parents. I am grateful to all my brothers for their support, but Vasco deserves my special thanks for his invaluable and material assistance on a wide range of legal issues. Kate Morais, my daughter, and Susan Agar, my wife, grow quite furious with me whenever I publicly express my love and thanks for their endless patience and support, but that is a cross, to use a Christian image, they must bear. Crowning this familial pile is Kay Pedrin, my mother-in-law, who happily defies the stereotype and has over the years earned my thanks and love. She has earned a special homage within the pages of this book: Meli is her maiden name.

Agent Richard Pine of InkWell Management is my wise guide through the jungles of the publishing world, swooping down from his Fifth Avenue office with a bit of encouragement or a challenge to do better, all according to need. The InkWell colleagues who, with Richard, have built my fiction career and earned my sincere thanks: Alexis Hurley (foreign rights) and Jenny Witherell (business manager); and William Callahan, Charlie Olsen, Nathaniel Jacks, and Ethan Bassoff, who have all similarly put their backs to the oar. Elsewhere, Juliet Blake and Mark Shepherd are much-valued and consistent supporters of my work.

Most of all, however, I must thank my Scribner editor, Whitney Frick, who gave me my first break in American book publishing, and has ever since only grown in my esteem, as have all the hardworking staff, such as Wendy Sheanin and Kathleen Rizzo, who stand behind Simon & Schuster. Whit is the real deal, with the requisite mix of professional grit and passion for good writing that lies at the heart of all great editors. It's been my immense privilege to work with her.

And to you, dear reader, I again express my heartfelt thanks for purchasing and reading my little book. May we all, in these hard times, find the Tranquil Light.

Richard C. Morais